LAST HOPE

--A spinoff from the work of Vengeance--

To strengthen my skin and sharpen my knuckles.

- CONTENTS -

- WORLD MAP OF XENAMUS -

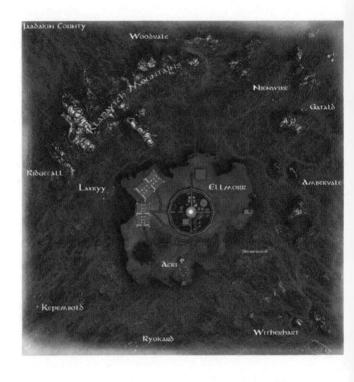

-ABBREVIATED GLOSSARY-

Babarin A fairly large race in the Kirbinian Galaxy. These people dwell all throughout The Galaxy. However, the majority inhabit hotter climates such as the planets of Xenamus, Weraxon, and Bactra. Unlike many other races, Babarins have high resistance to the heat that planets such as Xenamus serve.

Ellmorr One of the wealthiest cities in the Kirbinian Galaxy. The city sits atop the Fraygen Plateau and is guarded every second of the day by the Nizer Marine Corps. (N.M.C.) Ellmorr boasts gambling, skyscrapers, bars, museums, shows, and more. People from all of The Galaxy travel to Ellmorr to witness its elegance. Thus, it is a priority to protect Ellmorr from the horrors that occur below in Jaadakin County.

Fraygen Plateau The single raised region of land above the deserts of Jaadakin County. Atop this plateau sits Ellmorr, one of the wealthiest cities in the entire Kirbinian Galaxy. Additionally, the Fraygen Plateau is heavily guarded by N.M.C. troops and protects Ellmorr against wandering natives of Jaadakin.

Glithimite Small creatures that inhabit the deserts of Xenamus. They generally live in packs and move quickly. These critters carry the deadly Glithémien Disease.

Glithémien Disease A deadly disease that is plaguing the major cities of Jaadakin County on the planet of Xenamus. With a simple bite from a glithimite, one will begin to suffer from symptoms within a few hours. Symptoms begin with a slowed heart rate, high fever, weakening of muscles, bleeding eye sockets, and eventually the corroding of the lungs. Symptoms set in quickly, but it takes up to two days for an infected person to die. Currently, there is no known cure for Glithémien Disease. That said, there are rumors circulating that the Fraygen Plateau on the planet of Xenamus has a cure but isn't providing it to Jaadakin County.

The Great Fall The swift decline of Jaadakin County into turmoil after the Glithémien Disease plagued the cities and civilizations. Prior to The Great Fall, Jaadakin County was managing fairly; Commerce coursed through the deserts. There was enough food for the majority of Jaadakin County natives. However, the disease mutated so quickly, that Jaadakin scientists couldn't determine cure, or even its origins, before it ransacked the entire region. The Fall was relatively recent, thus the older generation of current-day lived before it, thus raising and educating their children during the chaos of Jaadakin County.

Jaadakin County The main region on the planet of Xenamus. Jaadakin consists of hilly deserts to flat stretches of sand. It houses five out of the six major cities on the planet. Jaadakin currently sits in extreme poverty and is being plagued by the deadly Glithémien Disease.

Jaro Another word for "year" used in the Kirbinian Galaxy.

Kirbinian Galaxy An immense galaxy that houses hundreds of thousands of inhabited planets and stars, mostly overseen by the galactic government. In comparison to the Milky Way, the Kirbinian Galaxy is quadruple in size and is divided up into five sectors.

Xenamus A Sub-Imperial Planet of the Kirbinian Galaxy. Technically, Xenamus is one of the wealthiest planets in The Galaxy because of the city of Ellmorr. Besides this bustling city, the rest of the planet, which makes up the impoverished Jaadakin County, has little food, water, and medicine to defend against the Glithémien Disease.

- PROLOGUE -

Deep in the Kirbinian Galaxy, an arid desert region named Jaadakin County on the planet, Xenamus, was impoverished and infested by an ostensibly incurable plague called the Glithémien Disease. It stole the life of every sorry soul that was unfortunate enough to catch it. Jaadakins were forced to fight for their lives and scavenge for food amongst the collapse of civilization of this desert planet.

Amidst the violence, one of the wealthiest cities in the Kirbinian Galaxy, Ellmorr, which sat on an immense plateau and was securely guarded by the Nizer Marine Corps. (N.M.C.), was without starvation or sickness. This metropolis bustled with healthy people, flowing commerce, groundbreaking sciences and technology, entertainment and a thriving society above the horrors of Jaadakin County below it. It was rumored that this city held a cure to the deadly Glithémien Disease that was carried by desert insects – glithimite – but the city wouldn't release it to the public. Down below, in the savagery of the deserts, inhabitants struggled each day to keep themselves and their loved ones alive while trying to get to safety in Ellmorr. This was where two men remained…

Vlayn rested the gun on the decaying wooden window sill and continued, "one day… jaros ago, when I was younger… cannibalism spread like the plague throughout my hometown, Witherhart. No food or water for days. So many corpses strewn across the roads, hanging from balconies, tossed in alley-ways… Cluttering the city. The hell were we supposed to do? Lay down and die like the rest?" Vlayn dropped his eyes to his feet. A tear ran down his face, but he quickly wiped it away. He cleared his throat, rubbed his beard, wiped his eyes, and spoke, "My brother and I… We ate our father."

Bardolf was shocked.

"Our mother…" Vlayn hesitantly continued with a gruff Babarin voice that had screamed too far for too long. A voice that had spoken too many hopeful words. A voice that was disappointed in the past. A voice that had learned time and time again that hope was never alive. Vlayn began with vexation, "Those fucking desert bugs. They stick to the goddamn ground and they *follow* your scent til they tear the skin from your eyes. It wasn't necessarily the hunger that killed her like everyone else."

Then, a heavy silence weighed the room down. The gallant lights from Ellmorr silently illuminated the shack and the depressed, empty settlement of Laxryy as it sat lonely in the desert. Vlayn's voice was clearer and calmer than ever, "We woulda ate her if we could," Vlayn said. "We didn't want to. We *had* to… survival… that's all it comes down to. It always comes down to that. After that, I killed my brother. He caught the disease, like my mother. He woulda suffered. I needed to put him out… had to. Ever since, I've been on the move. Without a family. Alone. Jumping from one place to another… it fit. I got used to it."

Bardolf tried to stand as he grasped his wounded leg. Vlayn took notice and paused until he asked a question that he had already answered himself long ago. And he knew this. "Do you needa kill in order to survive…?" he mumbled to a bewildered Bardolf. "Never forget who you are," Vlayn added. "Never let your guard down. Remember that."

Bardolf's C.C.N.T. 90 assault rifle still rested on the floor next to his feet.

Vlayn studied the weapon for a brief period of time, but long enough to see the words "Claeen Company Nabbuu Type 90," engraved sharply into the side of the barrel. He continued, growing irate once more, "See, those people in Ellmorr don't know how good they have it. They haven't had to do the worst kinds of things just to stay alive! Ellmorians haven't had to do things they never thought they would do! Major cities – close to death! And what does the Clansee do? Nothing! He continues to fund Ellmorr and leaves the rest of us to suffer!" Vlayn was out of breath; his long hair drooped in front of his eyes and the energetic lights from Ellmorr, over forty miles across the empty desert, caused his sweaty skin to glisten. He turned to Bardolf and sent him a piercing glare.

"This isn't about me," Bardolf said. "This is about *you*. *You're* damaged. *You're* weak. You want vengeance on Xenamus because of what has happened to *you*. This isn't about me. And you're alone, and I don't know you, but I *know* that. You lost anyone you ever enjoyed or loved. And those people outside – they're just foreign assholes who are following you into some dark fucking abyss. The county is falling all around us, but lunacy and rage isn't as unavoidable as you probably made yourself believe.""

Vlayn's breathing grew noticeably louder, "You speak of me as if I'm too far gone… As if I'm Altkin."

Bardolf waited a moment, then spoke softly, "Altkin is dead. But there's still people in this galaxy that are just like him… you *are* too far gone."

The two continued to make eye contact.

It seemed as if time had slowed.

-One-

HANDS ARE TIED

138 jaros earlier.

Vlayn Par'Wil sat tiredly in the center of his ravaged apartment room. The horrid stench of slaughter blossomed throughout the city in which he resided. His bloody hands trembled vigorously while he exhaled from a mouth that screamed for pure nutrients that weren't derived from his own species. Vlayn knew he had to leave his hometown, Witherhart. He understood that the terrors he withstood in this city had to be eradicated from his life. Vlayn rose to his feet gravitated to his haunted bedroom. Two lifeless bodies of his father and brother sat in the room, staring back at Vlayn with distress and disappointment. His father lay legless on Vlayn's battered bedspring. An axe whose blade was camouflaged in dried blood sat on the floor near the bed. A deceased fireplace was made with several dry logs and was catty-cornered in the meager bedroom where flesh was roasted and consumed by the same breed just a day ago: himself. Vlayn's eyes soon trudged back to his mutilated father, and his stomach sunk into his body as if he was going to vomit.

Vlayn had to. His brother, Tithen, had to. They would have starved.

Soon, his eyes drifted to his lifeless brother sprawled out along the grimy floor. Tithen's forehead was left with a gaping hole where blood once rushed to the surface and drenched his unusable face. Vlayn didn't want to budge any closer to the vile scene, but his legs moved forward instinctually, dragging along the rest of his body to the corpse. His eyes met with the despaired ones of Tithen's. Vlayn's jaw instantly dropped, but it seemed as if oxygen eluded him and he couldn't get air to his lungs. Tithen was in wicked, poignant pain just prior to his death, but when he was finally put out of his awful squalor, released from this cruel life on Xenamus, his empty face still urgently screamed with this agony as if Vlayn hadn't alleviated his brother's anguish at all.

Disgust and fear shrouded Vlayn as he stared at the appalling sight of he who he killed. But Vlayn had to. Tithenkeen was dying of the Glithémien Disease – the plague of Jaadakin County. He would have suffered at least two days before the sickness wiped out his immune system and slowed his heart to a stall. Tithen's lungs would've caved, his eye sockets would've bled, he would struggle to gain oxygen, but his lungs would cease to exist at that point. Tithen would have suffered if Vlayn didn't step in; these were the things Vlayn reminded himself of since the second he pulled the trigger after locking the sights of the pistol on his brother's head.

He tried to maintain expressionlessness as he stood enfeebled above his brother, but tears quickly swelled in his glassy eyes. As the corpses glared at him, he also studied himself. Who did Vlayn Par'Wil become these last few weeks? Was he a killer? Or was he a young man simply trying to survive in the decaying desert lands of Jaadakin

County? How could the leaders of The Kirbinian Galaxy let poor Xenamus simply fall by the wayside, and let it crumble through their fingers because of a killer disease?

Vlayn ambled through the apartment, flowing with the music of hopeless bellows and cries that repeatedly played through the parched walls. His body was hollow. He had lost everything worth living for. He was just a young man, and yet, the life was ripped from his bones. Vlayn left his home and began his lifelong venture.

The pain and loss burned inside of him, churning the plasma under his skin. He inhaled the tacky smell of innards that accumulated from his mother, father, and brother. It crafted a gut-wrenching stench that swam through his nostrils. Vlayn gasped for air, collapsed to the floor, and ran his hands through the debris that was collected on it. The lofty ceiling stood above him, observing a suffering Vlayn Par'Wil who had just witnessed his dying mother and father, and the necessary killing of his younger brother.

His surroundings grew watery, for tears bubbled in his eye sockets. Vlayn started to weep as he rolled along the floor with misery, as if a sharp blade was slowly piercing his skin. The pain was horrendous. For some reason, though, he inhaled the pain, almost feeling as if the additional suffering was well-deserved and much-needed.

A gentle, warm wind blew through the doorway that opened to the outside deserts of Jaadakin; it led to a quickly deteriorating city that housed an immense family of natives that suffered from a killer disease. The natives of this city starved day by day, fought each other to live, and ate their own people to keep their hearts beating. Their city was Witherhart, and every other city in the deserts of Jaadakin County suffered from these conditions as well, while the elegant city of Ellmorr sat lavishly on the Fraygen Plateau, watching the torture from up above.

Vlayn got to his feet, feeling his own anguish motivating him to leave this place of panic and fright. He opened this door and shuffled down the metal stairs outside that linked the apartment on the top story of the concrete building to the streets of Witherhart. Hunger struck him harshly, but this was nothing new. Fatigue battered his bones, but again, this was nothing new. Vlayn knew he had to escape his hometown. He had to be on the move. He had to keep pushing despite the recent horror.

But was Vlayn Par'Wil a murderer at this point?

He just had to survive at any rate, and he would continue to, even if performing dark deeds were necessary.

His palms moistened and sweat smeared his forehead as he sprinted defenselessly down a tight alley toward the main pathway that cut through the decrepit city of Witherhart. Vlayn peered both left and right when he made it to the end of the alleyway, making sure his path was clear of threats along the main cobble road, and pushed his legs even harder to escape the city. Hollow buildings towered over Vlayn as he sprinted by them. He felt scrutinizing stares of the starved and diseased natives of Witherhart as he tried to escape.

Cannibals dwelled in the alleyways of Witherhart, gnawing at flesh desperately. Marauders sauntered through the street behind him, wielding long machetes, scalpels, metal pipes, aluminum bottles tied to the ends of belts, and anything that could be used to inflict pain and see the blood. The remaining gazes of harmless onlookers studied Vlayn Par'Wil, searching for a clue of weakness. His legs kept moving, trying to escape the glares of these people who were stuck in one place their entire lives.

In reality, there was not one person looking at him the entire time, but Vlayn believed that everyone was watching and judging him.

-Two-

PULL THE TRIGGER

Vlayn coughed ferociously as the desert sand kicked up and entered his esophagus. He gasped for air, but the dust filled his parched lungs. A settlement sat calmly a half mile in front of him. Vlayn was crossing the distance between this unknown settlement and the depreciating city of Witherhart, which stood terrifyingly tall amongst the empty void that was Jaadakin County. The ominous buildings of the city towered behind Vlayn, gawking at him from afar. He kept turning his head behind as he walked, watching Witherhart, almost making sure the city wasn't trying to catch up to him to remind him of what he had done. Vlayn picked up his pace.

His boots dug into the deep sand with every step and his sweatshirt blew with the wind until a gust took it off his shoulders, exposing his blood-stained t-shirt. The young man stopped and turned around, only to see it dragging along the sand and getting swept away by the wind. He ran a few feet forward, attempting to retrieve it, but Witherhart was in that direction and he could see the rotting city grinning maniacally at him. He spun around and ran away, feeling the warmth of the breeze shooting him with grains of sand. Massive hills of gold sand surrounded him and there was an endless amount of these hills. Sand held its secrets in Jaadakin County. It was quick and simple to shovel it over a body and mask it forever

In front of him, the new settlement grew closer. He didn't have the first clue as to what this town was, what secrets it held, or what people it fostered. The only thing Vlayn did know was that it wasn't Witherhart.

Massive wooden planks circumscribed the small settlement, forming a thick wall to protect against intruders. Makeshift wooden stairs led to the top of this wall on the opposite side, where two rugged-faced men stood to keep watch against incoming marauders from the nearby city of Witherhart or nomads from the wastes of Jaadakin County. Both men were middle-aged, torn both physically and emotionally, but brawny on surface. They simultaneously stared Vlayn down as he slowly approached the open doorway to the town. They didn't look too friendly to Vlayn; after all, who was calm and understanding in the lands of Jaadakin County? People had been through too much and lost too many since The Great Fall of Jaadakin County to see the best in strangers.

Vlayn didn't feel too threatened, though. Naturally, he let his guard down. He stood five or six feet from the open passageway and peered up at the two guardsmen. The sand blew quietly and intimidatingly behind Vlayn as the hollow deserts screamed in dismay. In front of him, the sound of male voices filled the small village and overflowed into the thick, wooden walls, and from there, the sound traveled with the dreadful wind in the slowly darkening desert. Nighttime began to fall, and with it, the minute amount of civility Jaadakin County held during the day.

"Excuse me," Vlayn blurted out to the men atop the wall. His words came to an immediate halt, and he attempted to find more. Jaded, Vlayn had no idea what he wanted or needed to say next to gain entry. His mind and body were battered, weak, and craved sleep, especially after recent history.

Vlayn opened his mouth once more, ready to speak again. Before he could, a woman appeared in the gaping entrance and proceeded toward Vlayn. A grimy flak jacket gripped her torso with thick black pants dressing her legs, and bulky boots covering her aching soles from the desert. A rusty Dufe-102 assault rifle was roped around her shoulders. This rifle dated back hundreds of jaros ago and was commonly utilized amongst Nizer Marine Corps (N.M.C.) soldiers, or otherwise known as the galactic army. Newer models were born into the Dufe series throughout the jaros, thus making the eldest Dufe-102 fairly cheap and appearing frequently on distressed planets like Xenamus. In which case, this woman and many others like her had the 102 as their best friend. It was sturdy, reliable, and ready to swipe the soul from anyone. And she was ready to take Vlayn's if the need arose.

She swiftly approached the young Vlayn and grabbed him with her two bare hands and threw him into the scorching sand. "Who the fuck is you?" the Babarin woman shouted aggressively.

Vlayn responded with fear and dismay instead of words.

"You with that Akafayl Gang!?" the Babarin shouted. "Swear if you are I'll have no hesitation to make your head fucking *explode* into the sand you lay in. Don't need no suicide kid roamin' through my streets with a t-bomb attached to his hip," she said while standing, pinning Vlayn down with her heavy boot and pulling the Dufe-102 into her arms. She cocked the weapon's charging lever backward with force, and locked it sturdily on the young man's head.

"No! No!" Vlayn exclaimed. "I'm just a kid from Witherhart!" he bellowed with fear. "Please!"

"How 'bout the Blackguard, huh!? You some kid soldier tryna wipe us out!?"

"No!!! Please!! I don't even have a gun!"

"Get the fuck up kid!" she ordered as she lifted her boot from Vlayn's chest.

Vlayn scurried to his feet. His clothes were drenched with sweat and sand was stuck to his moist skin. The soldier took the Dufe-102 off Vlayn as her head spun around to the men on the wall. "See this lil' duster?" she shouted with a rich timbre in her voice while pointing at him.

The two soldiers chuckled uncontrollably and Vlayn's eyes dropped to his feet with sadness and loneliness. His short, soft hair blew with the wind and dried blood stained his fresh skin.

This ruthless woman was far more than just unsympathetic; she was trained in the meticulous art of savagery – To take the soul of anyone at the initial sight of one, and beat on with her life and continue to steal as if it was a ritual.

This young man, however, just began his training. Since glithémien were bugs that couldn't climb, they were limited to the desert floor. Vlayn's apartment in Witherhart guarded him from the disease and more so, many Jaadakin County natives that once had a heart, a family, and loved other people and themselves – Natives that then had to coat their own heart in a calloused determination to survive by doing whatever was called upon them by Xenamus. This woman was the master, and Vlayn was the newcomer to Jaadakin County and the new world that was created within the last seventy-or-so jaros by the Glithémien Disease. He just started to face the deserts both unpredictable and hopeless natives that clung onto an ounce of hope that came their way, and others that were submerged into insanity – Who killed for the fun of it, because their kill count was far too high to calculate.

The lives Vlayn took was for justifiable reasons. This was just the beginning, though. This woman, however, was thrown into the face of death many times. She was in the soil of Xenamus grappling with it and eventually submitted it. The soldier shot her gaze at Vlayn's face. "What the fuck do you want, kid?" she whispered with boozy breath.

Vlayn's lips quivered as he struggled to find the words. The Babarin's natural intimidation almost strangled him.

"You better figure out what the fuck you want to say before I shoot you!" she screamed with a fury that carried the words all throughout the deserts of Jaadakin County.

Vlayn began to back up, trying to leave submissively.

"Where you going?" the Babarin asked slowly. The bellicose words slithered through the air, snaked up Vlayn's legs, captured him, and disabled him.

"If you leave, I will slit your throat," she pledged. "Tell me why you came to my settlement. I don't know who you are… Pretty fucking suspicious you show up here without telling me what you want… If you leave, I will kill you. If you leave and get away alive, I promise I will find you. I know the sound of your heartbeat now, and there is no place I won't travel to kill you. I know every grain of sand on this planet. I've been everywhere. I've wiped out groups of Ellmorian Blackguards, survived glithémien bites, and mutilated more Jaadakins than you've ever met."

Vlayn faced his entire body toward the soldier at the sound of this Babarin woman boasting of these things as if they were achievements. "Tell me why you came to my settlement."

The words retched out of Vlayn's mouth as if the Babarin shoved her hand into Vlayn's throat and forcefully pulled them out. "I needed a place to stay."

And almost instantly, an ominous grin grew on the Babarin's face. "Oh, yeah?"

"Witherhart wasn't safe for me any longer. This was the first place I came across," Vlayn explained with the hope he could still have his life, even if he wasn't sure he still wanted it.

"Witherhart?" she repeated, "You came from Witherhart?"

Vlayn nodded with uncertainty, for he didn't know what to expect from this duster; a nomadic native to Jaadakin County.

"I know we're all sufferin'," she said while glancing back to her men on the wall, "every city in Jaadakin County is being fucked over by the Fraygen Plateau and Ellmorr... But Witherhart is the most destroyed... Tell me that lie again," she ordered, but Vlayn's eyebrows dropped. "Tell me again that you're from Witherhart."

"... I am from Witherhart..."

"Do I look like the type of duster you can bullshit!?" she howled as loud as she could that one could hear her vocal chords clapping together in her esophagus. Befuddled, Vlayn recoiled.

The woman exhaled, collected herself, and looked up at the two soldiers, then back at Vlayn with a smile that filled the lower half of her face. "I can let you in, yeah. But you gotta do one thing for me first, and if you are a true Witherhart guy, you can do this without issue."

"Of–of course," a panicked Vlayn stammered.

"Come," she ordered. "My name is Enver Rodge. What 'bout you?" she asked as Vlayn followed her inside the walls.

"Vlayn," he answered hesitantly. Vlayn was unsure of what he wanted from the world. He felt displaced after what he had to do to his family, and with every step he took during every minute of the day, he felt this overwhelming uncertainty. The only thing he seemed to understand was that he needed to live. In Jaadakin County, the norm was to find any way to survive. But did he want to be alive? At this point, Vlayn was coasting through life, skeptical of where he wanted to go or what he needed to do. He wanted to live despite his suicidal state – but what was the end goal?

Enver retaliated, "Vlayn – who?"

"Par'Wil," he corrected himself quickly, fearful of this mysterious, heartless duster. "Vlayn Par'Wil," Enver said for good measure. "This is Shorewood, my town," Enver stated dryly.

Vlayn looked around. About three or four rows of decrepit, wooden structures formed what was "Shorewood Settlement." Generally, small establishments such as this fell quite swiftly to larger, major cities such as Witherhart, Ryokard, or Woodvale. If these towns did stay alive, they were typically run by a brutish band of Jaadakins that understood the ways to living in a newly declining region of Xenamus: Jaadakin County – a region that only just a few decades ago was not prospering, but merely getting by; where commerce slowly but steadily flowed throughout the deserts. The necessities for life weren't abundant like it was in Ellmorr, but enough to substantially sustain life for a closely moderate life expectancy. Until the Glithémien Disease sprung out from the sand so fast that Jaadakin scientists had no idea what it really was. But over a short period of time, lowly Jaadakin natives either died or learned how to survive. Those who did were scraping by in the major cities, or formed their own villages, like Shorewood.

Here in Shorewood, men equipped with weapons slung around their shoulders filled the streets of Shorewood. With every glance, a callous man filled Vlayn's view as they would send menacing glares toward him. That was the thing, though. There were just men of the Babarin Race, no women. There was not one female in sight besides a strong woman – Enver Rodge; a woman so powerful that she could banish anyone she wished by a simple word, a pretentious breath, and that sorrowful soul would vanish eternally.

Just like most, the men in Shorewood once had people they cared for and supported. They had their own Babarin families riding on their backs. Since The Great Fall, they began living nomadically, fleeing from glithémien, locked in desperation, and some even collapsing into the anguishing mentality that could spin them to cannibalism. Whether it was a quick bite of flesh, or a feast, bloodlust was eventual and inevitable for many in Jaadakin County at this point in time.

This was where these men of Shorewood once were, and Enver Rodge could send any particular person far away from her town, and back into that hopeless world. If one set Enver off, or murmured a mere exhalation that crossed her incorrectly, it would be their neck, or an everlasting exiling. Vlayn only knew Enver for a short ten minutes, if that, and he was able to fully understand her authority.

Enver veered off the road with Vlayn following. The pair entered a tavern where drunk men crowded together. A mild blue light poorly illuminated the room, acting as a shield, masking the men's bruised, scarred faces with an expression of either repentance or anger. Either way, their facial appearances were drilled into their skulls. Still, the small crowd conversed with one another, discussing news that were as current as could be about the major cities, Shorewood, and speculations about the mysterious Ellmorr: the city that never spoke, nor spent any of its attention to those suffering below it.

Vlayn stood stoop-shouldered next to the authoritative Enver Rodge as he inhaled the dust that filled this perilous scene. A man walked up to Enver and shook her hand respectfully. Then, the man glared at Vlayn as if he would bludgeon him to a realm far from Allameen if the notorious Enver Rodge wasn't standing next to him.

The drunken men cleared a path for the short-statured Enver, with Vlayn trailing. Many looked into her menacing brown eyes with admiration of her authority and ability to rule this town, while others lowered their head, understanding their submissive position.

Eventually the two entered a small crawlspace with a narrow stone stairwell opening up to them. Enver stopped in place at the top of the stairs. She looked at Vlayn, then down into the dark stairway, motioning him to head down. Vlayn's mouth dropped open, attempting to find his way out of the situation, but Enver wouldn't even listen. Instead, she shook her head slowly, but kept her eyes locked on him. "No," she urged. "You said you were from

Witherhart, which means you're the toughest type of duster out there. No steppin' out now."

With that, he began down the stairs. An overpowering, ugly scent of mustiness and dry rot grew more intense with each step down. The dim light from the tavern and the sound of Shorewood's natives began to exit the air more and more as Vlayn went deeper underneath the bar and into a larger basement. When the stairs ended, he paused at the bottom, for he couldn't hear Enver's footsteps behind him, and he certainly couldn't turn around and see her – it was far too dark.

Vlayn's ears began to ring from the absence of noise, so he exhaled hard, ensuring he hadn't gone deaf. His body was as still as a tree trunk during the strongest of winds. His heart thumped – fearful of a genuine stab through his chest by this woman. But, no.

Enver came from behind Vlayn, and shoved him through the darkness with her hand. His heart pumped quicker by the second for all he could hear was the heavy breathing through Enver's nostrils in the blackness. Soon, she pulled her hand off of him and waded through the dark room.

Vlayn tried to sift through the darkness merely by his eyesight, guaranteeing he wasn't moving a muscle. He didn't want to startle Enver, wherever she was in the room, and end up getting slaughtered by her for literally stepping on her toes.

Out of nowhere, two bright, yellow spotlights turned on. They shined on two men and one woman that cowered on their knees with black hoods over their heads. The three panted heavier in front of the blaring light. Vlayn listened to their horrified, quickened breathing from under a tightly knotted cloth that covered their mouths under the hoods.

Enver smiled with excitement as she started to yank the hoods off them one by one. "You wanna stay in Shorewood, kid?" she inquired again.

Vlayn stood frightened and his jaw-dropped at the sight. He couldn't answer Enver this time. His legs instantly weakened and his arms started to flutter slightly while his eyes grazed over the horrific scene. Both wet and dried blood surrounded the three on the floor, with a few yellow teeth rotting away in it. His head turned from left to right, over and over again – his past was catching up to him.

Enver pulled out a pistol and pointed it at the woman, "I'm done using this lady," she said menacingly. Then, she pointed the gun at the man and untied the cloth that was shoved into his mouth, "This asshole tried to stab me in the back. And you can yell now. Nothin' will change this," Enver told the man, then drifted to the last man and placed the barrel of the pistol on the man's head, "And this asshole *actually* tried to stab me in the back!" she shouted. Then, silence filled the room. "Didn't work out too well, did it?" Enver said in his ear in a voice that was a little more than a whisper.

Finally, she glanced up at Vlayn, pulled the pistol off the man's head and tossed it to him. "Shoot every single one of these people, and you can stay in Shorewood for as long as you can stay alive."

The pistol rested in Vlayn's fresh palm with disgust. "Wh-Why?" he spoke through his labored breathing.

"Why?" Enver repeated in a raised tone. She responded as if it was obvious, *"Why!?!?"* she shrieked again. "Like I said, I'm done with the woman. And these other two assholes betrayed me, and if you're saying you can't do this for me, then you're betraying me too because you said you'd do it!!!" Vlayn stood behind the three with the barrel of the pistol pointed toward the ground. Water began to fill his eyes. He couldn't do this… not after what he recently did.

"Not behind them," Enver said. "Stand in front of 'em and shoot 'em. They need to see who's puttin' 'em down."

Vlayn's face transformed into deeper repulsion. He slowly revolved around the cowering woman and the two men and stood in front of them. Tears slowly ran down his cheeks. "I-I can't," Vlayn exclaimed.

"What was that?" Enver said. "I didn't hear you."

Vlayn gasped for air, "I-I can't," he repeated.

"*What!?* I still can't *hear you!!*"

"I-I-I-"

Enver raised his Dufe-102 to Vlayn's head. "You better fucking do it, or *I* will kill you."

"Please!!!" Vlayn shouted. "Just let me leave – *please!!* I'll do anything just to leave!!" he pled.

"No!" Enver screamed. "You came here for something! You not gonna do anything to get it!? You live on Xenamus, kid! You gonna have to do shit you don't like doing!!!" Enver shrieked. "Do it!!! Do it!!!" she yelled repeatedly, "do it!!!"

Vlayn cried as his wobbly hand raised the decrepit pistol. He could feel the warmth on the metal handle that was produced from Enver's tight grip.

"Do it!!!" she screamed again.

Not this again, Vlayn thought to himself. Vlayn didn't want to kill anyone else after his brother, Tithen. The sights locked onto the woman's head. Her face was beat red and covered in her tears. Her eyes were swollen and bruised, just like the two men. She whimpered from under the smothering cloth and tried to obtain oxygen, but it was almost impossible to achieve. The woman's eyes met with the innocent ones of the young Vlayn. Sorrow, regret, and fear filled his gaze. He didn't want to do this. He didn't want to live on this desolate planet of Xenamus, where circumstances forced inhabitants into cruelty – where the world proved to be a cage where every person warred against themselves.

But that was the point... that's what Vlayn had to remind himself. Killing for survival must be done in Jaadakin County. Running from hordes of glithémien to avoid the sickness must be done. Avoiding the blood-ravenous, haphazard militia that was the Ellmorian Blackguard was inevitable. Vlayn was slowly understanding that these things must be done just to keep his heart pumping.

And with that, Vlayn pulled the trigger. The woman's head snapped back, blood from her exploded skull, and white brain matter flung outward, splattering the living man next to her. The man gasped horrifically and spit the excess blood that landed in his mouth.

More tears ran down Vlayn's face, for he saw the image of his suffering mother in the now deceased eyes of this unfortunate woman. He missed his mother more than ever, and he continued to see her suffering eyes as the lifeless woman in front of him dropped to the floor.

"Next one!" Enver shouted grimly while stepping slowly behind the man.

Vlayn slowly looked up at Enver, but he knew what she was about to say. She shouted, "do it!!!" yet again with her stringy black hair falling into her face.

With that, Vlayn's head dropped to his feet, pistol slung in his right hand. Like a ritual, his hand raised again and pointed the barrel of the gun at the man, and pulled the trigger. Enver snorted, then cheered, "And that's what you get!"

This time, remorse overcame Vlayn, for he envisioned himself with his brother just a few days ago. The dead man flopped onto the cold ground. The sight instantly transported him back to that time when he was chopping his father's leg off so he and Tithen could eat. Vlayn could remember the words he once shouted with angst, "This is how we survive… We need to do the worst kinds of things just to stay alive! Doing things we thought we wouldn't ever do!" all while he severed his father's limbs. The world was battling Vlayn with hunger. Xenamus would've taken him into the sand if he didn't eat soon. There hadn't been water for days, but that was alright; Babarins had a water sac in their bodies called psarrolii that held water for days. But the problem was the lack of food. Tithen and himself hadn't eaten in days. The only way to escape death's cold hands was to eat. The world forced Vlayn to do something he never imagined himself ever doing: mutilating his father just to eat. Turning to cannibalism just to survive another day.

Vlayn peered up at Enver once more. He could see her hiding behind the sights of the Dufe. The last man crouched by Vlayn's feet, crying softly. He understood his fate.

"Make sure he's lookin' at you before you pull the trigger," Enver demanded in a low tone.

"Pl-Please," Vlayn begged.

"No," she responded rigidly. The harshness that covered the word was enough to force Vlayn to do almost anything.

Vlayn raised the pistol one last time.

He gasped, wiped his eyes, and pulled the trigger. The hole in the man's forehead ran deep and blood squirted out. The man collapsed limply at Enver Rodge's feet. Vlayn's legs gave out and he tumbled to the floor.

Vlayn could remember standing above his brother, Tithenkeen. Tithen lay sprawled out along Vlayn's bedroom floor. Dark bags hung under the young boy's eyes and he vomited blood just after consuming his father's own flesh, just like his older brother had. However, he wasn't suffering from consuming the flesh. He was suffering from the Glithémien Disease.

Vlayn was in this position just recently. His brother lay on the floor of his bedroom. His head faced the ceiling and the boy could feel his body slowly rotting inside from the Glithémien Disease. Tithen was suffering, and Vlayn needed to terminate the suffering. He raised the pistol to Tithen's head, told him he loved him, and pulled the trigger.

-THREE -

LIFE IS A TEST

The cold concrete nipped at Vlayn's skin as he came to his awakening. The bright star which posed as the sun contended to break through the dusty, cloudy skies, which generally veiled Xenamus from the rest of the Kirbinian Galaxy.

Vlayn's stomach continued to rumble excessively. He stood up from the sidewalk he had slept on and wobbled backward. A crooked-sitting, decrepit shack stared at Vlayn dauntingly. Then, Enver Rodge busted through the creaky wooden door. She strapped her belt tight and lit a paylian roll in the crack of his lips.

Enver looked over at Vlayn through the grey smoke, dissecting his quiet, docile state. Vlayn could feel her analyzation, so he hung his head low at the sight of her. Soon, a harlot exited the shack after Enver and began to strut down the main path in the center of Shorewood.

"Hey!" Enver called. The woman stopped in her tracks and slowly turned to her in utter fright. "Whas' your name again, kid?" she asked Vlayn.

"V-Vlayn."

"Ahh, right, right," Enver said as she drew her pistol, made her way down the stoop, and shoved it into Vlayn's right hand. "Take this slut to the back of the building and put her down. She's done with."

The woman began to back up as if she was going to take off.

"Stay there, lady, or I swear I will do worse things than make a kid shootcha in the face," Enver threatened with confidence and a malicious smile.

"Kid, I trust you'll put this dog down, right?"

Vlayn held the pistol in disgust. The memories of his past haunted him too much at the sight of a pistol or a weapon. Last night haunted him. His history nagged at his brain almost every minute of each passing day, irritating him as it drove Vlayn to the bottom of his life. But the abominable words of Enver Rodge were even more powerful.

"'Cause like I said, kid, I know the sound of your heartbeat, and I will find you, and I will kill you with no hesitation… so, you're gonna do it."

Silence.

"Good," Enver answered for him. "And take the body and put it in the building all the way at the end of this road and to your left," she said, pointing with her finger down the road. "Once you're down there, you'll know what I'm talking about… now, go," she ordered.

Vlayn and the prostitute slowly walked through the tight alleyway between the shacks. A warm wind blew Vlayn's hair back. He showed no care, though. A life was in his lap, yet again. How would he make this situation end this time?

"Please," the woman began to beg, "don't kill me. I needed the Credits to survive," she said, "and the only reason I'm in Shorewood is because the Glithémien Disease is taking down all the other cities."

Vlayn couldn't reply.

"I thought I was going to get lucky," she began, "this lady kills every woman she, or anyone else in Shorewood is finished with. I thought I would get lucky and she wouldn't kill me off. I just had to do whatever to get Credits."

The pair made it to the back of the building where Vlayn's face was still; he couldn't blink. He could barely breathe. He was terrified just as much as the woman was. Jaadakin County was asking far too much out of a young Babarin man of his age.

"Please don't kill me," she pled. "Just let me run… Let me go. Tell her that you killed me, fine. But let me live. I know you have a heart – you're young – you aren't as bad like the rest of us in Jaadakin."

Vlayn still kept quiet, afraid Enver was right around the corner.

"Do you have a mother? A family?" she inquired.

Vlayn's eyes watered, but he didn't want to let her see him in a weak state. "Yes… but she's gone. They're all gone, now."

"Gone?"

He supplied an equivocal answer, "They're all dead… dead from glithémien."

"Did you learn anything from them before they left?"

Vlayn nodded and began to sniffle, "I did. My mother taught me a lot. Taught me about the history of Jaadakin County, the Fraygen Plateau, and Ellmorr. Taught me about how life was before The Great Fall. She told me about the rest of The Galaxy and the leaders of it – the two High Clansees – Corvonn and Kirbside… she taught me everything."

"I'm so sorry," the woman said. "They lived before all this?"

"My father told me he was born just after The Fall. But his parents lived before it."

"Your parents sounded educated. They educated *you*. And that's what Xenamus does to us. It takes everyone we are closest to and fucking kills them," she muttered. "You need to get back at this world. Show it that you will never get kicked down. Always do the right thing. You can start now with letting me go."

Vlayn's eyes raised from his feet and met the ones of the despaired woman.

"Okay," he responded.

"Okay?" the woman repeated.

"Okay," Vlayn said with increasing confidence.

"But *kill* her," she said severely, "Save all the other women who will be raped by that woman, and get back at this world for the pain it caused you."

Vlayn sniffled while looking at her. He nodded to his right, motioning her to leave.

"Good," she murmured. Then, she snuck down the alley behind the shacks with her tattered blouse blowing in the wind.

Tears streamed down Vlayn's cheeks. His suffering from the loss of his family ate away at his heart. But at this very moment he needed to lock those thoughts away. A bigger danger stood in his way: Enver Rodge. Indulging in his own pain was over. He had to keep moving.

He analyzed the pistol while it loosely dangled in his hand. He examined the pistol grip's every crack and crevasse; each fissure displayed every merciless killing Enver Rodge had inflicted upon innocent lives. Vlayn almost shuttered at the thought and at the fact that Enver's weapon was in his hand. Finally, he fired at the ground and made his way back to Enver with a loose grip on the gun.

"Glithémien is ransacking all the major cities," Enver was saying to one of her men on the front stoop of the shack. "Not us, though," the man replied, "We're stayin' strong, I don't give a fuck what we gotta' do."

She nodded vigorously, puffed on the paylian roll, and turned back to Vlayn. "Put it down?" she asked him.

Her down, Vlayn thought as he nodded quickly.

"Is it in the warehouse?"

Acting as if he understood, he replied, "Y-Yes. Of course."

"Good shit," she said, then spun around to her soldier. "See?" Enver started, "told you this young guy could be one of us. *Could* be. Now let me give you a quick tour of the place," she urged to Vlayn as she tightly wrapped her arm around his shoulder.

The two sauntered down the main path to the warehouse. Enver walked nonchalantly while Vlayn walked with fear in every step. Men, some husky, some lengthy, some tattooed all over, and some with the purest, shiniest babarin skin walked passed the two, nodding to Enver with respect. The only similarity amongst every Babarin man was their tragic past; each man lost a family member or a dear friend to the Glithémien Disease, famine, or any other infection that bred throughout the unsanitary Jaadakin County.

"I know you saw the place, but thought it'd be right for the one leadin' Shorewood to show it to you properly." Enver rubbed her face tiredly, ran her tarnished fingers through her scalp, then spoke, "I was originally leading a settlement like this one called Gatald, north of here. But I eventually left because them glithémien buggers overran the place. Think it's still up an' goin' today, though."

Vlayn noticed a pocket-sized *Acts of Baleejus* stuffed in her back pocket, just below her oversized belt. A red ribbon bookmark fluttered in the warm, dusty wind, marking Enver's last reading location. Vlayn was confused; a woman of such brutality read a book about a God that was against senseless killing.

The pair reached the warehouse. Unlike all the other buildings and wooden shacks in Shorewood, this one was made of cement and concrete. A large wooden sign was screwed to the front of the building with the words: *Used/Dead* written on it in blood and innards: sinew dangled from the nails that hammered the sign in, with loins and psarrolii mashed up and painted hastily across it.

"I know it's strange," Enver said as she addressed the sign, "but it ain't like we're nobles living on Kirbidia where we can get the sign done the right way. So, like anyone else would, we took some blood from the dead and made it." Vlayn was disgusted but he shielded it from Enver. His head lunged forward, getting a better look at the peeling wooden sign and the suspended psarrolii from one of the loose screws.

"Let's head in," she said excitedly. "I don't do the dirty work," Enver began as she opened the heavy door, "My men put down those that aren't of use, and that includes you, kid. But this ain't just for men and women that we use, nah. Anyone who tries to stab me in the back will get the worst type of killin' and will be dumped here to rot." The immense building was home to a large pit, housing hundreds of dead people, both male and female, but all Babarin. Scattered yellow and black teeth were at the entrance, along with long, tendril slices of skin at Vlayn's feet. Babarin vertebra, snapped ribcages and other bones were stripped clean of its skin and strewn on the floor as the pair made their way closer to the immense pit of death.

"H-Holy *Baleejus*," Vlayn blurted out in repulsion at the sight. He didn't want to offend Enver, for he would put his own life at risk in doing so. But he couldn't hold his words at the sight. It was more than a nightmare. What kind of deranged, sick person would do this?

"It's my collection," Enver said passionately as she spun her head back to Vlayn. Her eyes slowly widened and a prodigious, genuine smile was on her face. "This – This is my collection," she told him again while chuckling lightly. "I hated every single one of these people, so I got 'em killed. But I love 'em now – they're *mine* now."

Vlayn forced a nod, despite his petrification.

"And if you betray me, I'll kill you and then you will be mine forever, in my collection," she promised him with her continuing smile.

Soon, the smell of coppery blood that stained the corpses, decomposing muscles, and the elastic tendons that sprinkled them harmonized into a beautifully nauseating odor that made Vlayn's nostrils cower. He coughed viciously and locked his index finger just below his nose. It was the smell of blood coupled with its rich topping of an iron smell that made Vlayn's mouth lurch forward. But he wouldn't vomit – he couldn't.

At the top of the pit, the carcasses seemed newer and fresher, with each dead person's last facial expression cemented to their rotting skull. While at the bottom, the bodies were mere skeletons and bones, suppurating as one whole bunch.

Enver was calm, as if the vulgar smell of death didn't control her like it did Vlayn. The smell was like an air freshener to her; the vile odor washed over her, reminding her of everyone either killed, or had ordered to be killed. She walked gallantly to the pit. A minute, yellow lightbulb hung over it, barely illuminating the terrible scene that made Vlayn retch silently. Maggots feasted off the bodies like it was an infinite buffet to them, while flies hovered over the pit.

How could Xenamus be suffering this much? How could the planet's natives live like this, where some had even lost their sanity and who they once were before The Great Fall?

Not all of Xenamus was being tortured by this disease.

The city of Ellmorr sat lavishly atop the wealthy Fraygen Plateau with N.M.C. soldiers and bases securing the affluence that the plateau held, while the rest of Xenamus – Jaadakin County – sat impoverished, struggling to survive as the Glithémien Disease pinned its people down. Jaadakin County suffered as its inhabitants fought each other for survival, and the sight that Vlayn stood before was the pinnacle of the perverse environment he was forced to grow up in.

"Where did you put the bitch?" Enver asked casually.

"What?"

"The prostitute you put down earlier today. I'm sure she's 'round here somewhere."

"Uhh, yes," Vlayn responded with heightening confidence. "I had to climb on th-th-the *that* group of dead people over there," he said, pointing to the corner hastily.

"Where?"

"Over here… I'll show you," he suggested boldly.

Vlayn's feet moved quicker. Adrenaline pumped through his body with every step he took. He studied the back of Enver's head as he walked with false confidence. His hands trembled. He was defenseless. No weapons. No strength. He was starving. How would he kill Enver?

But Enver would kill him anyway. Within that minute Enver Rodge would discover that Vlayn let the innocent woman go. He had to protect his heartbeat. He had to keep living for reasons he didn't quite understand yet.

Life was a test to see if people had what it took to live; to survive another day. Vlayn had to perform dark deeds that were necessary for survival – things he didn't see himself doing until he actually did them. At this point in his life, it was more than protecting all the women that may cross this sinister, perverted woman's path. It was a matter of protecting his own life, too.

And so, with all the might he could muster, he leapt toward Enver unarmed, causing them both to collapse into the death below their feet. Vlayn lodged his right forearm across Enver's neck and began suffocating her.

Enver squirmed and spun around immediately, as if being choked from behind was something she experienced daily. She stood, gripping the young Vlayn by his soiled shirt and throwing him a few feet away from her and into the pile of dead bodies. Enver drew her pistol while walking over the corpses and hastily fired one bullet, but she was unsuccessful. The bullet barely skimmed Vlayn and landed into a skull of a body. The head exploded upon impact, smothering Vlayn in lumpy, dark blood.

Vlayn noticed Enver ready to shoot another bullet, so he sprung to his feet and plunged toward her again. The two fell onto the bodies with Enver following up with multiple fists to Vlayn's face. She instantly bruised his eye socket and drew an endless rain of blood from him.

Vlayn ended up on the bottom of Enver, being pinned down forcefully; she pressed her hands into Vlayn's neck. He gasped for air but couldn't catch a breath. All he could see was the filthy, rugged face of a woman living in her sins – a woman growing close to the most ominous, evil man in all of the Kirbinian Galaxy: Nydek Urlon.

Vlayn managed to swipe Enver's hands from his throat, evading death. But Enver was consumed in rage, for Vlayn had the audacity to try to kill her. Enver didn't wait a second. She gripped Vlayn's right arm and swung it around his own neck. She pulled Vlayn's arm tight, choking him with his own limb. Then, Enver turned Vlayn's body over and shoved his face into the corpses, suffocating him.

Vlayn shrieked in pain as he was drowning in death. His cries were muffled, but he continued to shriek, trying to breathe through the bodies that smothered him.

Enver smiled malevolently at the sight from above him. Soon, Vlayn's body became still and almost lifeless. She exhaled sharply and stood above the young man. She looked at him shortly and began to walk off while holstering her pistol.

Vlayn's head was still submerged in the dead carcasses, controlling his breathing. He was living. But he didn't want to alert Enver that he wasn't dead. At the same time, he couldn't risk her escaping.

Vlayn slowly got to his feet, swaying slightly from the fight. Warm blood streamed down his face, but he showed no care. Vlayn turned around quietly, observing Enver walking over the mountains of lifeless bodies. He knew Enver was far stronger than he was. She could kill him in an instant. She was an astute survivor of Jaadakin County, while Vlayn was simply a young man, unexperienced in this harsh world. But he remembered his own journey and where he came from.

His mind naturally recited the long journey he was forced to take with his brother to find a doctor in Witherhart just recently. Blood didn't cover his hands at that time. He hid away from all the dangers of Xenamus in his seedy apartment complex with his family. But he was forced to venture off in Witherhart to find a doctor to save his mother's life. His brother almost got raped on this journey; Vlayn had to kill the rapist to save Tithen. He was forced to choke a doctor to death who stole from him. He had to brutally kill three marauders to protect himself and his little brother when they were trapped in a shack. Vlayn was pushed to face the cruel world of Xenamus. He had to grow up. However, after killing his brother to avoid suffering, he felt as if he retreated back under his skin to avoid the cruelties of Xenamus.

But Vlayn was alone.

No one would protect him. Only himself.

There was no avoiding the horrors of this planet. The only thing to do was face them. To be resilient. To overcome hardships and to navigate the calamities that would inevitably afflict him later. To try to find peace within himself in a world that was chaotic. To try to love, even after being heartbroken by the world. To keep moving, even if no one was there to support him. To strengthen his skin. To sharpen his knuckles.

Enver posed a threat to his life, and the lives of many others. It was time to rise up to the test of life.

Vlayn summoned all the courage within him, stepped over the corpses with speed and delved atop Enver once more. Vlayn screamed with all this might and mounted her. He unleashed a fury of punches to her face. He felt as if nothing could bring him down. Nothing could kill him.

Enver was shocked and certain she took Vlayn's life.

But she didn't.

Vlayn continued to beat Enver senseless.

She tried to break away, but Vlayn wouldn't give her an opportunity. His life hung in the balance, and if he even let the slightest chance of Enver getting up to her feet, his life was certainly over. And so, Vlayn yanked her hair and transferred his hands to her neck, beginning to block off oxygen to her lungs with a tight choke.

Vlayn had the eyes of a killer while glaring at Enver. His thumbs pressed hard into her neck, soon emitting traces of blood.

But Vlayn didn't let up.

He was close.

Vlayn screamed while on top of the killer and rapist. After some time though, Vlayn knew he wasn't strong enough to choke Enver to death. He swiped Enver's pistol that was holstered at her hip and stood up courageously with the barrel pointed at Enver's head as she lay sprawled out.

The memory of himself holding the pistol up to Tithen's head as he, just like she was similarly mimicking, lay on the floor of his old bedroom, dying, sprung into Vlayn's mind. This moment, with the pistol raised to Enver's head evoked terrifying memories. But it was in the past. Vlayn needed to pull the trigger to save his life. His brother, Tithen, was gone. His mother had passed, and his father starved, even though he was forced to mutilate him to eat.

Life was always a test on Xenamus. It tested its inhabitants to see if they had what it took to stay alive. To see if they would do whatever was necessary to save their own lives and to keep those they loved alive. The only way for Vlayn to pass this test was to pull the trigger at this moment.

Vlayn could see his little brother laying on the floor in a pool of blood as he suffered from the Glithémien Disease. He could see him coughing and dying. He could see the outline of him within Enver Rodge as she lay on the mountains of dead bodies that once belonged to the people that she sentenced to death. Vlayn knew he was hallucinating.

Vlayn shot the pistol, unleashing a furious shot. This time, though, he wasn't terrified like he was before. He was calm while he grew immune to the heinous planet, but more specifically, those around him.

He studied the corpse of Enver. Tithen's lifeless body seemed to disappear within it, for he no longer saw it. Vlayn inhaled quickly and exhaled heavily. He passed the test this time. But what was he living for? What was the point? He just saved his own life, but was immediately questioning the importance of it. Something was stringing him along. He didn't know what yet.

Vlayn slowly wobbled off the piles of dead bodies and onto the stone floor. He slipped over wet loins on the floor and plummeted to the floor. He yelped painfully then wiped his bloody cheek.

He knew Xenamus would continue to batter his soul – cornering him to kill and draw blood – compelling him to escape his inner sanctum of security and into the indulgences of the callous Jaadakin County. Life on this planet would continue to throw obstacles in Vlayn's path to ensure he was worthy of being alive. His brown eyes met with the dark, lofty ceiling above him.

What was next?

-Four-

LIFE ABOVE THE SAND

Seventy jaros later.

One jaro on Xenamus roughly equaled four months on Earth, but living in the ravished lands of Jaadakin County evoked the sense that Vlayn had been suffering for hundreds of jaros.

A thick, sagging beard dangled depressingly from Vlayn's aging face. He wore the same boots, with just a few more tears in them. Black pants and a long-sleeved shirt clung to his sweltered skin, both revealing and emphasizing his biceps and shoulders; muscles that were easily obtained from living the physical life of a Jaadakin.

His feet dragged along with the slow movement of his body. He breathed lifelessly as his eyes absorbed his typical surroundings. Each bloodshed and act of survival that was built upon the killing of Tithen made him increasingly cold and distant from the threatening world that showed no hesitation or mercy.

The city of Ridgecall welcomed Vlayn each day for the past two decades with the open arms of death, but he pushed those arms aside, and decided to stay alive.

Hopeless souls ambled through the Ridgecall streets, many were alone, some were accompanied by allies made since The Great Fall, and fewer had their family clung to their hips. Out of that group, almost all, including young Babarin children, were intoxicated on booze, paylian, or some other drug, simply to forget the pain of Jaadakin life. Some forgot what it was like to have emotion. The world around them was so unsympathetic, it made their faces freeze to an expressionless mold. They forgot what it felt like for a smile to form on their faces naturally, or for the feeling of pleasure to flourish within them. So, many that walked the streets around Vlayn looked for sex; something to remind them that they were still alive and not a walking corpse.

Vlayn displayed no care to these people, though. The death of his family still seemed recent, but it was over seventy jaros ago. He didn't accept what happened. He ignored the pain and proceeded onward into a seemingly barren landscape; it was an aimless one to anyone else. But to Vlayn, there was an underlying motive beneath all of his troubling anguish…

The Glithémien Disease haunted him. What was it? Where did the disease come from? How was it so powerful that it had the ability to wipe out a person's life within a day? Tithen was obliterated by it. It sprinted wildly through bodies and immune systems, wrecking everything in its path without hesitation.

Soon, a gun shot rang through the dusty atmosphere. Then another. Not one person on the road flinched, and Vlayn made his way to the sound.

There was Camrynn Ansheen, laying out five pillagers as they whimpered on their knees. A long, beige coat was tied around her waist, revealing a soddened tank top.

Boots clung to her feet and ankles. The long laces tightly gripped them and were tied all the way up her calves, protecting them from the filth and bacteria that inhabited the streets of this major city. She quickly glanced back at Vlayn, then raised the Clena 441 pistol yet again to the next person's head and shot him dead.

"Here, take this," Camrynn said quickly as she handed the pistol off to Vlayn. She then drew a sharp, small bloody blade from her hip. She bent down, grabbed the back of the man's neck, and slit his throat. She rose to her feet.

"Camrynn," Vlayn called, unaffected by this scene.

She swiftly looked back at Vlayn while proceeding to the next man. Camrynn was busy, but she turned to Vlayn quickly to keep him satisfied, "What?" she asked.

The last hostage jumped to his feet and began to run after noticing her distraction. Camrynn's head swung back around and ran full-force to catch the hostage. She jumped onto the man and quickly jabbed her knife into his torso. The man immediately fell to the street and writhed on the ground in agonizing pain. Blood spewed out of his chest, and with it, his intestines. He grabbed them as they dangled out of his body. His eyes widened, but he couldn't say a word, for he gargled on his blood. Camrynn took a few steps back. She wasn't even expecting this much of a messy killing.

Vlayn was intently watching Camrynn, but his eyes still wandered from the scene as his fatigue victoriously controlled his body. He studied the natives of Ridgecall as they walked passed him casually. Many sat alongside the road, and some turned to look at the scene. Many leaned against buildings and sat on curbs as they took their hourly gronotine-opium – a natural substance found in the cave networks of caves on the planet of Tabascuu. Mixed with opium, it yielded a very addictive narcotic, allowing these natives to live in another dimension that wasn't this one. Paylian rolls were simply used to chase these narcotics.

Vlayn's eyes perused these people until they ambled onward to the corroding buildings that had their foundations and frames snapping out of place. Window frames were cracked while concrete and dust particles drizzled from the sides as the structures withered away. The tired flames at the ends of the natives' sticks died out, while they desperately searched for hope on a planet that was hopeless.

Eroded tin signs were screwed into the sides of almost every building. Rust flourished on the corners and edges of the signs. This bronze corrosion advanced on the signs, covering the decals and words, but Vlayn was still able to make out what it was attempting to convey:

JOIN THE ELLMORIAN BLACKGUARD AND LIVE AWAY FROM THE HORRORS OF JAADAKIN COUNTY! LIVE THE LIFE YOU'VE ALWAYS WANTED!

Duplicates of this sign were posted all over Ridgecall and many other major cities in Jaadakin County as well. The Ellmorian Blackguard was a private militia that hailed from majestic city of Ellmorr. The group was radical and believed the Ellmorian people were sacred compared to the "feral beasts" who lived in Jaadakin County. The Blackguard was devoted to wiping out the Jaadakin people, but they were open to enlisting those from Jaadakin County into their army.

Vlayn knew this warped way of thinking. He understood that these scums truly felt that Jaadakin County natives were inferior to anyone living on the

Fraygen Plateau. He studied the heinous words from afar (*LIVE THE LIFE YOU'VE ALWAYS WANTED!*), knowing that in the minds of these radicals, Jaadakins envied Ellmorians, and the only way to gain access to the blossoming city was to join a group of them and murder innocent Jaadakin people.

Camrynn breathed heavily, which snapped Vlayn out of his haze. She stood above the man she had just gutted.

Vlayn was quiet. He wasn't in shock and exhausted. He looked down at the Clena in his hand. He pulled out the magazine. Empty. Vlayn sighed with frustration. "Camrynn," he called again.

This time, she answered his call. She looked over the seven men she killed and went over to Vlayn.

"It's time to leave," he said to her.

"No, no. Not yet. Not after I just protected this city from these assholes," she said, pointing back to the dead hostages as she made her way to him.

Vlayn ogled Camrynn, walking from the people she just killed. He couldn't keep his eyes off her. She was just a few jaros younger than Vlayn and there was a sly twinkle in her eyes that drew him in. She was captivatingly attractive and had a small waist that begged for Vlayn to wrap his arms around it. He wouldn't, though. He fought the urge to do this. He had to maintain his composure toward Jaadakin County and its inhabitants. But Camrynn was different for him, and she always was. Vlayn could never understand why, and his curiosity nettled him.

"Well you wanna' live, don't you?" he asked her tenderly. "This place is crawling with glithémien. Yeah, one or two crawlin' down the street is nothing harmful, but look down the alleyways… They're in herds of hundreds, eating corpses, chasing people down. They move quickly when they're together. We're not getting trapped by those little fuckers. I'm sure as hell not risking myself getting bit by one or two on the street."

Camrynn wiped the grime from her face and threw her sweat to the side. "I don't know where else you want us to go. We should've at least stayed in Kepembold twenty-something jaros ago," she answered. "Ambervale, Witherhart, Woodvale, everywhere else is just the same. Glithémien is tearing people down in every city. No place left to run, but Kepembold was standing, Vlayn. If we travel the deserts we'll eventually get bit by a glithimite. There's no more running, Vlayn. There's no hope."

Vlayn exhaled in disbelief, prompting Camrynn to continue, "We've travelled the deserts of Jaadakin for the past twenty-seven jaros, Vlayn. We jumped from each small settlement to the next. Hell, we met in the open deserts and I saved you from a pack of glithémien, don't you remember?"

Vlayn nodded slowly while glaring off into the distance.

She continued, "I fired wildly on all of them and freed you. Since then, we got so unbelievably lucky that we didn't get run down by another herd, or just got bit by one in our sleep. In the name of Baleejus, Vlayn, don't you remember Mayda Netsereen, Crasch Muron–Muroh – whatever his last name was? Do you remember those two?"

"I know what you're about to say," Vlayn muttered.

"They were in our group. Mayda was bit on her neck and went two whole days with it. Can't you remember *seeing* her open veins at the end of the second day, but she wasn't even bleeding because at that point her blood was *solid*. Crasch – you cut off his damn arm when he was bit on his wrist. This happened in the deserts. Like you just said, we can't take these risks."

Vlayn exhaled heavily. "We can go to Ellmorr," he said hopefully, obviously chewing on this thought for a while.

Camrynn chuckled. "You know they won't let us on the Fraygen Plateau. Even if we tried to sneak in, we wouldn't make it close to the walls. There's N.M.C. forts set up all over the plateau to watch out for people just like us who are trying to make it into the city."

"We need to try," Vlayn said. "Word is getting around that Ellmorr is being funded millions of Credits from Clansee Acuura. There are no glithémien. No sickness – glithémien can't climb the fucking plateau. There's food and water. They're living in luxury while the rest of us struggle to get by each day. Why don't we get to live that type of lifestyle, too?"

"Because we were born in Jaadakin County. Ellmorr isn't our home. We aren't like them," Camrynn replied. She naturally removed herself from the conversation and wandered away from Vlayn.

He gently took her arm and spun her toward him. "We're Babarin. Just like the people in Ellmorr. There's plenty of different people who travel from all over The Galaxy to live in the city, anyway. We'll fit right in."

"You're being too hopeful, Vlayn. It's not happening. We will never get in. You know the N.M.C. guards won't let in anyone from Jaadakin County."

"Because we're poor," Vlayn said.

"Yes. Also, because they won't risk anyone bringing in the Glithémien Disease."

"They have a cure."

"Who?"

"The Plague Doctors in Ellmorr. The ones doing medical research. They won't give it to us. They want us to fucking suffer, but they have a cure for the disease."

"How do you even know this?" Camrynn asked. "Rumors spread insanely throughout Jaadakin County. Who knows what's correct? People get angry and they make up things out of their anger."

"A doctor in Witherhart told me many, many jaros ago, Camrynn. My father made my brother and I go out and hire a doctor for my mother when I was younger. I wasn't too sure of it at first, but since then, I've only heard other dusters talking about this city and all of its medical information and this and that." Vlayn exhaled heavily as he rubbed his beard.

"Why would a doctor tell you this? I–I just don't follow–"

"Why not?" he answered. "What did he really have to lose? Think about it... he was a doctor before The Fall. If there was a cure in Ellmorr, doctors down here would be the first to know about it, right? They got it, Camrynn... And I need to find out what it is. I just need to know. I just need answers. My mother, my fucking brother, Camrynn. They fell to this disease. What could have I done to save them?"

"Nothing, Vlayn," she sprung in to save Vlayn from his worrying thoughts. "You had no idea what was wrong with them. You were just a boy." Vlayn was silent. He knew Camrynn was right. But these thoughts irked him. "You said there's no hope. Look, you're probably right. But the only place I've got left to check is Ellmorr. The only reason to live right now is to get into Ellmorr so I can find out what the Glithémien Disease is and why my family died." Camrynn was quiet, she tossed the idea around in her head, but then said rashly, "Why don't you just join the Ellmorian Blackguard then?"

Vlayn's head retracted in confusion. "Absolutely not. Each band of them is run by some cocky prick. I'm *never* going to take orders from someone like that," he declared. Then, Vlayn stepped closer to Camrynn. "I never want to purposefully put you in danger, Camrynn," he struggled to say softly, but his gravelly voice took over. "You can handle yourself in Jaadakin County, probably better than me. And I know this trip to Ellmorr most likely means death to the both of us, and who even knows if we will get anywhere close to the city. But anything is better than staying in Ridgecall, or anywhere else in Jaadakin and just waiting around to die. And I will never join the Blackguard and be controlled by some other duster, either. You'd never see me again."

Camrynn stood in silence. She peered at the decrepit, rotting buildings of Ridgecall. Natives still walked through the city without a destination in sight. Others marched through the streets, though, rushing to their families or those newly created to protect them from the dangers of the desert and this city.

"I need you to come with me, Camrynn. I can't go alone, or at least I don't want to travel alone," he pled. Vlayn took the Clena, examined it for a second, and stuffed it into the back of his pants where his belt strapped the weapon tightly to his body.

Camrynn breathed louder and looked up at Vlayn with panic. He softly placed his hand on her shoulder and forced a smile. She nodded slowly and her hair fell in front of her eyes. "It's deadly Vlayn –" "It'll be the deadliest trip of our lives, Camrynn. What else do we have down here, though?"

"We'll be cautious – plan our moves. We'll try. But death is likely."

"It's our last hope," Vlayn urged.

-Five-

BROKEN CLOCKS

Asbestos coupled with ohbrizorne festered in the decrepit walls of Vlayn's childhood apartment. The chemicals leaked from the holes in the ceiling, emitting toxic, invisible fumes. He monitored his breathing, taking note of the amount of toxicity he was inhaling. His head hung low, stretching his neck to its full extent. He grazed his coarse hands along his unkempt, overused face then tiredly looked at his fingertips, then his forearms. He noticed every little unevenly healed scar and his resistant skin that endured through each day of battle.

"Were you dreaming, Vlayn?" a voice asked him. "No," he answered quickly.

"Do you ever dream, Vlayn?" the voice asked suspiciously.

"No," Vlayn replied, still keeping his head low.

"You don't?"

"No, I don't," he retaliated as he found himself sitting on top of his ruined bedspring.

"Do you ever dream of other planets?"

"I told you I don't dream," Vlayn said.

"What about The Mother Planet? Or Konlax?" the voice asked further.

"I don't dream," Vlayn responded; "I think, though."

"Well, do you think about those planets? Do you think about how amazing life is everywhere else *but* Jaadakin County? Do you think of how dull life is? How dark and bleak everything is here?" the young voice inquired curiously.

"Of course I do. I—I think of other planets. But that's not the life we have. This is what we have. It's not much… Hell, it isn't anything. But it's what we have," Vlayn said as he stroked his thick beard – a souvenir of becoming an educated survivor of the wastes.

"So, you do dream."

Vlayn lifted his head slowly toward the figure at the opposite end of his outgrown, childhood bedroom.

The young boy sat innocently. His soft, pale Babarin skin gleamed radiantly. His bright eyes spoke softly as he admired Vlayn Par'Wil: a man who appeared to be heartless by his exterior. The boy's sinless smile diffused happiness; a rare trait in the depressed deserts. His clean, shiny, light brown hair flopped freely on his forehead where a deep bullet hole was dug into the center of his forehead. A stream of dried blood stained his shiny skin, once running from the cavity on the top of his head, down to his cheek. The boy displayed his blithe disregard for the conditions he was in; he was smiling, as if there were boundless things to be cheerful about on this lonely planet that stripped its inhabitants of all love and hope.

Vlayn's eyes boiled with tears as his head began to tremble with fright and overwhelming sadness and despair.

"Ti-T-Ti," Vlayn stuttered. He tried to complete his words, but instead he inhaled heavily to collect himself.

The boy was still seated across the rugged, aged Vlayn angelically, and the bright sky shined upon the boy. "Ti-*Tithen?*" Vlayn gasped as the control he had over his life was immediately swept away from him. His left cheek quivered a bit, and he surrendered all the energy within him to his surroundings; he didn't even have the audacity to wipe his tearing eyes.

"So, you dream about better places... better times," Tithen assumed.

"I don't dream, Tithenkeen," Vlayn answered to his hallucinated brother through his tears, "I *think*... I think about you... About our family... I think about the things I could've done differently," he exclaimed through his watering lips, "I think about the things I could've done... Things that may have kept all of us alive. Things I could have done to not be alone today."

"So..." Tithen uttered softly, "you do dream."

Eventually, Vlayn nodded quickly. His head slowly shifted toward the fractured window frame. Through this window he could see the ominously tall buildings of Witherhart as they surrounded the apartment complex in which he once lived. The buildings were clean, polished, and thriving. But his apartment was ragged, filthy, and broken.

Vlayn rose to his feet and drifted toward the window. He peered down below to see bustling crowds of natives. They were all fresh and bright with a destination and a goal. The whole city was draped with elegance and its people held occupations. They were free from illness of any kind and smiled frequently, for there were reasons to be delighted. It was prospering, and this was a rare sight, especially in the real world.

But the clock in this realm was broken.

Vlayn spun his head back to Tithen, who remained seated and still; he smiled joyously with the bullet hole in his head, while showing satisfaction that he was in a better place. Vlayn tried to smile through his thick, rumpled Babarin beard and grungy skin, but nothing showed. Deep down, he was glad.

He retreated back to the window and admired the shocking sight of Witherhart. He smiled slowly until all the color of the buildings and the people beneath him were pulled apart, like wet paint dripping off of a canvas. Then, Vlayn's mind rebuilt this scene into one that was far more sinister and desaturated. He gasped for air without realizing the oxygen wasn't even real.

The buildings faded into spoiled, aged structures, hunching over from numerous jaros of inevitable erosion. The crowds of lively people thinned and their abdomens were sunk into their body. The silky sky converted into the realistic dusty one that revolved with fury around Xenamus. The vile smell of illness and death instantly filled his nostrils.

"No," Vlayn murmured under his breath. He looked down below from the safety of his cramped bedroom. He glanced down below at the narrow alleyway between his apartment building and the neighboring one. A group of cannibals inhabited the alley and huddled around a dim fire with a grate standing over it.

Vlayn recognized this scene. He was here before.

He spun around, looking for Tithen.

His room was empty.

Vlayn slowly raised his hand to his face. He rubbed his chin. He was beardless. Then a rough, gritty cough screamed from another room in his apartment.

Vlayn leapt off-balance at the recognizable noise. He slowly navigated through his bedroom with a fearful, naïve gait of a young man. He was an experienced survivor. But this wasn't real. It couldn't be.

Vlayn made his way down the hallway and into a larger room, where he found Tithen sitting in desperation against the wall with the deep bullet hole no longer in his head. Vlayn's mother sat across his brother on a chair above her own pool of blood. Vlayn's eyes fell back to Tithen. He struggled to call his name. He felt as if he was opening his mouth to shout for his little brother, but not one word escaped his lips.

"How's... how's Mom?" Vlayn asked instead. It was as if he was in his own younger body, trapped like an animal, watching everything unfold from the side.

"She's fine, Vlayn," his father replied abruptly, "now, please, go back to your room."

Vlayn understood why his father would want him to exit the room; a father wouldn't want his son to see his mother suffering. "No, Dad I want to stay –" "Vlayn!" his father shouted with irritation. "Please go back to your room – Tithen, you too."

At that moment, his mother gagged and threw up blood, adding to the wet pool below her feet.

Vlayn retreated to his bedroom, with his father following. "Vlayn," his father began while stepping into the doorway of his bedroom, "you have always been such a strong, brave young Babarin. You have always faced and overcome obstacles that stood in your way. You have shown your little brother how to be – how to be in this world of Xenamus… you know how life is… how to survive –"

"There is no survival, Dad! This is our life… we are fine," Vlayn said forcefully, cutting his father off. It appeared as if he was trying to reassure his father, but deep down, Vlayn was trying to convince himself that what he was saying was true.

But the older Vlayn – the spectator – knew everything he was saying was all wrong. He knew that no matter how bad it got, no one was ever fine, and no matter how great life may have grown to become, it never lasted very long. But at this moment in his past, as a young Babarin man, he was hopeful.

"Son, I know what it is like growing up on Xenamus. Survival is life." He lowered his head and got closer to his son. "I have always done what I needed to do in order to keep this family alive. That…" he hesitated and looked around the bedroom hastily, "that is life. That is my life. That will be *your* life. And it will come sooner than you think."

Vlayn was confounded; he already knew that was how life was. He had experienced all of the horrors of Jaadakin County already. Why was he back here in his childhood?

There was a pause.

Vlayn moved from this confusion to somewhere close to placid. He was silently absorbing all of the information his father was spewing out.

"I have had to do certain things for us to live – I took the lives of others to protect us. I have sacrificed my meals and gave it to you and your brother so you could have food in your stomach. I have literally given the clothes off my back and gave them to you and Tithenkeen, even if they were just torn rags, so you two were warm during the night. I have done these things just so we could all be *alive*," his father said, "Life is a test. Xenamus tests us. Sees if we got what it takes to survive. To keep those we love alive."

Deep in his mind, Vlayn didn't want to respond. But the course of history seemed to be predetermined. "That isn't all of life, Dad," a youthful Vlayn shot out. "There's a whole different lifestyle outside of Jaadakin County. The Fraygen Plateau, where the city of Ellmorr is, the life there is completely opposite. They don't wake up each day and fight to stay alive. Fight starvation, fight thirst... and fight others. The people who live in Ellmorr don't need to do that."

"Son..."

"You don't need to kill to survive, Dad."

"I never used the word kill," his father said correctively.

"That's what you implied, Dad. I'm young, but not stupid. I know the people of Xenamus kill to live. But we don't need to. There's hope for all of us. There has to be." A strong mix of impatience and rage surged in his veins, but it wasn't apparent on his face. As an older Vlayn, hearing what his younger-self was saying, he immediately grew frustrated at the words he once said many jaros ago.

Of course one must kill to survive. *Of course* there was no hope. These were all clear facts that nomads and survivors of Jaadakin witnessed each passing day. Vlayn was one with Jaadakin survivors and he knew all these notions to be true. So, if he was in his right mind and correctly-aged body, he wouldn't dare murmur such words. It was almost a sin to. But peculiar feelings sparked in his subconscious mind. Vlayn knew he wasn't where he was.

His father wiped his face and cleared his throat. A younger Vlayn explored his father's face; each crevasse, scar, and how his stagnant facial expression withheld a silent agony.

"Vlayn..." he spoke gently, "I was just like you. I didn't want to believe that life on this planet could be as cruel and harsh as it is... but it is. You will come to realize that. On Kirbinian World, where The Palace is, their life is different. In those cities, life is better than ours. Planets like Reft, Dexaan, and Flom, for example, are wealthy planets. The people live there comfortably. Not in fear. But it's what we have to deal with, son. The life we have... is the life we have. We can't change it. We can only accept where we are and fight every single thing that tries to take us down. Whether it's starvation, disease, or people. I understand it's harsh, Vlayn. One day you'll change and adapt. You will. You are so strong. Don't confuse pure survival with pure evil. Don't become like those people down below. Kill only to protect yourself and those you love. Many lose their sanity when they're out in the deserts for too long."

"Dad... we don't need to kill."

His father didn't respond. He knew his son wouldn't understand quite yet. However, experiences would mold this young man into a keen survivor. "Your mother," he began to tell his son, "as you can tell, isn't looking too good... I don't know what's wrong with her. She's dying, son. Listen, there's a medicine shop about a quarter of a mile south down the cobblestone road... you're old enough. Vlayn you need to get there, see if there is a doctor for hire." His father paused and pulled out a small wad of Credits. "This is 100 Credits. This is everything we own – right here," he said, "get a doctor here. It is the best opportunity for your Mom to live."

"Dad, I'm not going down there. I... I–I can't. It's way too dangerous," Vlayn responded timidly. The present Vlayn simmered with annoyance at the sound of those cowardly words.

"Son, I believe in you. You will survive," his father said. He walked out of the room for a moment and came back with an old Nabbuu 88 pistol.

Vlayn saw the gun and exclaimed, "No, we don't need to kill!"

"It isn't killing, Vlayn. It's protection," his father responded.

Vlayn's face fell into the sweaty palms of his hands and he shut his eyes powerfully. His surroundings were now black and everything was silent. A small orange light danced in the darkness that was spawned by the absence of his sight. Vlayn could feel his face relaxing. His breathing slowed and calmed. His eyes were still closed, and it seemed like he wasn't alive.

The supposed world around him kept quiet for a short while, diffidently observing Vlayn's examination of the tiny orange light that skipped throughout the darkness.

Is that a fire? Vlayn thought to himself.

Suddenly, a strong, warm wind blasted Vlayn, carrying sand particles that punctured his skin like miniature daggers. He immediately lifted his face from his palms.

His father was gone. Vlayn wasn't in his childhood bedroom, but he certainly wasn't back in reality.

Two buildings sprouted upward from the ground below him, standing intimidatingly tall above him; one to his left and one to his right. A tight alleyway was drawn out before his feet and an intense scent of blood and gore harmonized with the stale smell of the dusty atmosphere. Vlayn recognized this scene, though. It was a matter of minutes since he had left his apartment with his younger brother under orders from his father to retrieve a doctor to aid their dying mother.

Vlayn was a young man. He was uncertain of the treacherous surroundings that was Jaadakin County. He was safe all his life prior to this event, behind the safety of the apartment complex; it was masked from the perilous fright, disease, and raw survival that everyone else in the County had to face. It was a matter of time, though, before Vlayn had to face all of it, and he was forced to face it at a young age. Vlayn was reliving the moments.

His memory grew more vivid as his past began to load quicker. Corpses began to clutter the alley and the vile stench of death contaminated the breathing air. Then, as his brain reloaded this memory, a clear picture showed a tall babarin man thirty feet in front of Vlayn. He wore a black hood with slits cut out for his eyes, and Vlayn could smell the man's murky stench steaming from his skin.

It seemed as if the ground was rumbling. Vlayn gasped for air as his legs wobbled with fear. He recognized this demonic man. He couldn't exactly recall the events from his past, but he knew it had something to do with Tithen.

What're you two boys doin' out here all by yourselves? Vlayn could hear those words echoing in the air of Witherhart, but there was no source. He tried to move closer to the man who stood solidly, not moving a muscle. Vlayn's legs couldn't move, though. It was as if they were locked in place. The course of history had already been decided.

What're you two boys doin' out here all by yourselves? he heard again. He recognized the voice. But at this moment, it seemed as if the entire Kirbinian Galaxy and every life-force – both almighty and mortal – were uttering these words.

Then, the memory hit Vlayn. He turned around to find Tithen, but Tithen wasn't there. His eyes fell back to the menacing man in front of him, only to see Tithen captured by this hooded marauder with a pistol on Tithen's head.

Vlayn tried to scream to Tithen, but his lips wouldn't budge and his vocal chords were mute.

Everything grew increasingly quiet. The wind halted. The voices from the main road behind Vlayn grew quiet. It was as if Xenamus ceased its rotation on its axis. Then, the play button was pressed, and his history resumed.

"You going to stay there... right?" the man asked.

Vlayn wanted to say "no" to this babarin and pull out a sharp blade and cut this psychotic man's limbs off and feed them to him. But he wasn't that bold at the time. He was merely a young man and most certainly not a killer yet.

Instead, Vlayn nodded quickly, petrified. His head quivered slightly as his eyes submerged in tears. He stared at the man with disheartenment, and the deranged killer returned the look, but his eyes were filled with madness.

The door fell off its hinges, and the man pulled the gun off Tithen's head and fired a bullet into Vlayn's leg.

Immediately he collapsed to the ground in pain, shrieking with terror. "No!!!" Vlayn could hear Tithen shout.

"Now I know you won't be going anywhere," the man announced joyously while yanking Tithen away by his neck.

Vlayn scrambled on the ground, trying to cover the gaping hole in his leg with just his bare hands. Blood drained from the crater in his thigh as the dirt from the pavement below him clung to his sticky, almost paper-thin skin. An overwhelming pain pumped through his skin and crashed right into his heart. He couldn't even move his leg at first. But the pain of losing Tithen was far worse and more motivating for him to move. Through his dimming eyesight, he could make out the Nabbuu 88 his father gave him ten feet ahead, but it was too far of a crawl for him.

He glanced to his left, noticing a rusty machete hidden behind a dumpster and a number of corpses. Vlayn knew the weapon was likely stashed behind the bin for someone who would need it at a later date. But Vlayn didn't care.

He made way to the blade.

Vlayn extended his arm as far as he could underneath the steel dumpster, trying to obtain the machete. He could feel his energy and life being swept away with the blood that gushed from his leg, but he wouldn't give up. While sprawled on his back and half his body submerged underneath the dumpster, he raised his head every so often to keep watch on the main pathway of Witherhart. He knew that any natives of the city would see Vlayn's vulnerability in this alleyway and could take advantage of it if they wanted.

Finally, he obtained the machete, and he could instantly feel himself coming back to life; adrenaline coursed through his veins as he hopped to his feeble legs. The bloody mess below him was terrifying, but he couldn't mourn over it. There was no time. A small, rectangular note was tied to the handle of the old machete, but Vlayn pulled it off the handle and stuffed it into his pocket.

He limped over to the back of one of the buildings where Tithen was taken hostage. He tightly gripped the handle of the weapon, for it was the only thing he could truly feel. A series of metal stairs led up to a door at the top that was left open a crack. Vlayn began to hobble up the stairs that sizzled in the desert heat. He could feel this blistering warmth from the Xenamus sun being soaked up by his resistant skin. He made it up five steps until he collapsed in pain, gripping his gunshot wound while glaring at the top of the stairs. Only a few more to go, but it seemed to be as high as the Klapaytch Mountains.

He inhaled sharply as his head revolved in circles. The sun stared at him blaringly. Vlayn squinted, trying to look away from the brightness, but he couldn't take his eyes off the rays. Everything around him finally descended back into its colorless state of grief that was always encumbered by a determined wind. Vlayn persevered, though, knowing Tithenkeen was in that room and in imminent danger.

He climbed up the next few stairs and, without hesitation, threw himself into the room.

Tithen was pinned down to a torn mattress with the man standing above him with his pants unstrapped, and the hood still masking his face. With all his might, Vlayn shrieked and exerted all his power into one slash of the machete. The blade precisely sliced through the man's torso, splitting it into two chunks, creating a torrent of blood and guts.

Vlayn tumbled to the floor and the man's legs collapsed next to him. His vision turned black and muted. The orange light danced around the darkness of Vlayn's mind again. This time, though, it was accompanied by a soft voice. "Vlayn," he could hear it call in the dark. Vlayn recognized the voice. He felt a sudden shot of compassion and safety at the sound, but he couldn't seem to place a finger on who it was, and he couldn't chase it, for he wasn't in the realm that the voice originated from.

Vlayn could smell musty air before his eyes even reopened. His head sprung backward at the pungent odor. His eyes popped open, only to find himself hiding under a table with his brother to his left and a foreign man laying prone to his left. Vlayn was growing more confounded as his memories pushed him to skip through his past.

Then, it hit him: it was a mere thirty minutes after being shot in the leg by the maniacal rapist with the black hood. The man laying prone next to him on the floor was Greth Madeen, the Babarin doctor the brothers found for their mother. Events changed, though. Upon entering this medicine shack on the side of the cobblestone road in Witherhart, Greth broke the news to Vlayn and Tithen that their mother was dying from Glithémien Disease based on the symptoms Vlayn described. Being unfamiliar with this disease and hearing it for the first time, Vlayn asked for more information. Greth told him there was no cure in Jaadakin County, and further said that Ellmorr had obtained a cure but wouldn't share it with Jaadakin County.

Greth persuaded Vlayn in telling him his mother would die regardless if she had a doctor inspect her or not, and Vlayn would also die from his gunshot wound's blood loss. Vlayn paid the doctor to patch his wound with the Credits supplied by his father. After doing his best to fix Vlayn's wound with the minimal medical supplies he had, he snatched the entire wad of money instead of the agreed upon amount. Vlayn threatened Greth to return the Credits, until a group of marauders on the street banged on the front door. Vlayn, Tithen, and Greth retreated to the back room and hid under a table, ready to fight for their lives.

The memories hit Vlayn like hurling rocks. All these events occurred jaros ago, but reliving them was painful.

"I'll kill you both after this," Vlayn could hear Greth promising.

Vlayn's blood boiled. He knew he could mutilate this man if he came across him in current-jaro.

At this time though, he was still very young.

In this dream-world, neither Vlayn or Tithen said a word. The young Vlayn plotted his next move to survive, while Greth Madeen continued to seek his vengeance on this cruel planet through his words and his violence. Indeed, Xenamus had tortured, harassed, and inflicted various forms of pain on this aged man, and it was just beginning to assault Vlayn at this time.

"We need to move. Can't stay here," Vlayn spoke furtively to his brother.

"No point," Greth interjected. "You'll both be dead anyway."

Vlayn crawled closer to Greth underneath the table. "What the hell man? You fix me and then you kill me??? What kind of logic is that???" he whispered aggressively even though he could feel his wound slowly bleeding, sullying the numerously swathed bandages.

"Yes," Greth responded curtly.

"What??? What does that even *mean??? Why???* That's so stupid. It's a waste of your materials," he attempted to persuade. Lacking fighting skills, Vlayn would try to say anything to keep himself and Tithen alive.

"Sure, it is, but at least you'll be saved from the horrors you'd be experiencing the rest of your life on Xenamus. I'm tellin' you kid, whatever you've witnessed so far..." he looked to his left at the prone Vlayn, "it only gets worse," Greth promised.

He crawled back over to Tithen.

More banging on the front door echoed throughout the hollow shack.

"What are we going to do?" the voice of the innocent, young boy asked.

Vlayn hesitated a moment and turned to Tithen. "I'll– I'll kill him," he whispered so low, he almost mouthed it to him.

Greth got to his feet and slowly made his way to the open doorway that led to the front of the wooden shack.

The young Vlayn held a tight, long piece of cloth in his sweaty palms that he tore from the tablecloth that dressed the table he was hiding under. He swiftly rose to his feet and skipped weakly behind Greth. Without a thought, he wrapped the long rope around the man's neck and choked him, exerting all his energy into this killing.

The choker and the choked subsided to the floor. Vlayn inhaled deeply, calibrating his mind to kill this man and protect Tithen. The pair rolled on the floor. Greth squirmed and tried to fight back to defend his life, but he was pinned by Vlayn.

Soon, his face altered to an increasing blue tone, and his life swiftly belonged to Vlayn Par'Wil.

Vlayn jumped to his feet, staggering over his weak leg, observing the dead man below him with a cold face. He immediately looked back at Tithen to see if he was safe. At the same time though, he wanted to ensure Tithen wasn't mortified of the animal he knew he was transitioning into.

Vlayn! a raised, female voice cried.

Vlayn spun around in circles in the shack, looking for the voice's source.

No one turned up and Tithen remained locked in place underneath the table, as if he wasn't real.

Something prompted Vlayn to reach into his pocket and retrieve the note that was on the machete; almost like a spiritual, almighty figure was with him in this room, lifting his arm and moving it to his pocket. His bloody, mucky fingers slowly unfolded the soft paper in front of his eyes. There were a few words written hastily and lopsided on the small page:

EaT HIM aNd YoU caN leave

Vlayn! the voice called again. Vlayn's head perched up at the sound. The same orange light appeared in the corner of the shack. It drew Vlayn closer while serenity washed over the shack.

What happened to the marauders trying to break in?

Everything paused.

The orange light blurred until it completely faded. Soon, his vision dimmed. He knew the routine; he was being moved to another point in his history.

Vlayn shook his body and kicked his legs back and forth in response, as if he was trying to wake himself. He felt his right leg kicking with force, but in this dreamscape, not a single bone in his body budged.

His surroundings descended into the earth below his feet, and thick walls emerged from the ground up, quickly circumscribing him and creating a cramped bedroom. Ohbrizorne grew inside the walls, a snapped bedspring appeared behind him, and the rest of his quiet apartment complex greeted him. This was his old home. Vlayn walked cautiously through his bedroom, scanning his surroundings until he noticed something.

His thick, scraggy beard was back. It veiled his face, protected him, and instantly gave him the strength of a Jaadakin survivor.

Was this even a dream?

Or was he actually here?

Vlayn exited the bedroom and drifted toward the den.

The entire apartment instantaneously entered darkness. A grey, eerie light mysteriously illuminated the room while his boots clicked against the hardwood floor with each step. Vlayn carried himself confidently; if his beard was back, he was no longer a boy. He was no longer in his nightmares. He could carry himself with confidence in his ability to protect himself and draw blood with ease.

Suddenly, as the den took shape in front of him, his dead mother sat in a wooden chair that was warping in toward the center, accompanied by the odd grey light slightly brightening the scene.

Mother, he thought to himself, seeing the light partially casted on the slouching corpse in the center of the dark room. A pool of dried blood absorbed her feet. Her disheveled, parched skin stuck to her decayed bones. The Glithémien Disease had taken her down, just like Greth Madeen said it would.

Jaadakin County won.

Ellmorr won.

They were taking innocent lives with their overwhelming arrogance. Only if they sent the N.M.C. out into the deserts of Jaadakin with the cure, then people could live. The people would have a chance for a better life than the one they battled with every passing day. The deserts would slowly become civilized again and would return to how it all once was before The Great Fall.

Vlayn's mother could've lived.

His father could've lived.

Vlayn reached for his face and softly tugged on his beard. But soon, his thick facial hair slipped through his fingers and sunk back into his skin, revealing his young Babarin skin. Then, he glanced down at his legs. His pants were soiled with dry blood and his wound was fresh again with bandages wrapping it.

He spun around and glanced at his bedroom doorway.

He was back.

Vlayn ran into his room.

There his little brother sat on the floor, leaning against the wall. His head hung with loneliness. Their father lay on his bedspring with a note next to his side. Vlayn knew exactly what the note read. He saw this note countless times, both in person and in his thoughts over the jaros of his life after this event. He had read it time and time again.

Still, though, he picked it up and read it:

To my dearest sons, Vlayn & Tithenkeen,

I cannot express how lucky and proud I am to be able to say you two are my sons. You both are a blessing in my life. Everything you both have done has made me very happy, proud, and lucky. You boys never cease to amaze me. I am not able to begin to tell you both the guilt I feel for leaving you two behind in Xenamus alone. Hopefully the High Clansees of the Kirbinian Galaxy will support you two as you grow up. When the county bounces back from the disease, I know you both will grow up to accomplish wondrous things and you will assist Jaadakin County in reviving itself.

I wish I could see you two. I am confident you boys will make it back here safe from the medicine shop. Your loving mother unfortunately passed away fifteen-or-so minutes ago. Whatever illness she had killed her. I am next to go. It is starvation for me though. That is what will take me down. I'm sorry I can't be around to see you boys. No matter how hard life is here on Xenamus, always stay true to yourself because it is so easy to let the life we live change us. Because it can change us instantly without us even realizing. Just know that in my last waking moments, I am thinking of the two of you.

Love, Dad.

Vlayn looked closely at each word, observing the characters that dressed the words. Tears swelled in his eyes and he glanced over to Tithen, sitting quietly, submerged in the sadness of Xenamus until he coughed viciously.

"Hungry, right?" Vlayn inquired while wiping his eyes. He knew the answer though. He had been through this once before. He knew what he was soon going to do. What he *had* to do.

Tithen didn't respond.

"I'm hungry, too," Vlayn told him.

The white sky precipitated into its pragmatic, dull atmosphere, dusting the planet's surface with its dreariness that fertilized the land for its violence. It was late-evening, but the sky moved at an alarming rate toward an overlying darkness that nighttime brought; a speed that was impossible in real time.

Tithen sat quietly without noticing the abnormally altering sky above the apartment. Vlayn noticed, though, because this was his world. He ambled toward the shattered window frame of his bedroom. A group of men and women huddled together down in the alleyway. The group stood five feet from a ferocious fire to avoid the dipping temperatures of the night desert.

Beside the fire, a man hacked away at a dead body while two women assisted the man in maiming the cold corpse. Finally, the man severed a limb, lifted the heavy flesh, and tossed it on a metal grate that stood above the large bonfire. The flesh roasted in the energetic flames. And above the mutilated body, more cannibals gnawed at flesh to keep themselves as far away from starvation as possible.

Just like the Glithémien Disease, cannibalism plagued the major cities of Jaadakin County. Genuine food ran scarce throughout the deserts. One of the remaining things to do to keep the people alive was to feed themselves with the last thing they could get their hands on: themselves.

For jaros of Vlayn's childhood, he hid behind the windows of his bedroom, observing the barbarism and cruelty of the streets of Witherhart below him. He always analyzed everything from above. At this moment of Vlayn's life, even though he was above all the horrors, he was alongside them. Throughout the jaros, the person Vlayn became was similar to those that were down in the alley.

Vlayn spun around. Tithen sat tiredly on the floor, for hunger had stricken him and had sucked all the energy from his bones. Vlayn's stomach rumbled, too. His eyes drifted to his deceased father, then to his little brother.

He had to protect Tithen's life.

His feet trudged forward slowly, scraping the debris on the floor. Vlayn knew what was about to transpire. He did everything he could to stop himself from walking forward, but there was no changing the events.

His slow-moving legs accelerated into a weak jog into the other room. Across Vlayn's brittle mother was a gaping hole in the sheetrock. He dropped to his knees and scrambled for a set of dry logs. He retreated to his bedroom and laid the logs on the floor. He immediately ran back over to the bed and retrieved a book of matches.

Immediately, he bent down and attempted to ignite the logs on the floor. "Vlayn there's only three matches left," his brother warned him with a weak tongue. But Vlayn ignored Tithen and proceeded to light a match quickly. He scratched it swiftly over the box repeatedly until it struck. The match head sizzled and casted a fumy orange light over Vlayn's face. He wobbled over to the catty-cornered logs and attempted to light it, but before he could bend down, the match died.

"Vlayn – you're going to waste the matches!"

Vlayn turned around, "So help me!" he yelled back in despair. His eyes were red and watered relentlessly. The young Babarin man's face was covered in filth and a small splash of dried blood was underneath his chin– a true survivor.

"How do you want me to help you!?" Tithen responded with an equal amount of desperation. There was nothing left for the two of them. Nothing. Vlayn felt the loneliness of his life. The extreme pain was premature, and it overcame him without hesitation. Vlayn knew what he was about to do and what he was going to do after these events.

Vlayn felt himself observing from the sidelines of his own body. It felt even worse, though, because Vlayn knew for the many jaros later after these events with Tithen, there was seemingly nothing for Vlayn, beside an almost unattainable loophole in the single rule of Jaadakin County since The Great Fall: draw blood, or someone will drain yours. This loophole was simple, and every duster knew of it, but not many were daring enough to even try.

This way out was sneaking into Ellmorr. There were very few ways to gain entry without being spotted by N.M.C. patrols; one way was to have an insider in the N.M.C on Xenamus. Someone who could obtain intel regarding patrol routes and times on the plateau, where to steal land vehicles and receive makeshift Division B Recognition Passes to gain entry into the city. One mere

N.M.C. soldier would do. But Vlayn hadn't any connections. Still, he would rather risk his life and try, then to stay in Jaadakin County where there was truly nothing to live for.

Vlayn dropped to his knees and sprawled toward his bedspring. He stretched his arm underneath for old magazines that his father passed down to him. Without even glancing at them, he crumpled them up and fashioned them underneath the logs. He lit one of the last matches and slowly lowered it to the paper. The paper immediately caught flames, and soon the logs lit. The fire grew larger by the second as Vlayn blew on the flames.

"Why are we lighting a fire?" Tithen asked. Confusion and hunger overwhelmed the poor boy to the point where his eyes teared. Vlayn didn't answer right away, though. He stood above the fire, staring down at his feet.

"Vlayn!"

Vlayn remained silent. Noise from the cannibals in the alleyway grew louder, cluttering the air in the bedroom. The bonfire from outside continued to hauntingly illuminate a portion of this room that casted an uncanny feeling in their darkening hearts. Vlayn left the room and came back with a dull axe the family once used for additional protection. Every household in Jaadakin County had something similar to this. Commonly, families had a few guns and a substantial amount of ammunition. Almost all had started their weapon collection before The Fall, but since life declined in the deserts, households would get their filthy hands on a sharp object, in case ammunition ran scarce. Vlayn looked at his family's sharp object: the axe. He knew the axe's life was over.

"Vlayn," Tithen called again.

Vlayn walked over to his dead father. He gripped his father's left calf with one hand while the other firmly held the splintered wooden handle. His sweaty palms slid along the wood, creating a weak grip.

"Vlayn... what're you doing?" Tithenkeen asked cautiously.

Vlayn stood to the side of his bed, still pinning his father's leg down. He stared back at his brother, with the bit of the axe head resting on the man's hairy legs. The growing fire behind him illuminated half of Vlayn's face. He continued to stare at his younger brother with guilt, remorse, sorrow, fear, and coldness – feelings he would hold on to for jaros and jaros later. He didn't blink. He didn't breathe. Nothing was left for the two siblings. Vlayn wished he could give his little brother more. He felt horrible that his father had passed away and that he couldn't give his youngest son the life he knew he deserved – a life he deserved, too.

Vlayn was swelling with pure anger toward Xenamus. He was infuriated with the Kirbinian Galaxy. What did Vlayn Par'Wil do to get such a cruel life of squalor? *Vengeance* was inflamed within him... *Vengeance* was necessary on this planet and its people.

He peered down at his father's calf with depressed eyes. "*Vlayn! Vlayn! Vlayn!*" Tithen called over and over, but Vlayn was too focused and horrified at the sins he was about to commit that his hearing was dulled. In his peripheral vison, Vlayn saw Tithen rising to his feet and swaying from his hunger. Vlayn turned his head to Tithen. "I'm sorry," he said grimly. He wished he could say more to Tithen. He had so much more to say. But the past did not speak that way.

Vlayn swung down at his father's leg. Then again. Then again. Blood jetting out of the leg, soaking Vlayn.

"Vlayn!!!" Tithen yelled. The boy jumped onto Vlayn's back, attempting to make his brother stop the mutilation he was performing. Vlayn pushed Tithen aside and refocused; he could see the calf bone, so he swung even harder, attempting to snap it. But blood quickly filled the gash, masking the bone once again. Vlayn kept swinging, though, knowing he was hitting the calf. He paused in the middle of his chopping and turned to Tithen, who was hysterically crying, sitting repelled. Vlayn too was beginning to shed tears, but he spoke steadily, "We gotta do things we don't see ourselves doing! That's the only way to live, Tithen!" His voice was hoarse, as if the last day and a half made him age significantly. He persistently continued to chop the leg. "We need to eat!" Vlayn shouted while mangling the leg. "This is how we survive! Doing things we never thought we would do!!"

He continued to hack away as his brother stared at him. For a brief moment, Tithen saw the growing monster in Vlayn.

The bloody axe dropped to the floor at his feet. Blood covered his hands and face while he exhaled heavily in fear of himself. The sky grew darker with each drop of blood from Vlayn's fingertips to the floor. He tried to breathe through a mouth which was going to subsequently consume the flesh of his own kind. Several hours passed by within seconds as he limped backwards from his bathing session of his father's blood. He quickly found himself sitting quietly against the wall of his bedroom that once housed a sinless Babarin. Their father lay in the bed legless as Vlayn breathed heavily. Blood from the last day and a half covered his hands and face.

Vlayn, a soft voice called within his mind and amongst the dark room.

Tithen lay on the floor in his own blood. He continued to cough until he vomited more blood.

Vlayn, the voice whispered from the unreal skies from up above.

The bitter cold from the deserts of Xenamus encompassed the boys. "Glithémien," Vlayn suggested as tears streamed down his face. Tithen squirmed viciously as the chilling air bit his skin.

"You'll…" Vlayn hesitated, but couldn't seem to speak. Oxygen coursed through his airway and to his lungs. It seemed, though, that even air wasn't satisfactory for his body. "You'll die within the hour," Vlayn continued. He gripped the Nabbuu 88 pistol he retrieved from the other room earlier. He studied the gorgeous, classic weapon that dated back to the Early Jaros. The grip had taken countless beatings. The synthetic wood that constructed the grip held ravines of scratches. The framework of the iconic pistol was crafted from tempered gavellum with a barrel made of thick tocsin; both of which endured many battles over the hundreds of jaros since its original creation, proving its toughness. This pistol could sell for thousands on the market, and maybe even more because it was fully functional. Unfortunately, there wasn't a genuine market in Jaadakin County. Either way, the Nabbuu 88 was going to function properly for the act Vlayn was going to commit.

He continued to not only loathe over his parent's death, but from the actions he had recently committed. "I can't see you suffer, Tithen," Vlayn said softly as he dropped his head against the pistol's barrel in agony.

Vlayn, the soft voice grew sterner in his brain. A brighter orange light danced in his vision.

Tithen coughed and gasped for air. The boy's face was swollen with black bags hanging under his eyes.

"Life is a test… life is a test on Xenamus. It sees if we got what it takes to stay alive… to keep those we love alive…" Vlayn knew he wouldn't get a response. But he continued to speak in the dark anyway. "I have failed this test." Vlayn shut his eyes and all he could hear was the heaving coming from his sick brother and the same soft voice calling to him from the universe. He couldn't pinpoint the source of this voice, so he tried to ignore it. "This is survival now. That's what life is. It's what it has always been," he paused for a moment to clear his throat, then continued to speak grimly, "I've been a fool not to realize that sooner. We don't have the life people have on Kirbinia, Reft, the city of Ellmorr, or anywhere else in the Kirbinian Galaxy. We just don't. This is our life. This is life. Our circumstances. This is what I need to cope with… the worst kinds of acts must be done just to live… because…" Vlayn shut his eyes again as tears ran down his face. "Because there is no hope. For any of us."

The orange light flickered brighter, then brighter, then brighter. It almost entirely filled Vlayn's vision. He could see it gravitating closer and closer to him. Vlayn could almost reach out and grab the light. For some odd reason, an intense motivation spawned in his mind; a motivation to get to this light. If he got to it, maybe he would escape this nightmare. But his stomach growled ferociously. His father's meat wasn't satisfactory for his stomach enzymes. They longed for something more stable and substantial, but the flesh of his father was already consumed. He dug into his pocket and pulled out the same note:

There was only one source of food that remained in this room. Vlayn unwillingly drifted toward Tithen. He still lay on the floor. The young, optimistic boy looked up at his brother. "I can't see you suffer," Vlayn murmured. The brothers stared at each other.

"I love you," Vlayn said sincerely. "But I–I have to do this."

Vlayn dropped to his knees and his eyes onto his brother's. His breathing was inconsistent and his eyelids trembled as he shed tears. "Tithen," he uttered softly. Tithen struggled, but he lifted his head to look at Vlayn, then reached for his older brother's hand.

Vlayn squeezed Tithen's sweaty palm tightly, as he reached to his right for the bloody axe that was underneath the bedspring. He looked at the young boy once again, then quickly swung down on Tithen's arm.

Tithen's body shook and the boy cried in horrific pain. Vlayn still held his hand, ensuring the arm wouldn't budge. He chopped down on the inner elbow again, and again. After mutilating the limbs of his father, the axe started to grow blunter. Blood emptied from Tithen's veins, but the bone was stubborn; Vlayn chiseled away at it, but it wouldn't break. Tithen was still alive, trying to wiggle his arm. He was able to move his shoulder, and the dead, half-severed, portion of his arm dragged along the apartment floor with his writhing movement.

Vlayn sobbed, but he proceeded to unevenly chop away at the bone, feeling that this maiming was necessary.

The orange light flashed again, prompting Vlayn to sit back from his mutilated brother. His tears ran down his face and mixed with Tithen's blood that splattered on his cheeks. Vlayn sniffled and looked left and right for the light in the center of his dark bedroom, but it was nowhere to be found. His hands and forearms were smothered with dark blood, sweat and tears soaking his cheeks, but he couldn't find the voice or the orange light.

His current task sprung into his unconscious brain again, reminding him of what he must complete. Vlayn leaned forward, grabbed Tithen's palm with one hand, and the other grabbed his bloody forearm. He started tugging this half, trying to rip the half-severed elbow apart. Finally, it split, and Vlayn fell on his back with Tithen's forearm in his lap.

He saw his second dinner in his arms. Vlayn didn't want to eat his brother; he had to. It was the only way to survive.

The orange light shined from just outside his bedroom and Vlayn scurried to his feet, blankly staring up at the ceiling. Tithen's forearm dangled from Vlayn's right hand like a barbarian ready to feast on his long-awaited prey. Blood dripped unflinchingly from the dead arm, and Tithen, to Vlayn's left, was seizing, rolling across the floor as the boy held his unevenly-chopped arm. He could feel his deflated tendons and veins freely hanging from his inner elbow.

Vlayn was hypnotized by this light, only caring for it and its source, not of his dying brother who was in a horrific, mind-numbing pain.

Vlayn, the soft voice called.

The small, orange light grew larger in the boroughs of his unconscious mind.

Vlayyyyyn, the voice said again.

The orange light grew more vivid, sparkling in the darkness of his bedroom. He felt a sudden shake, and soon his mind bled out and the orange light transformed into a meager fire in his fuzzy eyesight. He then found himself laying on a filthy wooden floor, and his eyes met this fire.

"*Vlayn.*"

Vlayn sat up with his heart racing and sweat clogging his pores and his shirt sticking to his chest. "Is everything alright?" a panicked, soft female voice inquired.

"Y-Yes. Of course," his tired voice answered. His brother's blood once drenched his skin, but only the filth of the deserts tainted his skin now. He turned his face to study Camrynn's as she sat worriedly next to him. His pupils widened and his heart began beating a bit quicker. His voice transformed from ice cold, to warm and gentle, "I'm alright," he added, assuring her of his safety.

"Were you dreaming?" Camrynn asked quietly.

Vlayn scanned the disheveled, abandoned room the pair had camped out in for the night. He felt his face; he could feel his long, tousled beard, the dirt and grime covering his skin, and the coldness that radiated from his animalistic survivalist's body. Tithenkeen felt close to Vlayn, as if he was sitting next to him in his childhood apartment in Witherhart. Vlayn never severed his little brother's arm in real life. So why was he forced to do so in his dream? – a graphic realm that the mind went to find tranquility during idle times.

But none of that was true. Peacefulness was impossible to find even in a dreamscape.

He sat up farther to get a better look outside: Jaadakin County. Nothing new. "Vlayn," Camrynn whispered, "were you dreaming?"

Vlayn grew silent for a moment. He looked to his feet and sighed. He rubbed his forehead and looked back up to her. "Yes," he responded. "I was dreaming."

-Six-

ONLY LOVE

Vlayn shrieked powerfully as he tackled a Babarin man to the ground. Sand splashed upward from his scurrying feet, like a wake following the stern of a boat. It was a mere four hours since the pair spent the night in the hollow shack, where Vlayn went back into his past.

To his left, another foreign man pursued Camrynn. Vlayn noticed Camrynn in crisis while he mounted his own opponent. His heart thumped quicker, his palms moistened, and his mind started sprinting with nervous thoughts. Sitting on top of the man, Vlayn grasped the man's neck and smashed his head into the sand. Again. Again. Again. The man was still breathing.

Immediately he spun the resistant man to his backside. Growling, he scrambled to get ahold of the man's skull with his feet slipping in the sand while hearing Camrynn forcefully shouting. Vlayn's opponent was starting to get to his feet, but before he could, Vlayn grabbed his head and spun it left and right, back and forth. He knew if he did this religiously and as powerfully as he could, the neck would snap. But the muscles in the man's neck were just too strong, and he began fighting intensely with Vlayn to get to his feet. Vlayn tried to hold him down, but he was a burly man of at least two-hundred fifty pounds. Noticing a bright necklace hanging from his neck, Vlayn quickly grabbed the chain and began choking him with it. After a few seconds, the chain snapped.

He realized the waves of the battle shifting, so as a final attempt, Vlayn shot a fast punch into the man's esophagus. The man collapsed into the sand, struggling to breathe. And Vlayn punched him in the throat again, then again once more for good measure.

Vlayn jumped to his feet; he was sure he took the man's life.

Camrynn was standing her ground against her enemy. Vlayn knew she could take this marauder, but he didn't want to risk it. He took the man by his back and threw him to the ground. He lurched onto his back and started choking the killer from behind.

The man struggled to breathe. Vlayn exhausted himself; he sliced his forearm across his throat and clinched it as hard as he could. Camrynn got above the man as Vlayn was still underneath him, strangling him mercilessly. She stabbed him in the chest once. Blood jumped out of his chest and began drenching the man and Vlayn beneath, but the man was still holding onto his life. She stabbed him again, then again until his heart was massacred and blood slowly oozed from his chest.

Vlayn heaved while he shoved the heavy, lifeless body off of him. He slowly rose to his feet, putting pressure on a pair of knees and soles that bawled in agony. The journey to Ellmorr was long and treacherous; the distance between himself and the exalted lands of Fraygen were immense. Vlayn and Camrynn were ready to battle anything to get to Ellmorr; Vlayn needed an answer to his family's death.

"Thank you," Vlayn murmured with a forced grin. Camrynn stepped closer to him and rested her filthy hand on his face. She ran her fingers through his beard and gently pulled his oily hair off his forehead. After Vlayn lost Tithen and his entire family – after *reliving* the horrors and the loss in his past just five hours ago, he needed Camrynn with him.

Vlayn pulled away from Camrynn and rubbernecked at the dead bodies. "Who do you think they were?" he queried while bending down to retrieve the glistening necklace.

Camrynn shrugged. "Who knows," she answered.

"And why does it matter?" Vlayn supplemented. "It doesn't – I don't even know why I'm asking."

"It matters. We can lose ourselves in the desert–" "We can lose ourselves in the cities, too," Vlayn interjected. Camrynn nodded while she followed him as he toured the bodies. "But we can lose ourselves in Jaadakin County. It's good to know there are others out there who are sane, like us," she added.

Vlayn snorted and looked up at her. "Well, we just killed 'em," he said. "Well, we had to. It was us or them who was to go." He inhaled almost noiselessly, "Let's go," he urged with a heavy exhale.

The two began marching on their way. The crooked city of Ridgecall stood miles in the empty desert behind them as a continuous void of sand lingered in front. The Fraygen Plateau was not yet visible, but it was there. Their feet sunk into the warming sand with every debilitated step. A grimy Clena 441 pistol was steadfastly strapped to Vlayn's hip with only a few deadly rounds remaining.

"Maybe they were Ellmorian Blackguards; trying to take out Jaadakins like us."

"They weren't," Vlayn said. "They wear the logo on their clothing, I think."

"And how do you know that?" she asked, but Vlayn shrugged. "Not sure if it's true. But maybe they were people like us, travelling to Ellmorr."

Camrynn was silent.

"There are others like us," he agreed while gazing off into the distance. Camrynn chuckled, "Maybe there are. But they won't survive like we will – we have the magical 441," she remarked.

Vlayn's face loosened, "What're you talking about?" he asked while swiftly glancing down at the Clena 441 attached to his hip.

"You haven't used that pistol since you traded it," she said through her heightening laughter. Her filthy, blonde Babarin hair flopped angelically into her eyes while she stared at Vlayn, who was finally shedding a smile.

"No, no," he began justifying himself, "there just hasn't been a reason to use it."

Camrynn's laughter slowly declined, while she watched her walking feet submerge into the sand. "Tell me that story again," she insisted.

Vlayn snickered. "Why do you always ask me to tell it?"

"It's funny."

He looked off into the hollow desert, and began, "Okay so I was in a trade shop in Kepembold with your Noc Exzero and we were out of ammunition and we needed more. I didn't have any Credits to buy any–"

"Well, we still don't have any Credits so you don't need to mention that," Camrynn giggled.

"I told the shopkeeper that it was an empty Nabbuu Type-V pistol and that I was willing to trade it in for her Clena 441 pistol. Of course, she didn't believe me that it was a Type-V, but then again no one on this planet has ever seen a Type-V. But when she called her man to the counter to take a look, I quickly thanked her and walked out with her pistol before the guy showed up."

Camrynn broke out into more laughter. "The duster probably thought he made a fortune off it, meanwhile he lost so many Credits."

Vlayn smiled, "It ain't that funny," he assured her. "I don't know why you love the story so much, but if it makes you laugh…"

The two pressed on in the hopeless deserts. Every conflict that could strike in the future would only be resolved with Vlayn's bare hands and Camrynn's blade; those few bullets in the Clena 441 would only be considered an absolute last resort; it would be the final opportunity to stay alive if his makeshift fighting skills failed him.

"We don't have many happy times," Camrynn murmured, "that's why I make you tell it – to remind me. To remind you." Vlayn forced another grin, which Camrynn enjoyed seeing. She knew it wasn't genuine, but her heart lit up at Vlayn's self-awareness of his increasingly cold nature, and how he attempted to slow it down. She looked into the golden horizon. She was entertained by the mountains of sand that conglomerated into communities, while they sluggishly grew larger as the pair got closer to them. "We stop at the next settlement we come across," Camrynn said as her face hardened from lassitude, "we should stock up on any food and water we can scavenge."

"I agree," Vlayn remarked as his eyes slowly started to warm to the sight of Camrynn Ansheen. He chewed on his lip, yawned ferociously, and stared off. *Not too much longer,* Vlayn thought to himself, even though the exalted lands were farther than he imagined.

Camrynn returned with a smile.

"Thank you, though," he said.

"For what, exactly?"

"For being there for me," Vlayn pointed out. "For being *here*. After everything I've been through, smiling and being the slightest bit happy didn't seem possible. But it is the real thing with you… so thank you, Camrynn."

"Don't thank me," she said. "I once saw you as a dead man, Vlayn. When we were first getting to know each other, you were in so much pain on the inside that you couldn't talk about *anything* but survival," she said. "But now, Vlayn, you have a heart and it's beating. You know that and I don't want you to forget that. And I know you better than anyone you may've known before, and I see you right now. You're living." She sent him a big smile, but Vlayn couldn't smile back quite yet.

As if recluses, the two walked away from the rest of Xenamus and the Kirbinian Galaxy, only interested in each other and not of the other people who dwelled on this planet or anywhere else. The beaming star in the gloomy sky shot down on the pair. Its extreme heat didn't even dare to alleviate its strong rays of light as it set slowly, but surely, behind the two. Camrynn held her blade tightly in her hand, and this star casted a crisp shadow of it on the sand behind her. This grim sunset was uniquely dazzling and oddly peaceful. But these two Jaadakins that walked into this sunset were deadly. And Vlayn watch the sunlight softly pillow Camrynn; it emphasized the curves of her hips and reflected her lethal stride of a warrior.

"Don't you wonder how they could do this to us, though?" Camrynn inquired blankly. She observed the emptiness and listened to the quietness of the deserts. If she didn't cross paths with another Babarin besides Vlayn for the next ten jaros, she could be convinced she was the last person on Xenamus.

Vlayn's head cocked toward her confoundedly.

"How could the High Clansees leave us to die like this?" she continued, "They're the leaders of The Galaxy-"

"*Leaders* isn't an accurate word," he said with a tired grin.

"My mother taught me this, Vlayn – Clansees rule over a group of planets in The Galaxy and every so often they meet on Kirbidia with their superiors, the High Clansees, to talk about matters of the Kirbinian Galaxy. All of the Clansees and the two High Clansees are what makes up The Council. They have a say in what goes on in each planet. They have the ability to change the conditions we live in every day. *Me and you.* I just don't understand why they don't."

The wind picked up for a moment, carrying horned grains of sand and blew against Vlayn's rugged face. He squinted, but didn't flinch. He simply let it bathe over him and allowed the grains to get caught in his hair. They trekked through Jaadakin County at a slow pace. There was no rush. In fact, rushing wasn't the best idea; nomadic dusters needed to take their time, stop at every settlement they spotted to stock up on food and ammunition, and most importantly, reserve their energy.

It was as if Vlayn and Camrynn were in their own private orb; no outside force could inflict any level of pain or hurt upon them. This was far from true, and it was simple to allow oneself to slowly slip into death's destructive hands if they grew weak or merely fell under the desert's deceptive spell; convincing travelers that they couldn't be hurt by a glithimite or another traveler just because they were seemingly alone out here. They weren't.

Camrynn proceeded intensely, "They can grow Jaadakin County and make it just as beautiful as Ellmorr and the Fraygen Plateau. They can find a cure for the disease and save their people. Don't you want that, Vlayn?"

Vlayn exhaled tiredly and lowered his gaze to his feet. "Yes," he said surely as he rested his hand on the handle of the pistol that was still holstered securely. "I just know they have a cure to the disease," Vlayn murmured, glancing at her as the pair walked. "It'll cost too many Credits to save us – to save Jaadakin County and *all* the cities in it. They gotta have the Credits to do it. But knowing the greediness of our Clansee, they'd rather fund Ellmorr with it and keep it running like a tourist attraction. It's what brings outsiders to our planet. Without Ellmorr, no one'll care about Xenamus," Vlayn said with inflamed words. "The Clansee only gives a damn about the wellbeing of Ellmorr."

"But if they found a cure to the disease-"

"They did," Vlayn said. "Like I told you, Camrynn, they're keepin' it locked up behind the walls."

"But what if the cure leaked out?"

"It wouldn't be."

"But what if it *did?*" Camrynn snapped back. "Then people like your mother and your brother wouldn't have died."

"The cure will never be released," he shut down her thoughts. "The Ellmorr society *must* know the cure to the disease behind those damn walls. I just need to understand *why* she died. I just wanna know if I could've saved her or my brother, or could have just prolonged their lives."

"I know. But I don't think they'll let in people like us."

A potent grief overcame Vlayn. He knew what Camrynn said was true. But he wanted to keep hope alive even though there was a miniscule amount of it. "Glithémien isn't the only thing we should be wary of – the Blackguard," he suggested.

"We'll be *fine,*" she articulated confidently.

"The Ellmorian Blackguard patrol these deserts looking to kill any Jaadakins, just because they think we're animals," Vlayn stated.

"Now you're just getting beside yourself, Vlayn."

"It means they think we aren't royalty like the people of Ellmorr. We aren't good enough," Vlayn said while flailing his hand as he spoke. "It's not true, though. It's not real. We're not animals. If I see a group of them cruising the deserts I'll kill them all," Vlayn said.

Camrynn glanced over at his arrogance.

"I'm serious," Vlayn said as his Babarin face grew pale with fury, "I'll do anything to kill them all. No one's above me – we're all on the same killing field. Truth of the matter is we're all stuck on Xenamus. One half is safe behind a fucking wall with Credits while the rest are dying from glithémien and starvation just below them."

Camrynn rested her hand on his shoulder gently. Her presence gradually calmed Vlayn's expanding rage. "Everything will be fine," she whispered through the gentle winds of the wastelands that stood before them.

Camrynn's eyes scanned the nearby area. The radiant star was just above them, notifying Camrynn of its slow travel to sundown while it still brightly illuminated the barrenness of these wastes. The two were of the Babarin Race, so they naturally absorbed the harmful rays of the blazing star up above. Any marauder pursuing them would been seen for at least a mile away.

Any other race would die within mere hours of being exposed to this much "sun" without the protection of a U.V. Suit. So, the star and its brightness had no effect on them. The only oncoming threat was darkness. When the star revolved to the other side of Xenamus, the deserts were shrouded in absolute darkness, for the nearest moon was far away. Cities, especially Ellmorr, were safe at night, but being stuck outside in Jaadakin County after dark could result in death. It was like being stuck out at sea without a life-preserver. There was no civilization for miles, and without any source of light, someone trying to walk around would not be able to see ten feet in front of them. At this point though, Vlayn and Camrynn had nothing to worry about.

"You never really told me about your family." Vlayn said, changing the subject as he scratched his cheek and wiped his sweat.

"What about my family?" Camrynn inquired.

"You know about my family," Vlayn replied, "how they died... what happened to your family?"

"I'd rather not talk about it, Vlayn," she said defensively.

"It means something to me," he said. "It would help me."

"Why would it help you?"

"To know I'm not alone. That I'm not the only one struggling. It's been seventy jaros but I still think about it every passing day as if it just happened."

Camrynn sighed as she glanced over at Vlayn's tired, sluggish face. "We lived in Gatald," she started. "North of Ambervale. It was a small village. Only about fifty to sixty Babarins. Everyone knew each other, and my father and I were the newcomers. They didn't despise us, they just had their eye on us. We stayed for several nights until everything went downhill. They allowed us to stay together for the first two nights. They made us feel safe and welcomed until the next night when they separated us. They put us in two different windowless rooms. They locked the metal doors behind us and every night I felt as if the walls were caving in on me because I couldn't see them. It was so dark. The only air I was able to breathe was whatever was left in the room after they shoved me in there and closed the door. There were no mattresses, so I slept on the stone floor. I breathed slowly each night, controlling my heartbeat. I was afraid I was going to run out of oxygen before it got light outside."

"Why'd you stay if it was that bad?" Vlayn asked in a rasping voice. "Why didn't you try to find a way out. That's what I would've done."

"They fed us," Camrynn replied. "You know what it's like – when you starve for days, you'll take what you can get. But it wasn't much. They measured it so precisely. They gave us just the right amount of food to keep us alive."

"What about your father?" Vlayn was inquisitive, but he was more so vexed with something else.

"My father felt weak and helpless. I knew all he wanted to do was protect me from the dangers of Jaadakin County but instead he was thrown in the room like some inbred creature just like me."

"So, what ended up happening?"

"Fifth night... I remember it exactly. There was a small light shimmering from under the door. I looked at it for a few hours as I controlled my breathing. I wished that I could be on the other side of the door in the fresher air. Then, the light went out, and the locks on my father's door were opened. Footsteps rushed into his room and I quickly heard punches and my father shouting in pain. I heard all their feet shuffling, and I knew he was fighting back. But there were just too many of them, Vlayn. After a minute, I heard him getting raped. He screamed and screamed and tried to force his way out. I know he tried."

Vlayn faltered to say something, but his words were fumbled.

"My body was still. I was shocked. I lay almost lifelessly for the majority of the night until my stomach started growling. My cheeks were sticky from my tears. Then, my father's shouting stopped, and he started shouting my name. I heard my door beginning to open, I got up quickly and ran to the corner of that box. My heart was beating quickly," Camrynn paused as she began to weep. She glared off to the left into the desert, away from Vlayn.

Vlayn put his hand on her shoulder, stopping her. She felt the warmth of his hand and continued. "It was that terrible woman," she said, "she was the leader of Gatald. I saw her once before when we first entered. She eyed me when I walked in. I was suspicious of her, but I knew my father would protect me if things got bad. When they did, he wasn't there. The woman stood in the doorway of my dark room. I could see the image of her darkened profile, and I'd tell you her name, Vlayn, but I honestly cannot remember. I've completely erased it from my brain. She watched as a group of men grabbed me by my arms and threw me into the wall. I tried to defend myself but I was weak then. I was young. My head smashed against the stone wall. I saw black, but I was still there. One man grabbed me by my neck and pinned me to the floor and started unstrapping his belt. I heard my father banging against the wall in the next room. He screamed as I just heard big booms and thumps against the wall. I knew he would do anything to break down that wall and save me, but he couldn't." Camrynn paused while she clasped her trembling hands together. The awful agony of her past sickened her.

She stammered, "Th–The room was pitched dark. The light in the hall wasn't there anymore. But I could see the man's face through the darkness as it hovered above my eyes. I–I still remember it. The only thing I was able to do was choke him with my nails, digging deep into his neck. Blood dripped onto my fingers but I kept pressing them into his skin until he leapt off me and looked over at the woman in the doorway. It was the only thing I could do, Vlayn."

"I know… I know," he said soothingly and placed his hands on her hips, staring into her eyes as she shared her pain with him. Underneath his false serenity was infuriation. He wished he could've been there to sever their horrid bodies.

"The woman told the men to exit and crouched low, telling me it was only a matter of time before she got what she wanted. I survived that night, but I knew she would get *someone* to try to rape me again."

"Were you?" he asked slowly.

"Next morning –"

"Were you?" Vlayn pressed in a raised voice.

"Vlayn, let me finish," she said as she took his hand. "The next morning she gathered the entire settlement of people. Everyone was there. I can remember all their faces of greed and misery – stuck in place. The woman put my father down on his knees and I stood right behind him. Her hands were dripping of blood from another person. She gave some bullshit speech to the crowd… talking about how she always got what she wanted and nothing less… that nothing would stand in her way. I stood there in the center just shaking. My legs trembled so much I thought they were going to snap. Then, she reached down and took out a machete. I still remember the sound it made while coming out of the sheathe. I took a step back, thinking she was going to kill me. But instead she gave the blade to me. She whispered in my ear, *take your father's head, or I will hold you down and rape you in front of everyone.* I knew even if I did kill my father, I would still be raped. I cried. The woman took a few steps back, watching me, enjoying the sight. I looked at the long blade in my hand. I cried and cried, and I couldn't stop crying. The woman just kept yelling *do it, do it, do it,* over and over again, Vlayn."

Vlayn's eyes dropped to his feet. Enver Rodge sprung into his mind and how she chanted the same two words over and over until his young-self shot every kneeling person dead in that cellar. He had learned so much since then; he wasn't fearful of Jaadakin County like he once was. He made it one of his goals to keep the ones he loved alive. He wouldn't fail the test of Xenamus ever again like he did with his own family. He grabbed Camrynn's hand tightly.

"My father shook on the ground. I knew he just wanted to get up and kill that woman and every single person in the crowd. But he couldn't. I hated that he couldn't. I was mad at him for a long time afterward. But I knew it wasn't his fault," Camrynn said. "I screamed, *I can't*. And the woman fucking swelled with anger. She walked over, took the machete from me and pushed me to the side. The crowd transformed and started watching happily. They all chanted *do it* a million times over. With no hesitation, Vlayn, she just took the machete and swung at my father's neck. It split in half and my father collapsed next to me on the ground. He wasn't even dead yet. He was still conscious with a half-severed neck. He rolled across the sand, his body dragging his skull with it," she said through her cries. "That asshole picked me up and dragged me along by my hair. I know my father saw me being taken away. That was his last sight. It had to have been."

"Did she rape you?" Vlayn asked with growing anger.

"She tried to, but I was able to run away. I got as far away from Gatald as I possible could. Baleejus only knows what they did with my father's corpse. I just needed to get away, Vlayn," Camrynn started sobbing. Vlayn moved closer to her and hugged her – pulling her close to his chest, and she listened to the somber music of his heart.

Vlayn shut his eyes momentarily, closing out the scorching Xenamus sun. He could feel the warmth of her body even in this declining heat. The two stood in the empty Jaadakin County deserts. The perilous landscape of this world deteriorated each day, but Vlayn was going to do anything to keep Camrynn safe. He didn't want to let go, but she pulled back and looked at Vlayn's rugged, bearded face.

"I will keep you safe," Vlayn promised with a vindictive voice. "I know you will," she replied with confidence. "But you don't need to. We keep each other safe – or, as safe as we can possibly be on this trip to Ellmorr."

Vlayn looked down into her eyes, then admired her grungy, yet soft Babarin skin. He could see how she had aged over the past twenty-seven jaros, since they initially met. And as he adored her, he could begin to see the once younger face she had; it had less grime, sweat, and less blood on her hands. She was the same soul, though. Camrynn was mostly unaffected by Jaadakin County's oppressiveness. "You're stronger than me," Vlayn whispered to her, as she settled in his arms and he could feel the lump in his throat expand. But Camrynn was confused. He continued, wearied, "It doesn't matter how many dusters you killed, or how many lives you saved – or, even how many people you're protecting. It's about being able to never change – to never *decline*. To be a stronger version of yourself. You're stronger than me because you can still see the good in people. You can still see hope in everything, while I can only see hope in one thing: Ellmorr."

"Vlayn," Camrynn interrupted, attempting to mollify him from his chest that she leaned her face on. "No," Vlayn said softly, bearing the weight of her resting head. "After everything you've been through, you hadn't gone cold, and you can still smile freely. After everything I've been through, I know I've gone cold. I don't see the good in people. I know that. I accept that. I didn't see the good in you at first, even though you saved me from glithémien when you didn't need to. But you saw the good in me right away." And from those words, Vlayn started to tear. "I wish I could be like you," he said. Then, he leaned in and kissed her. The two stood solidly in the sand, kissing each other, her running her fingers through his glossy, generous hair. Him with his eyes closed, feeling the shape of her hips. It seemed the only hope worth living for was just this. This was the only love and genuine affection Vlayn had felt since the fall of his family, but he still couldn't smile as candidly as she could. He was slowly coming back to life, though, and Camrynn was indeed reviving him. He never wanted to let her go, and so he didn't. He pulled her closer by her waist; so close that the structure of her body molded to his, and they became one. Camrynn pulled back momentarily, idolizing the way the dying sun sparkled into Vlayn's eyes; a set that was so frigid.

He let her study his face, but not for too long. He loved Camrynn. He loved that she cared for him and how she understood his grievous pain. She knew when to not push too far with him, and when to press him to be unguarded of his heart – something he didn't trust. But he couldn't let Camrynn watch the movement of his eyes and the harrowing configuration of his face – not for too long, and certainly not this close. So, Vlayn moved for her lips once more, slowly lifting her by her waist again. Camrynn advanced to the tips of her toes, one hand firmly grasping the back of Vlayn's head, the other planted on his chest. His heartbeat quickened. He needed her. He wanted her. His tongue salivated at the flavor of her lips. The pair slowly declined to the cooling sand, where Vlayn ran his fingers underneath her shirt, his index and middle fingertips painting on the left side of her torso. Their tongues met, their lips secured.

Vlayn pulled her coat from her shoulders, throwing it to the side, then moving his lips down her neck, breathing down it. She moaned softly at the feeling of warm, wet lips surfing down her skin. On all fours, Vlayn pushed her shirt up to her neck with his left hand, where the tip of his tongue travelled down the center of her chest and down to her belly button. She exhaled, for she surrendered her body to him.

"*Vlayn*," she mumbled through another exhale. A cool breeze washed over them, prompting her to pull on the collar of his coat. She needed to feel the heat of his chest on top of hers. She needed him to be closer. Closer than this.

Vlayn met her eyes; both of their pupils enlarged and neither blinked; their curious love fascinated them – how could one love in such desperate times? But they both did. And it wasn't just them. Many others across Jaadakin County fostered relationships during this era. No one else mattered, though. He was in control of Camrynn's heart, and she was in control of his. But neither would shatter something so fragile. Vlayn ran his thumb over her closed lips, feeling the ingrained lines in her bottom lip, and studied how these lips accompanied her face so perfectly.

"How could she be so beautiful?" he thought at the sight.

"Come here," she whispered amongst the breeze that casted over the desert. He moved for her lips again – slowly puckering, gently kissing her, feeling her lips press against his, listening to the sound of the wet kiss, then slowly retracting, allowing his lower lip to be the last thing to leave her face. His left palm held her right cheek, his right hand gripping her round hip. She was solid. Someone to hold down. Someone who could keep him alive and mentally alive. He could learn from her; Camrynn was healthier, stronger, and braver than he was.

He unbuckled her pants and pulled them passed her hips and down her thighs. Vlayn then went for his belt, quickly unlocking it, but Camrynn broke up his scurrying hands and undid his pants for him. *"Vlayn,"* she murmured, pulling him close. And after she pulled one pant leg off, Vlayn's chest rested atop hers, and Camrynn wrapped her arms across his back. He slowly pressed into her, and they were closer than they were before.

✱✱✱

Night set in rapidly. Darkness overcame the pair and imminent death was awaiting them if they didn't evacuate the barren deserts quickly.

Intense lust was a recent topic, and more importantly, it was an infrequent topic. When lust did arise in a duster's life, it could tamper with their head – their priorities of survival. Vlayn looked at Camrynn differently. The love he felt for her was indeed stronger. But it was changed. They had a different connection. Nothing seemed to overpower the feeling of lust. And sex derailed his plans and his focus of Ellmorr – but only for a short while. Once the pair were back on their feet, he could feel the pain in his chest again.

A small settlement was on the horizon and they managed to make it there before being stranded in the middle of nowhere. It was two or three tiny wooden shacks. They were warped and half-sunken into the Xenamus sand. It was decrepit and unsafe to stay there for the night, but it was far better than the remaining options Vlayn and Camrynn had. The two retreated to the top story of the tallest structure.

When getting to the top, Vlayn migrated to the nearest window. The bright lights of Ellmorr gleamed over the horizon. The massive city itself couldn't be seen from this distance, but the shining lights of this lavish metropolis had the ability to illuminate its perimeter, flashing in the desert sky. The pair were close to the Fraygen Plateau, but if they were any farther from it, the darkness would absorb them completely.

"Ellmorr," Vlayn hummed to himself as he observed the lively luminescence. But there was no joy. Only angst and rage rippled in his body. The disease: the city had the cure. All of Jaadakin County didn't need to be in such turmoil. Resuscitating Jaadakin County was possible.

"Camrynn," Vlayn called. "At the first sight of the plateau, we find a place to hunker down for the night and figure out how we'll make it up there. There's gotta be paths that N.M.C. land cruisers take to make it up to the plateau, don't you think?" Vlayn spun his head around cautiously, scanning the room. He slowly drew his Clena 441 pistol with ease and patrolled the room. Gun in his right hand, he squatted low to the floor. He sifted through the light debris until his fingers met with a plastic picture frame. He began analyzing the frame, but something else caught his tiresome eyes – underneath the frame on the floor was a charred *Acts of Baleejus*. He scoffed at the sight, disapproving the thought of the God named Baleejus.

He put the frame down momentarily to study the book. He opened to a random page and narrowed his eyesight onto a certain sentence in the middle of three other paragraphs that filled the ruffled pages. He lifted the book into the distant moonlight. *If a mortal soul robs the life of another, then later loses their own to the hands of a different being, then they shan't be forgiven.* He heard the words being spoken in his own voice, so he read it again. But the words overlaid the silence and the blue hue from the moon brightened the page, only causing Vlayn to shiver. He bit his bottom lip in disgust at the sentence. Vlayn thought, *what if you gotta kill to live? Will Baleejus make me die a filthy death because I had to kill dusters in my life so I could stay alive?*

He threw the book into the wall lividly, brushed his hair back with his hands, then lifted the picture frame close to his eyes, trying to make out what the stained picture was beneath the gritty glass. Suddenly a figure emerged from behind him. Instinctually, Vlayn sprung up and raised his pistol onto the stranger.

"Woah! Woah!" a young boy begged with his arms raised in innocence from a doorway, revealing his dark babarin skin and his shabby hair. Camrynn tip-toed out of another room behind Vlayn and gently placed her hand on his right shoulder.

"Step out," he directed the boy, and when he walked from the doorway, Vlayn continued to order him, "knees." "P–Please. I'm with a group," he whispered, "a–an–and when you're with these types of people y–you *lose* who you are – your identity." The boy tried to swallow the nervous knot he had in the back of his throat, but it wouldn't pass. Vlayn bypassed the boy's cries, "I said *knees*, kid." Finally, the boy dropped to his knees with his eyes clouding, and Vlayn could easily read not only the evident heart-brokenness displayed on his face, but also a strong sense of loneliness.

"Vlayn," Camrynn mumbled. Vlayn glanced back at her while scratching his beard. He repositioned his finger tighter on the trigger while he contemplated what to do. The boy started to sway from his growing cries; *"Pl–Please– Please,"* the boy bellowed, choking on his salivating mouth. He didn't want to meet death quite yet. He wasn't ready –

but Vlayn was steady and stoic with his weapon's sights locked sturdily on the boy. "P–Please, sir. I can help you. We're stronger together. N–No one can survive out here alone."

Vlayn's eyebrows lowered and his mind wiped away all of his deliberating thoughts when he heard that sentence. "No," Vlayn stated, "anyone can survive out here alone." He took one more deep breath and shot the boy dead. The boy's neck cracked after his head sprung backward after taking the shot. The body spiritlessly plunged to the floor and Vlayn stared at the boy momentarily, watching the blood slowly paint his futile face. He then lowered the pistol with an empty look. "V–Vlayn," he could hear Camrynn's now jagged voice.

Vlayn looked at Camrynn without a shimmer of emotion, "Please," he muttered. "Don't say anything. Not right now." Then, he began walking into the other room with the picture frame shattering beneath his walking feet. Almost immediately and habitually he redrew his pistol and started surveying the room until his dreary eyes met with a scene that wasn't like the typical monotony of the deserts. Camrynn trailed Vlayn into the room sorrowfully. And when she entered this room, the disturbance she felt from the dead boy paused, for what was in front of her terrified her even more. But it wasn't just this scene that stunned her.

She covered her mouth with her hands, as if they were magnetically drawn to her lips. She patrolled the room until she ended her walking on the opposite side of a naked, blood-stained mattress, farthest from Vlayn. "I–I can't believe this," she spoke quietly through her fingers. An elderly man lay headless on the empty bedspring and his head resting on the floor, next to Camrynn's feet. The skin was decaying swiftly, leaving behind the brittle bones of the skull. Next to the bed frame was a very young boy, just a little younger than Tithen had been. The boy was sprawled out along the filthy floor in his own blood, mimicking Tithen. This floor was once saturated with the combination of both corpse's blood. At this point though, the floor was steadily withering away and was brittle from Xenamus' powerful heat.

"Baleejus," Vlayn exclaimed with a weighty gulp. He slowly walked over to the young boy and eyed the body mournfully. He knelt down above the body, inhaled sharply, and rested his forehead on the barrel of the pistol. Vlayn closed his eyes and exhaled onto the warm metal. Camrynn made way to the aged man. She squatted at the edge of the bed and clasped her hands together. She teared as the uncanny blue moonlight partially casted its light in the room. Vlayn's entire world began to spin as he observed the scene. He was always able to keep his stoic persona, even in the brutish of situations with swinish people.

"Camrynn," Vlayn whispered with fright. The lights of Ellmorr gleamed into the room, deviously illuminating the two bodies. He could see the gaily lights scrutinizing him. He lumbered over to Camrynn and placed his hand on her cheek affably.

Suddenly, a rich, bullheaded voice filled the room, "Stay where you are," it demanded. Vlayn immediately spun around and raised the pistol. He locked his sharp sights on the foreigner, ready to pull the trigger. "No, no," the voice said. "Put it down." The stranger was shrouded in the darkness of the night with a hood over his head and mangled clothing. He stood in the doorway with a heavy machine gun pointed at the two, ready to unload. Behind him, Vlayn could see a dozen additional dusters filling the entire second story of this shack. There was no sense in fighting. Vlayn and Camrynn were outnumbered. He slowly lowered the Clena 441. Camrynn stood behind Vlayn cautiously. "I see you x'ed-out that kid. Not too shabby," the man complimented sickly. "It's all good, though. Not like he was of much use… You, though. That may be different." Vlayn stood tall, shoulders cocked back, held his eyes steadily on his enemies, and was prepared to fight for his life and Camrynn's.

-Seven-

THE CAGE

Darkness filled the cage that Vlayn was trapped in. Hunger overcame him. His stomach growled with fury as his hands tightly gripped the metal bars that boxed him in. He breathed heavily with sweat beading down his sweltered forehead and cheeks. His hair was sticky and was gummed to his wet forehead. Tears filled his eyes. The survivalist within him came to the forefront, making his tongue salivate at the smell of flesh.

Piercing shrieks came from down a dim hallway, echoing amongst the walls and repeating a few dozen times over again. The blackness was foul and it shrouded Vlayn's vision, making him dizzy. He kept his eyes locked at the small light from down the hall and he wouldn't look away. He felt his warm breath escape his dry mouth and warm his scarred hands that grasped the bars. Listlessness weighed heavy in his body, but animosity boiled within him.

Another bellow of horrific pain echoed in the stone hallway, reaching Vlayn's cage. This time, it was louder.

And soon, it was silent.

***

Two hours earlier.

The man tugged Vlayn along by his arm; he grumbled and tried to force his way out, but he was unsuccessful each time he tried. Vlayn knew Camrynn was behind him in the darkness of the stone hallway. He knew she was in danger, and he made a vow to himself he would always keep her safe, even if she could keep herself safe.

Nonetheless, he failed.

The group stopped for a moment. The man let go of Vlayn and proceeded through the darkness to a small metal cage. He unlocked the gate and turned back to Vlayn. He took him by the neck and threw him into the cage.

Compared to a male human, Vlayn was of moderate height. And yet, the ceiling of this cage skimmed the top of his head.

Through the darkness, the man stepped inside and shot a fist into Vlayn's ribs, knocking him down to the stone floor. The man squatted down to him. "You're just like those Ellmorian Blackguards – thinking you're all tough. Even though, behind that whole window-dressing, you're weak," the man said with a low, grating voice. The stench of his stale breath crept into Vlayn's nostrils, making him recoil backward.

The details of this duster were initially blurred and vague to Vlayn, but he could tell he was a mid-aged babarin with sparse hair and adorned with a ragged grey top and grey pants. A deep scar ran down the right side of his haggard forehead and reached all the way to the corner of his cracked lips. Small cuts and bruises decorated his filthy cheeks and his spectral face with fragile, white skin tissue circumscribing each old scar. His grungy hair was seemingly blown out by the desert winds and some fell onto his face. He didn't attempt to swat it out of his eyes, though. He simply stared at Vlayn without flinching.

"Why are you doing this?"

The man chuckled slowly as Vlayn could hear Camrynn beginning to whimper in the darkness several feet in front of him. "*Food*," the man said slowly with his dry vocal chords straining.

"F-Food?" Vlayn responded.

"*You*," he said. "You and your girl are the pleasure and the food," he added sinisterly, then followed it with a grin, revealing his grey teeth and the yellow plaque that dressed them.

Vlayn's eye twitched energetically in correlation to his brewing anger. If this was happening seventy jaros ago, Vlayn would have cowered and begged for his life. But he had struggled. He battled. He bled. He cried. And just when he thought he cut the heart of the devil herself, he had met the devil once again; he was half a foot away and he was far too close to the woman that he loved dearly.

If there were loved ones, then there were people Vlayn was automatically dedicated to protect; it was in his nature. At this moment, it was one person.

Vlayn sat up undaunted. His eyes firmly lingered onto the man's. His face was as cold and impenetrable as fractrin to where it seemed the blood in his body stopped flowing. He inhaled through his nose and exhaled slowly. "I'm going to kill you," Vlayn said carefully just to ensure the man heard every single syllable that he murmured. "There is no hesitation. There's not a *shred* of thought when it comes to the worth of your life. And I'm sure as hell not gonna stop and think before I take yours."

The man returned the look. A supreme smell of bitterness and rabidity was exchanged between the two, without a word being said. The man slowly exhaled through his mouth and strained to let out a brief, squealing cackle. The sound screeched over and over in Vlayn's head. It got louder and louder in his brain, almost to where his eardrums bled even though the cage he was trapped in was absolutely silent.

Camrynn quieted momentarily and sniffled a few times. She tried to keep silent though, for she couldn't see Vlayn and the man through of the darkness, but she tried to hear the pair.

"You're a funny guy..." the man responded slowly.

Vlayn didn't flinch. He didn't even blink. The two were intelligent, loyal students of these killing fields. They were ready to sacrifice each of their limbs in a fight for their lives. "...Funny that you're the one threatening *me*. Listen up: never let your guard down... because if you do, there will always be badasses like me right 'round the corner ready to snatch you up, just like I did, and kill you, which I am about to do. Never let your guard down," the man repeated, "*never*." With that, the man stood up, took one last look at Vlayn and exited the cage. The gate shut quickly, and three locks secured the door.

"Throw the girl in the other cage, too. We'll start with her tomorrow," the man ordered his slaves. One woman took Camrynn by her arms and threw her into the cage directly adjacent Vlayn's. She started crying uncontrollably as she retreated to the cage wall nearest Vlayn.

"I'm going to fucking kill you!!!" Vlayn shrieked.

The man snorted hysterically in the darkness and slowly disappeared with his people.

"I am going to protect you," Vlayn whispered to Camrynn through the metal bars. "I will not let you die."

Camrynn wiped her tears. "Vlayn, I will kill him."

"I know this may remind you of your past, but it will not end the same way," he promised.

"I know it won't, Vlayn," Camrynn responded as she stuck her hand through the bars. Vlayn took her hand and raised it to his lips and kissed the top.

"I love you, okay?" Vlayn forced the words out of his mouth. He was beyond upset; he was sick – sick at this whole situation. He was sick that he allowed Camrynn and himself to be stuck in this type of danger.

Camrynn nodded again as she cried heavier, "I love you too," she said sincerely, followed by a brief cough. "If we die tonight–"

"We *won't*," Vlayn emphasized. "Vlayn..." Camrynn started softly, "I need to know why you killed that boy earlier." Her eyes gleamed with faltered fright. She was trying to force herself to avoid seeing the man Vlayn was truly transforming into.

Vlayn's head tilted with question while his eyes squinted, trying to see her through the darkness, "Who? What *boy*? What are you talking about, Camrynn?"

Camrynn inhaled through her nose and shut her eyes. She examined the familiar gloomy blackness that her closed eyes served, then finally opened them to meet the same thing. "The boy, Vlayn," she answered tiredly, "the kid – the *boy*, from before. He was on his knees, begged you to spare him, and you shot him clean dead, Vlayn."

Vlayn propped himself upward against the metal bars and ran his fingers through his hair. "He wasn't a boy, Camrynn —"

"Vlayn, he was just a boy," she rushed the words out with true worry. Camrynn loved Vlayn, and more importantly, she loved the man he was at the core of his heart. However, the deserts of Jaadakin County habitually altered the original, weaker souls of its natives into feral creatures that were stuck in their pain from losing their loved ones. The stronger souls like Camrynn never wavered from who they were. They killed when it was necessary, but they understood the value of every Babarin's life. Vlayn had a weak soul, and Camrynn was fearful of his alteration. "I can't see you change into a man you aren't. I can't see it. I don't want to see it."

"Camrynn," he began, "it has nothing to do with that."

"It does," she countered.

"No. No, it doesn't. He wasn't a boy. It was a heartbeat. That's all it was," he told her. "I don't care what his age was, his past, his potential fucking future… all I care about is me, you, *my* future, *your* future, and how much ammunition he had in his gun and what he could've done with it. That's it. I couldn't risk keepin' him alive," he looked down at his fingers in the dark and began picking his cuticles anxiously. "You're still here, right?"

Camrynn looked at him emotionlessly, then let out a short cough to clear her throat.

"Right?" he asked again.

Finally, she nodded.

"That's all that matters," he said. "And I hate to mention it, but you laid out seven men back in Ridgecall."

Camrynn countered, "that's different."

"How?" Vlayn said. "It's still a life. You took lives just like I did. It isn't much different."

"I was protecting Ridgecall," Camrynn replied. "I *had* to kill to protect those people. No one else was going to. Those men were going crazy in the city. They would've killed people if I didn't do what I did. You know this, Vlayn. Don't try to turn it into something that isn't."

He sat still, thinking about Jaadakin County and the savagery of the lands. Vlayn tried to understand how to survive and not lose the seemingly insufficient amount of empathy that his declining soul had. It was far too difficult for Vlayn to understand, and Camrynn seemed to understand it fluently. Instead, Vlayn nodded silently.

"We've both lost people, Vlayn." "I know that," he quickly responded.

"I don't want you to feel like you're the only one. In case something happens to me tomorrow or tonight—"

"Camrynn—"

"Listen, Vlayn. If something happens to me tomorrow, I want you to know how my mother died. You know that she passed away."

"I asked you plenty of times over the jaros. I didn't want to pressure you into telling me."

"I want to tell you now. I want you to know that I understand that pain inside you…"

Camrynn was silent, so Vlayn began nodding. "So…" he started, "how?" She was still quiet, hanging her head low. "*Camrynn*," he whispered.

"Sun poisoning," she blurted out, then looked up at him.

"Sun poisoning?" Vlayn was confounded, and Camrynn nodded. "That doesn't affect Babarins. We're the only race that can withstand Xenamus heat like this."

"I know. My mother was mixed – Kirbinian and Babarin."

"But what about U.V. Suits?" Vlayn asked, "She didn't have one to protect her from the heat?"

"Well, she did," she said curtly.

Vlayn's eyelids squinted together. "So, what happened, Camrynn?" he questioned caringly. Still, though, she didn't respond quite yet. Her face lowered again into sadness while the absence of light nipped at her sweaty skin.

Vlayn nudged himself to the bars closest Camrynn. "We all have skeletons – a *shadow* that follows us. Whether it's something we did, something we *had* to do, or a messy past. Everyone in Jaadakin has that in common. I certainly do and you know it."

"She had a U.V. protection suit, but the suits are made in Ellmorr," she said even though her face was locked sturdily in a position that was aligned with the cold floor. "The ones they actually sell to Jaadakin County aren't really created with *care*, if you want to put it that way. They're thrown together and they don't actually protect people from the rays. The exposure'll just penetrate the suit and you'll get poisoned from too much."

"Another way for Ellmorr to make money," Vlayn put in.

"Yeah," she mumbled. "It's Ellmorr; *slippery*, *greedy* Ellmorr. They can do anything they want, Vlayn. You know that. It's probably cheaper to throw together a U.V. suit and give it to people like us, and then put the Credits they save into making real, protective suits and give it to the wealthy in Ellmorr or the N.M.C. on the Fraygen Plateau."

Vlayn studied her face through the darkness. It seemed the outlines of her face started to fade as he continued to focus on her. Then, Camrynn cleared her throat. "You may just think Ellmorr is screwing Jaadakins by ignoring our cry for help with the Glithémien Disease." "I may not have the same type of angst toward Ellmorr as you, Vlayn. But the people of that city only care about Credits. We can see that clearly from down here. They make Credits off us."

"I'm so sorry, Camrynn."

"No, no," she responded, "it's fine," she added as her eyes gravitated back to the floor. Then, her voice lowered, close to a whisper. "I've accepted it. I have you, now. That's all I need."

"I am *going* to get us out of here," Vlayn assured her. "Don't worry."

Camrynn's breathing slowed and she forced a smile. An intense pressure overcame her – making her head spin. Maybe it was the heat? Maybe it was hunger? But she looked up at Vlayn drearily. She eyed him from the other side of the bars.

Vlayn studied her with shock. "What's wrong?" he asked her nervously. Camrynn inhaled, feeling the knot in the back of her throat. "I love you, Vlayn," her words mixed with apprehension and regret. "But I didn't want to have sex with a monster." Vlayn's heart was jolted with devastation. "Camrynn…"

At the root of her heart, she didn't want Vlayn in that moment – that period of dusk in the desert. "It happened naturally, Camrynn –"

Her voice slowly grew hoarse, "I was, and *am* scared of the man you're becoming. I–I– *maybe I just wanted to feel something…*" She coughed wickedly, and her hand covered her mouth until she pulled it away from her face only to see blood had splattered her palm.

"Wha–What is it?" he asked her anxiously.

She swallowed hard, but didn't respond.

"*What is it?*" Vlayn pressed.

"It's nothing, really."

"*No,*" Vlayn pled.

"Vlayn…"

"G-Glithémien…" Vlayn murmured as he could feel his heart instantly shattering with pain galloping up his chest. "P-Please Camrynn. Don't –"

"Vlayn, I won't go."

"Please!" he screamed as his eyes watered. "Ellmorr is *torturing* us!"

"I will live, Vlayn," she said mildly.

"I *won't* let you die from this, Camrynn," he promised. He jumped to his feet and ran to the metal bars. He gripped them as tight as he could until his skin stretched and almost blistered and bled. Vlayn was ready to draw blood to protect his own. His eyesight reduced; all he could see was the end of the hallway and nothing else. Nothing else but the man that stole him from near valueless life.

-EIGHT-

ROPES IN THE MIND

An undefiled silence was the only true heartbeat in the room. Camrynn's head hung low, weeping sadly on the cold, stone floor. The only sound in the metal cage she could hear was her heavy breathing. Her forehead thumped loudly, concurrent with her migraine and her rising temperature.

She pushed her light hair out of her face and turned to Vlayn in the cage next to hers. It was the deadest of the night, and he was curled up in the corner of the cage. His eyes were closed, evidently sleeping.

Camrynn glanced over to the end of the stone hallway, envying the light at the end that shined luminously. She dropped her head to the metal bars behind her in defeat, closing her eyes slowly as the feebleness overtook her body. Her tiresome mind began to fade away into the empty blackness as she progressively fell farther into sleep. Camrynn was at peace with herself at this one, very moment. It was surprising that she could allow her mind to enter a state of peacetime while being trapped like a homeless dog in a horrifically mind-bending scene.

Though her mind rapidly dissolved into a lightless oblivion; she could feel her overheated brains turning to molten muck. Anxiety slithered around her placid mind and its thoughts and strangled it without a pause. Her eyes sprung open and her body lurched forward from the metal bars she leaned on. Camrynn heaved while tears began to fall from her face and onto the stone floor beneath her.

Her warm tears felt like freezing raindrops as they slid down her steaming cheeks.

Her sight grew fuzzy, her ears rang, and her head rotated three-hundred-sixty degrees, over and over again. She searched for a shred of light, attempting to ensure the darkness hadn't made her go blind. But she couldn't find any within her cell, and she couldn't see the dim light at the end of the hallway any longer.

Her palms grew clammy as she gripped the cold floor beneath her, but she couldn't quite feel its coolness either. And soon, the floor lost its mild touch, for her entire body went numb.

She tried to call for Vlayn, but her words simply couldn't reach the surface of her tongue.

Then, a loud thump on a wall broke the once steady silence, causing her ears to howl in agony. A male scream echoed in the room and Camrynn's head spiraled in circles, trying to find where this scream was coming from. She searched more, until the shouting grew more familiar as she listened to it.

It was her father.

"*No, no, no, no,*" she mumbled to herself.

Camrynn peered over to Vlayn's cage. However, the metal bars that separated them hastily transformed into the bare white wall that enclosed her jaros ago when she was trapped in Gatald.

Another thump smashed against the wall followed by a loud scream from her father again. Camrynn knew what came next: the man with his baleful glare would enter her room and try to rape her.

Her eyesight still sat under a hazy fog and her surroundings turned increasingly lopsided, but Camrynn still retreated to the corner of the hallucinated room. Then, a woman entered the room. She knew that her mind fell deep into a state of self-bondage as the ropes of her own mind entangled her to near death. It felt real.

Was this real?

Camrynn recognized the woman that barged into the room and let the group of men inside. She still heard her father screaming with all his might, knowing his daughter was in terrible danger. But as the men progressed toward her, it immediately changed into someone foreign.

Her sight became vivid, her hearing grew real, and she could feel the intense grip that this man had around her arms.

This wasn't a hallucination anymore.

Her father's cries quickly transformed into Vlayn's screaming. He kicked the metal bars that kept him locked in his cage. His disheveled hair flopped into his eyes and his sweat flung from his cheeks. He shrieked powerfully and lunged forward, kicking the bars. From the floor, Camrynn knocked the man with a powerful fist, then leapt to her feet. She swayed from side to side from her increasing fever, giving the man an opportunity to pursue her again. A woman came in to help subdue Camrynn, but Camrynn turned and punched her before she could do anything.

Camrynn was exhausted and ill. Any strength she had, she just used.

"*Let her fucking go!!!*" Vlayn roared as he reached his arms as far as he could through the gaps of the bars. Camrynn was dragged out of the room by her arms as she cried and begged for her life. "*P–P–Pleeeeaseee!!!!*" she roared.

"*Hey!!!*" Vlayn howled. "*I'm going to fucking kill you!!!*" He stood in the center of his lonely cage, watching Camrynn being hauled off into the light at the end of the stone hallway. He couldn't do anything; he was helpless. His defensive shoulders lowered, his heart shattered, and his rage heightened. Vlayn continued to ponder how one could survive in Jaadakin County and still see the goodness in others. But he quickly started to learn that this wasn't possible.

-Nine-

KNOW MY NAME

Kicks were shot at the metal bars in front of him. He screamed as tears filled his eyes and ran down his face. His ruffled hair flopped onto his forehead. He gasped heavily as his sweat mixed with his tears and he could hear Camrynn pleading for her life in the room down the stone hallway.

Then, he heard the same malefic laugh by the man.

Vlayn kicked the bars and shrieked again, trying to force himself out.

Then, the earsplitting crack of Camrynn's screaming echoed amongst the cave. This time her voice was smothered with a fevering pain. She screamed again, again, and again. Vlayn could almost hear her torture; the sound of the lacerations made by sharp blades and scalpels coupled with a rhythmic pounding against the wall or a table. Vlayn was almost able to smell the stench oozing from the sadists in the other room, along with the repugnant odor reverberating from the stone walls.

Camrynn continued to wail from her suffering, until it was silent, but the thumping continued for a good two minutes in the silence, until it was over.

Vlayn's legs were feeble and he plummeted to the ground, sobbing. He tried to catch his breath, but it seemed the world around him was sucking the air from his lungs.

The man entered the hallway shortly later, taking every single dramatic and threatening step, mocking Vlayn's visible pain. He hummed to an odd tone as he strolled through the darkness. Finally, he returned to the cage, observing Vlayn from the outside. "It was sad," the man began, "I *liked* her. She was cute. My people painted on her chest with knives while I *stuck* it in her. But this is just how it ends, I guess."

Vlayn couldn't even listen, for he balled his eyes out. The man smiled; enjoying seeing Vlayn in his weakest state he had ever been in. Then, after observing for a bit, an overwhelming fury stirred within the man. He swung open the gate, picked Vlayn up and threw him against the bars. "Grow up, you little bitch!" he howled as he punched Vlayn in the face multiple times.

Vlayn fell to the ground and the man kicked him in the ribs. "Never let your guard down!" he screamed, "that's why you're stuck here! The strong dominate the weak on Xenamus. It's just sad it took you this long to realize that." The man rubbed his eyepatch, "take all your clothes off, guy," he ordered tiredly.

Vlayn glanced up at the man confused, "W–What?" he asked through his wilted face.

"You understand the words I am speaking!!!" the man howled back, "do what I said!"

With hesitation, Vlayn began to undress himself.

The man studied the naked Vlayn for a short while until he finally formulated his sentences, "See," he said, "now the only thing you got is yourself and your brain that's gonna recalibrate to only know my name. Nothing stands in between now," the man stared at Vlayn briefly, until suddenly he advanced toward him. He grabbed Vlayn by his neck and pinned him against the bars in the dark. Holding him by his throat, he jabbed him in the chest, then grappled with his pants to get them off.

Vlayn struggled for air from underneath the tight grip and tried to get the man off him. His emotional pain was far too superior, and he couldn't find the strength that was required.

The man started to pull his pants down, ready to rape Vlayn.

He was vulnerable and he continued to shed tears. A piece of Vlayn died with Camrynn, and at the thought of her, Vlayn knew she wouldn't want him to die like this. But Vlayn was losing all sense of control; he was about to be used like an object – a man stripped of all the qualities – both positive and negative that made him Vlayn Par'Wil. He was going to lose his identity and surrender it to this primitive man.

The pants dropped and he forced Vlayn against the bars even tighter. He breathed heavily in Vlayn's right ear and smashed his palm into his face as he struggled to force himself into Vlayn.

Enervated, Vlayn yelled, feeling this man getting closer and closer into him, and he was even closer to losing himself. The man continued to press his hand onto Vlayn's face, but he wouldn't give up quite yet. Vlayn opened his mouth and chomped down onto the man's pinky. He continued to stab his teeth into the finger, until he felt his two front teeth shatter the bone, so he retracted his head, tearing it from the man's hand. The man instantly backed off and bent over, holding his bloody hand. The bare bone was visible, and his torn skin dangled freely in the air.

Blood squirted out, impetuously flowing and painting his palm. The man began screaming in a stifling pain.

Vlayn's tongue was coated with the crumbs of the broken bone, and he spit the remains of the finger and the blood out of his mouth, feeling the man's blood dripping from his lips and through his beard. The nauseating, tangy iron taste of the blood made Vlayn's head spin.

In excruciating pain, the man retreated out of the cell with the door closing behind him. A few armed people came into the hallway. "Deal with that fucking duster!" the man ordered. A woman threw her Dufe assault rifle to the side. She got into the cell and demanded Vlayn to sit in the corner. And so he sat in the corner silently with the blood of the man dribbling down his sweaty, naked body. His beard was soaked of it, and all he could really feel was the sharp remains of the bone caught underneath his tongue. He glanced to his left into Camrynn's cell.

It wasn't a race to the end, but she won.

A few hours later, the same man walked slowly through the dark hallway. Stained linen cloths were swathed over his hand.

"What's your name, guy?" he asked, approaching the cage door.

"Vlayn," he uttered with a gruff voice.

"That's a kinky name." the man responded peculiarly with guttural sounds coming from the back of his throat. "I'm DaRoone," he said irately. "And that's the only name you need to know from now on," DaRoone stated as he stepped closer to the locked cage. Vlayn watched the man as he rose to his feet. "When I tell yuh something, you respond with: *yes DaRoone*. If I order something, you say: *yes Daroone*. See? It's pretty simple. So, forget about the *chapters* and *verses* you lived by before all this," he said grim-faced. "Forget about your own name: Vlayn, or whatever the fuck that awful name is. *DaRoone* is all you need to know." The man paused. He sucked air through his cracked lips, creating an odd, squealing sound. Deranged, he grinned through the stabbing pain in his hand. "Do you understand?" he asked, testing Vlayn.

Vlayn didn't answer.

"Do you understand?" the man pressed.

Still nothing.

"You're pretty stubborn aren't ya!?" DaRoone shouted. "We'll work on it, aye? You've got no other choice but to obey me," he declared. "And when I need sex, I get sex. No more fucking fighting – I'm not having any of that," his face was solid. But then he let out another small grin with his eyebrows dropping. Then, the deranged man spun around and walked down the stone hallway and into the light.

Two days later

The room spun around Vlayn as hunger defeated him. He was in darkness for days. His stomach stuck to his bones and churned adamantly. His tongue was shriveled. The droplets of water he was given every twenty-four hours just weren't enough. The silence engulfed him every passing minute. His eardrums rang incessantly; the absence of even a little noise evaded him. From time to time he would gasp as loud as he could just to make sure he didn't lose his hearing from this silence.

The planet of Xenamus was known across The Galaxy for its excruciating heat. It could burn through every race with the exclusion of the Babarins. Despite this, Vlayn's naked body shivered on the stone floor. He curled into a ball in the corner of the metal cage, attempting to generate heat, but his body slowly broke down from the cold.

Footsteps called from down the hall, making Vlayn's ears scream with agony. "Time to eat!" DaRoone shouted. "Can't have yuh all munched-out in that cage."

Vlayn grunted with pain as he covered his ears, "Guess you ain't killing me after all," he said beamingly. "Want this?" he asked as he held a dead, raw pramius – a fish-like creature that was found in the oceans of Reft, Siskilian or Sayt-Lok, planets that were very much comprised of large bodies of water. "If you don't eat, guy, you're gonna die. Just say yes. C'mon, make it easy on the both of us."

Silence.

DaRoone gravitated closer to the cage, waiting to hear the words, *yes, DaRoone*. But not a word was murmured from Vlayn's lips. Frustration swiftly conquered DaRoone. He threw the pramius into the cage and dirt and mud stuck to the raw fish as it flopped onto the ground. Vlayn simply eyed the pramius, then observed DaRoone marching down the hallway.

After DaRoone's exit, Vlayn immediately crawled to the pramius on all fours like a cat. He picked it up and analyzed the muck. He scrubbed the scales with his left hand, then raised it to his mouth. His stomach screamed and he knew what needed to be done. He placed the fish in his mouth, slowly biting down into the pramius. His teeth met with the cold flesh, but he bit down harder and his teeth slowly punctured through the scaly surface. Once his teeth were inside, he slowly retracted his face, slowly stripping the foul flesh from the bones. Vlayn spun the flesh around in his mouth with his tongue until he finally began to chew. He could feel every particle of the food tainting his mouth. His stomach sunk inward before he even forced a swallow; even the organ understood the kind of sludge Vlayn was going to force down his throat.

He chewed on it again. Then again. Then again until the pramius was merely bones. He dropped the slimy, meager bones through his fingers and crawled into the corner of the cage, curling himself into a ball. His breathing was labored as he felt the raw fish arguing with the enzymes in his stomach. His body stunk of filth and his growing beard held most of the awful stench. Dirt filled his pores, transforming his identity. Vlayn didn't care, though – the pain he felt was traumatizing. He glanced into the cage next to him quietly, then his face dropped solemnly. Camrynn was *right there* it seemed. His hallucination was cut off, though, by the continuous swirling of his stomach as it tried to digest the raw fish. He knew he was going to vomit, but he tried to keep it down. This was the only food he was getting for a while.

He glanced over at the empty cage to his left again. He could see Camrynn sitting in the corner of her cage, too, crinkling together just like Vlayn.

Vlayn shook his head suddenly, attempting to wake himself. But unfortunately, he already was awake. He ran his fingers through his raunchy beard, experiencing the tormenting agony of being truly, truly alone. He couldn't cry. He needed to, but his body was wilting.

-TEN-

FORLORN FIGURES WITH SCARS

Seventy-one jaros earlier.

The Klapaytch Mountains stood devastatingly high
above the rest of the lowlands of Xenamus. The enormous
peaks scowled silently with a woeful face, the terrors that
transpired all across Jaadakin County; the things the
Jaadakin people were compelled to do under the invisible
laws that these unruly deserts created.

Ellmorr cocked its shoulders back, chin raised, trying
to size itself up against the mighty Klapaytch Mountains
with the lowlands of the deserts staring up at the two
monstrous figures tremulously. The city of Woodvale
cowered at the foot of the mountain range, sitting far away
from Njenwire, the closest city to Woodvale in Jaadakin
County. There was such a great distance between
Woodvale and any other city that it was as if this city was
its own world, surviving all by itself. The Jaadakins that
totaled the waning city's population knew one another.
They had their own language – a language of facial
expressions. One particular facial expression could alert if
there were deadly newcomers to the city – and each person
explicitly understood this expression.

Woodvale was a quaint city; it held a hilly landscape
with a chillier air temperature as opposed to the incredibly
hot climate the rest of the entire planet endured. As
always, food was scarce, but glithémien were even scarcer.
This gradual dip in climate didn't agree with the desert

critters, thus very few numbers crawled throughout the city. Still though, this didn't hold back the extreme barbarism of Jaadakin County.

In the center of Woodvale was a rowdy bar that was full of natives to a city that ceaselessly strived to escape from their unendingly painful life.

The cylinder-shaped glass spun counter-clockwise in the mud-caked hands of a grimy duster as he sat atop a feeble barstool. The glass reflected a dying sunlight that shimmered through the mucky window panes. The bar was poorly lit, but no one cared. This young man stared deeply into his glass, dawdling behind it, and studying the thick alcohol that stagnantly weighed the glass down: Allameen Blaze. It was a heavy drink that was filled with numerous ingredients that could get any lightweight into a state of mind that was far from typical. People filled all the barstools and tables that were available and occupied the floor space. The people spoke of rumors that circulated all over the deserts: the cure for the disease, The Council, and Ellmorr. This man was adorned in a cumbersome, puffy coat and denim-like pants that clung to his calves. He stuck a paylian roll into his lips and lit it slowly, like he had no place to be. But suddenly, he sucked in the smoke and quickly blew it out, as if the smoke in his lungs nettled him, or something underlying made him so pettish, his bones rattled.

"Let m'ask you something," he could hear two men chatting a few seats away from him. "We smoke paylian rolls, but why do we always use DarkWagen Paylian Rolls?"

The other person scoffed, "Who cares what brand paylian rolls we smoke. Jus' shut up and smoke a few till you get high."

"Zander," another man called, shoveling people out of his way.

He took his eyes off the two men speaking of paylian rolls and turned to the muscular, broad man. "Drux," Zander responded drably through the noise of the people.

"We're heading out," Drux ordered.

"Out of Woodvale?"

"Not yet. We have some things to get done here first."

Zander gazed at him, knowing of Drux's loose-lips, his derailed mindset, and his beguiling words that had tendency to drive just about anyone to his level of lunacy. Zander was glad he hadn't continued his sentence; he downed the strong Allameen Blaze and slammed the glass onto the counter. He rose to his feet and met the malignant eyes of Drux. Zander squinted slightly, observing the man's shuttering stare and the abhorrent twinkle that his right eye delivered. Finally, Zander sifted through the mob of people with Drux following.

The pair made it outside the bar and met with about ten more rugged-faced men and dull-faced women. Each one awaited Drux's next command, and more importantly focusing on when they would get their next fix of bloodletting. Zander felt the cool breeze exhaling from the mighty Klapaytch mountains that stood lofty a mere few hundred feet from him. Woodvale was constructed on the doorstep of this mountain range, making its streets broken and hilly. This bar was at a high point in this town, giving Zander a view of this declining town.

Every member in the group was dressed in a leather coat with a logo stitched on the upper right sleeve. The logo held two intimidatingly long letter "L's" with a dark, navy blue tint encompassing it.

"Zander!" Drux called again. Zander ambled through the group and walked to Drux with his head held high. The entire group locked their eyes steadily on Drux, displaying their respect toward the man. Drux leaned in closer to Zander, "That long, *unseemly* scar on your forehead is damn-fuckin' ugly!" he said vigorously while he analyzed Zander's coarse face. "Those scars won't be too lonely anymore," he promised while he unstrapped his belt. Zander glanced down at the belt, then up again at Drux's gleaming, sinister eyes. "What are you waiting for?" Drux inquired. "*What are you waiting for!?!?*" he screamed with spit flinging from his bottom lip and splashing Zander's face. But Zander didn't even flinch; he blinked calmly.

"You know what to do," he told him. "*You* came to join *us*. Entering the Ellmorian Blackguard isn't *simple*," he began, "I promise you it will be the most challenging thing you do. But if you survive your initiation, it will be the best damn-fuckin' thing for you. Now, get on your fucking knees."

Zander's head slowly revolved in circles; studying the men and women that circumscribed him, then listening to the music of raving dusters inside the bar. Each person in this group showcased a wide variety of scars upon their face. There were so many scars that their initial face was altered into a new form; a new personality – a new *person*. This transformation came from the leader of this Ellmorian Blackguard group: Drux.

Finally, Zander dropped to his knees but kept his head cocked upward and his back erect.

"Sure you want to be sitting up that confidently?" Drux asked him.

Zander didn't answer. Instead, he took one deep, heavy breath.

Without a thought, Drux whipped Zander in the back with all his might and the noise of the slap rang for miles. "Sure you want to be that confident?" he asked again. Zander's body was lunged forward, gasping in pain. He still didn't respond.

Drux slashed him again, "Sure 'bout that!?" he hollered forcefully. He whipped him once more in the back and squatted in front of him. He gripped his chin and cheeks and forced Zander to look at him deep into his eyes. "Tell me why you want to join the Blackguard," he demanded with a heavy voice.

Zander forced a swallow to clear his throat and began, "M–My life – my *family* – they banished me. They lived in Ellmorr, but I couldn't live up to their expectations of what a true Ellmorian was, so they ordered the N.M.C. to take me from the Fraygen Plateau."

"So, why the Blackguard then?" Drux asked as he loosened his grip on Zander's face.

"Saw the signs," Zander replied, "saw how fucked up Jaadakin County was. Figured this was my best shot for survival."

A malevolent grin casted upon Drux's face with the tormenting sun gleaming right into his eyes. "You shot right," he said. "But I gotta make sure you're strong enough to make it with us. Your last name is Valem, right?"

He nodded quickly, and Drux rose to his feet above the kneeling Zander. "Alright, everyone!" Drux shouted to the rest of the group. "We *may* have a new addition."

Zander's face and body began to loosen as he calmed down.

"But I'm not too sure yet," Drux spoke as he paced back and forth, "not too sure he's got what it takes – what it takes to live in this group. What it takes to *wipe out* the abominations of this county – the Jaadakins." Drux paused to glance down at Zander's developing confusion. The wind started to roar a bit louder, as if it was foreboding to something far more sinister than mere words. "He's too pretty," Drux added with a lower voice. "He's too… *fresh*," he stopped in place with the belt drooped in his right hand. He was silent and thinking quietly. The chilly winds hailing from the Klapaytch mountains made the belt flutter softly with the breezes and his hair flow freely in the air.

Finally, he spun around and landed a firm smack of the belt onto Zander's innocent face. Drux admired the pain flourishing from Zander's poor heart. He swung again from the left side, settling another hefty blow to his face, and immediately countering with a final whip to his right cheek.

People started flooding out of the bar with drinks in their hands and women in the laps of the men's. They were petrified beneath the surface, but they smothered it; each one knew that this was the wicked Ellmorian Blackguard; a bevy of baneful people that had the caliber to put heads on pikes. If they were set off, mass slaughter would ensue throughout Woodvale.

Zander's face was immediately red and puffy and his right cheek ruptured, beginning to bleed. He turned back to the crowds of inhabitants outside the bar, then at the Blackguard group in front of him. Through the fuzzy eyesight of Zander, he could see the men and women's scarred faces that were transformed into the faces of demented zombies.

Drux grinned and knelt, getting into Zander's face. "There we go," he uttered as he ran his finger sover Zander's face, spreading the blood about his cheek. Zander felt an enormous electrifying pain all across his body; he couldn't even focus on Drux's eyes. "We'll be adding more scars to that face," Drux promised him. He quickly jumped to his feet and shouted, "let's roll out!"

***

The group wandered the deserts with ease, knowing they had the firepower to exterminate even the most dangerous people if the need arose. The deserts of Jaadakin County were silent, acting cowardly at the hands of this Ellmorian Blackguard group. Like the desert, the group members were just as quiet. The men would rub their gnarly beards from time to time and the women would pull back their greasy hair.

Zander staggered behind the group, dragging his aching soles with a mere P.A.G. pistol with half a clip. Very often he would glance down at the pistol. As he would walk, he would slowly turn the pistol in his palm and watch the sun's brilliant rays not only stupefy himself, but illuminate each crevasse of the handgun. To entertain himself, he would turn the pistol in such a way where the sunlight would perfectly outline the engraving on the barrel:

PAG 0082

Drux walked closely behind him, intently studying the back of his head. Just like the entire group, Drux was benumbed from fatigue and hunger, and was in an overwhelming daze from the scorching heat of the Xenamus desert.

"Zander Valem, right?" Drux asked again.

Zander glanced back at him twice before answering. His heartbeat quickened at the question and his powerful enervation evaporated immediately. "Y–Yes," he replied.

Drux simply nodded as he raised his Ctudd 8 assault rifle from his right hand to his left. The magazine of the weapon sat in the back, toward the stock. And every so often, the stock would poke him in the chest. The white metal of the advanced firearm glistened with confidence in the Xenamus sun. Indeed, the Ctudd 8 was fairly popular throughout The Galaxy, but this weapon was far more superior than the typical weaponry that was commonly used throughout Jaadakin County; this particular one hailed directly from Ellmorr, and many who saw Drux carrying it would stop and glance for a moment, simply to see what it was.

Zander refocused on the grim landscape in front of him: the many heads of unforgiving marauders, endless sandy hills, and a minute settlement slowly growing into fruition over the horizon.

The silence settled back in, but not for too long. "*Group!*" Drux roared. All the dusters halted in place and Zander's face immediately entered not only a confounded one, but one that was far stronger than fearful.

Drux grabbed Zander by his left armpit and dragged him through the group. He threw him forward and Zander tried to keep his bearings but he tripped over the sand and fell to his palms. "Get up!" Drux ordered. Zander scurried to his feet but fell once more in the sand. Drux bent forward and scooped him up with exasperation and threw him forward again. The pair walked fifty feet ahead and the group watched intently.

The winds increased for the sky was briskly alternating to a stormy one. The small settlement watched timidly in the horizon in front of a dying sunlight, with the group of Blackguards standing in the opposite direction, stone-solid. Drux rigidly eyed Zander without a blink and without a sheer flinch of his face – he knew his people were observing him.

He could see Drux's trigger-happy fingers reach for his belt and unstrap it. "What're you waiting for?" he asked. "A–A–Again?" Zander responded anxiously. "Get on your fucking knees," he demanded.

The wee amount of hope that Zander held was swiftly and shamelessly sucked from his brain by Drux. "*GET ON YOUR KNEES!!!*" he howled potently. Zander's eyes lost their hope as he morosely lowered to his knees. His head drooped low and he glared at his knees digging into the sand. He studied each grain, wishing he could be one of them and not in this situation.

Drux squatted low with the blood-stained belt in his right hand and the rifle in his left. "You know," he started with a whisper, "my father always said if the blood on the belt is dry, it's time for another strike," he admired the solid blood coating the belt and cackled, "Are you a sinner?" he asked him through the developing winds.

Zander lifted his face to Drux's.

"Are you a sinner, Zander?"

His eyes watered at the new epiphany of the hopelessness of Xenamus.

"Well," Drux added, "are you?"

"Y–Ye–I–" Zander tripped over his words, unknowing of what Drux wanted to hear. "N–No. I am not," he replied, exacerbating the situation.

With the belt still dangling in his hand, his face filled with impetuosity that made him reply with confidence, "Then I believe we oughta change that, don't you agree?"

Zander's head fell low yet again. He was confused in these deserts, just like many others were. He was aimlessly wandering, without a glimpse of what a life with a goal was like. He disappointed his family and was estranged from them. He believed he could handle himself in a world that was full of forlorn figures.

"I asked you a question," Drux urged.

"I–I–"

"Don't you *agree?*" Drux's eyebrows dropped and his pupils grew firm and furious. "DON'T YOU *FUCKING* AGREE!?"

"Y–Y–*YES!!!*"

Drux leapt to his feet and released his fury with the swinging of his belt in circles a few times for good measure. He looked over at his group in the distance, isolated from civilization in these deserts, then back down at the cowering Zander Valem. "Alright, then," he began, "let us add some more scars to that face." With that, he winded his right shoulder back and flung the leather belt as hard and as fast as he could swing at his face. The belt whipped Zander's left cheek and swung around the back of his head, simultaneously slapping the right side.

Drux cocked his arm back again and lashed Zander without hesitation. Zander's body flinched and blood and teeth shot out of his mouth. "*Baleejus*," Drux gasped in amazement. He then kicked Zander into the sand then looked back up at his group with his boot resting on Zander's chest. "Everybody join in!" he waved with a smile.

The group hurried over to their leader and started pouncing on the young Zander. They threw kicks and jabs all over his body while Drux was in the center, swinging down with the belt at his chest. His t-shirt was ruffled about, almost tearing from the sudden jerks of his arms as they swung up and down, over and over again.

Zander screamed in agony, writhing in the sand. He scrunched his body up and dug his head between his forearms for protection. He howled with every landed blow, and he could feel the sweet taste of blood filling his mouth and staining his teeth.

The group continued to beat Zander into the sand, until Drux called it off. "Enough!" he shouted while he leaned over into his face. He closely examined his face for scarring. "Hmmm," Drux pondered. "Give it some time." He stood up and erected his back, swinging his rifle into his hands and gazing off into the distance toward the settlement. Sand particles hailed from the sky and it seemed they were bobbing nervously in front of a dying sunlight and quietly in the empty deserts.

"There," Drux murmured. "Zander, if you aren't a sinner now, you will be in due time. As long as it beats, then I will make sure you are one." He wiped his nose and cocked back his rifle. "Get the kid up," he ordered the group while wiping his nose with the top of his palm. They yanked him up by his arms and placed him on his feet. Drux slapped Zander's bloody face playfully and sent a grin.

Soon, the twelve men and women voyaged onward toward the settlement. As usual, Drux was heading the group and Zander was timidly standing in front of him and the rest of the men. The settlement grew slowly in front of their own eyes as they gradually came closer to it.

"Drux, It's Njenwire," a man suggested after long study of it.

Drux quickly spun back toward him. "What was that?"

"The settlement – It's Njenwire."

"I don't give a single goddamn what village it is or whatever the hell its name is. It must be corrected and conformed to the Ellmorian ways. You know that, DaRoone," Drux said, but he continued to toss thoughts around in his head. Suddenly, he stopped walking, prompting the entire group to halt as well. The group was quiet, the deserts quieter. The wind whispered, and so did Drux, "Or, do you?"

"Wh–Why, *of course*," the man assured his leader. But Drux hummed, "*Hmmmmm...* not *entirely* sure if you understand." The sun was nearing its close, casting a dark silhouette around Drux. A portentous wind predicted something far more dangerous, though.

"I was just saying–" "No, you weren't just saying *anything!!!*" Drux shrieked, spitting in the man's face and letting his fire wash out of him by the force of his tongue. "Seems to *me* that you don't understand our duties here in Jaadakin County! Seems to *me* you aren't as *solidified* with this group like I thought you were! Seems to *me* that *we* all have a non-believer in the Ellmorian Blackguard and we cannot allow it!!!" Drux started to pace around DaRoone, glaring at the man from all angles.

Zander stood behind a few men and women. The thoughts that once occupied his mind reprioritized themselves at this one moment. Before this he thought:

When is our next meal?

I wonder how they are in Ellmorr?

Do they think of me?

But soon his mind overheated with new fluttering thoughts:

What will Drux do? And am I next? His eyebrows lowered in bewilderment, watching from a few feet away.

DaRoone uselessly pled, "N–No, I–I–" with the wind lifting grains of sand from the golden hills off in the distance, DaRoone started hacking up the morsels that flew into his throat. Then, Drux took him by his neck and threw him into the sand, "*Who told you that you could fucking speak!?*" he wailed, then mounted him and quickly glanced up at his group that swiftly circled the scene. "Knife!" he commanded. A woman surged into the action of supplying him with a rusty, chipped blade.

He loomed over DaRoone's face, whose head was slowly sinking into the fluffy sand. "And meanwhile, I thought you had enough *scars* to fill that entire face. No, no

I was too naïve," Drux said. He brought the tip of the blade close to DaRoone's eyes. "Shall we start with the eyes, or the face?" Drux's voice rippled softly.

"P–Pl–*Please.*"

"Does this haunt you?" he asked formidably, but DaRoone wouldn't answer; his wide eyes focused on the rusty, jagged knife edge that dangled right above his left pupil and Drux's ragged, leathery cheeks stretching backward from a menacing laugh that revealed his cracked teeth.

"Then I will make sure this is the most goddamn terrifying thing you've ever experienced." With that, Drux dug the tip of the blade into his skin, finely slicing through DaRoone's filthy cheek. Blood ruptured from the wound, but Drux dug deeper; starting to dissever his cheekbone. Finally, he pulled the knife from the cut, and went to the other cheek and replicated the same carving. He did it twice more on both cheeks until he pulled back and admired his work like a painter.

Blood streamed down DaRoone's face like tears and Drux glanced at his hands, admiring how the county begrimed them. He began to laugh, then moved these palms to DaRoone's face, digging his fingers into the cuts, pulling them further apart, then spreading the blood all over DaRoone's face as much as his own. "You thought I was going to cut your eyes out just then?" he asked while rubbing DaRoone's blood on his own cheeks and grinning maniacally. Drux looked over at Zander, observing his scarred face from the whipping and beatings he took from the Ellmorian Blackguard group, then back at DaRoone. "Now for the eyes," he said dauntingly. Without hesitation, he shoved the tip of the blade into DaRoone's eyeball.

The eye erupted, letting out innards and sludgy, dark red blood. It squirted onto Drux's face. DaRoone's entire body seized in accordance with his awful screams. But Drux pinned him down into the sand as he snickered through his own blood-covered face. "Take *one* more good look at this *gorgeous* planet because your eyesight is about to be absolutely extinct!" he shouted happily as he punctured the other eye and started scraping the sludgy eyeball remains from the socket with his bare fingers. *"Ha-ha-ha-ha-ha-ha-ha!!!"* the man snorted in true joy as he started stripping the eye sockets clean and yanking dead nerves from the brain. DaRoone screamed, feeling Drux cleaning him out.

Drux looked up at Zander while he sat on top of a convulsing DaRoone; DaRoone's blood poured from his cheeks and eyeball remains stuck to his skin while he glared at Zander with a huge smile. DaRoone howled while he reached for his eye sockets. He was able to feel the two empty cavities on his face where his eyes once were a minute ago. Drux energetically hopped to his feet and kicked the bloody mess on the ground. "Zander," he summoned. "Yes," he responded promptly with fear as he made his way to Drux.

Drux rested his hand on Zander's shoulder and gave him a brief grin. Then, he raised the bloody knife to him. "I asked you if you were a sinner," he started, "and you said you weren't. And that's fine, because you will be soon. But take this knife, shut the lights off for this poor, miserable man and you'll be one step closer to entering this Blackguard group."

Zander studied Drux's darkening face in the newly nighttime desert. He was swiftly becoming desensitized to the terrors of Jaadakin County through this man. Finally, he took the knife from Drux and proceeded to DaRoone who was still whimpering painfully in the bloody sand.

"The neck," Drux suggested. "Easiest way to reach for them lights and *flick* them off." Then, he added candidly, "the blade won't really get through the skull," he said while scratching his cheek.

Zander glanced back at him and nodded in dismay. His eyes returned to DaRoone. His face shrunk in disgust at the eyeless face of the man; entrails of his eyes scorched his cheeks and decorated the rest of his face. He heaved painfully, waiting to die.

Finally, Zander knelt above the pain, pulled his arm back and swung at the neck. His own fear conquered him and made his swinging arm weak. The blade barely punctured the man's neck, so he was still alive but struggled to breathe.

"What's going on?" Drux asked suspiciously.

"N–Nothing," Zander quickly stabbed DaRoone's neck.

"There it is," Drux congratulated joyously.

Zander stepped back from the corpse; streams of blood started from the empty holes in the body's head, and continued to fall into the sand beneath it. The gashes on the cheeks dangled open and Drux smiled senselessly at Zander. "It's an ugly sight to you, I know," he said. "But you killed," Drux said, "you drew the blood of another Blackguard in this group. Therefore, you aren't Zander Valem no longer, no, no. You have stolen the name. You must identify yourself as DaRoone." Drux glanced over at his group, "Everyone!" he shouted, "Meet DaRoone!"

The Ellmorian Blackguard group clapped like drones. Zander scanned the group with nervous eyes, knowing he was slowly fitting into the horror.

***

The small settlement of Njenwire stood right before their toes. Small structures accompanied the sandy pathways that cut through every corner of the village. Despite its meager size, the town boasted a dense population with its people packing it to the brim. Njenwire was a northern village, relatively close to Woodvale. Similar to this major city, Njenwire's chillier air temperature held back much of the glithémien critters. However, people still scurried about in fear of a deadly bite.

The group, including Drux and the new DaRoone, stood before the apothecary and the crowds of bustling people surrounding it. The Blackguards stood sturdily behind their leader and DaRoone, understanding what was going to soon occur. DaRoone quietly observed the natives while planting his two aching feet into the sand. "The Ellmorian Blackguard is simple," Drux told him, "our main objective is to get rid of the scums of Xenamus – the Jaadakin people. The organization tends to take on Jaadakin people, however, because we feel even the worst of devils can change. My group – the men and women right there –" he pointed backward, "*I* was a Jaadakin… we all were Jaadakins. Now – we are *Blackguards*… Now listen, I'm crazy."

DaRoone peered at Drux's bloody face from earlier.

"I'm crazy," he repeated with a grin. "I lost my old self when I entered the Ellmorian Blackguard. I'm self-aware, I know this. There are many others that lead Blackguard groups, but I just lead mine differently. I've gotta *whip* the concept of the Ellmorian Blackguard into people's minds.

I must have people be afraid of me, so they follow me. I teach through example…"

DaRoone continued to analyze the people in front of him; Jaadakins going about their daily lives, trying to survive, trying to keep their families together, trying to find love in a world that was so loveless. "You told me you weren't a sinner, *DaRoone*," Drux said as he began picking his teeth with his index finger, "but the only way to enter the Ellmorian Blackguard is to sin." He watched DaRoone's face; a face that was thoroughly ingrained with filth and far more covered in fresh scars. Finally, he pushed his Ctudd-8 assault rifle into DaRoone's chest, "Empty that entire clip into this crowd of people," he whispered, "and your initiation will conclude."

DaRoone grabbed the weapon and glanced into his eyes, "Drux," he said, petrified. "Do you want to end up like the *real* DaRoone? A man whose name *you* conquered?"

DaRoone was silent with his mouth slowly creaking open. Drux's brawny shoulders flailed forward, "*Kill them!!!*" he screamed with rage as he pointed to the crowd. The mob of people in the sandy, cobblestone road stopped almost immediately and snapped their eyes on the group. They examined them until they finally understood who they were: the killing machines – the Ellmorian Blackguard. "I–I–I don't know if I–I *can*," he insisted.

"Do you enjoy your eyesight, DaRoone?" Drux asked, looking down into his eyes. "Pull the trigger on these people," he said frankly, then migrated back to his group, observing.

"P–Please," a Njenwire native stepped out of the crowd, begging DaRoone.

Both DaRoone's and Drux's attention snapped onto this woman. "I know who you are," she said, "*we* know who you all are. Please – we are *good* people," she insisted. "Njenwire is falling, just like the rest of Jaadakin County. We have no hope left. Please, we will eventually die from starvation or glithémien. So, *please*, by the name of Baleejus allow us to live the remainder of our days with our families," she begged DaRoone, the man behind the trigger, and the man who was about to execute a crowd of innocent beings and impose an untimely death upon them all. "Please!!!" the woman cried, stepping forward. "You *all* can change. There is a way back!" a tear ran down her face, but she pressed on, "we all started out somewhere! A heart! A family! We all were innocent Babarins at one time or another!" and soon, Drux grew very, very silent, listening to the woman from afar. His face loosened, and so did DaRoone's. The woman gasped heavily as more tears streamed down her face, "We–we have all done some–something at one time or another! Done something we never thought we would *ever* do! And we did it for the benefit of ourselves or–or for someone else! We are all the same!!! So please!!!"

Drux exhaled heavily and his face transformed into a softer one as he listened to her voice and her words. "DaRoone…" he called through the wind. The Njenwire woman looked over at Drux with hope, and Drux could feel her gaze. "Kill em' all," he ordered with a voice whose tone was unchanged, undismayed by the woman's words. Drux paused a few seconds before this, but he was far too deep into his own sadistic mind; no one could shine a candle into his soul.

"*Please!!!*" the woman shouted. Drux's face grew red and his palms and forehead sweaty. "*DaRoone!!!*" he could hear him call yet again. "*Please!!!*" the woman shouted back.

Drux chuckled, *"DO IT, DAROONE!!!"* he roared. And finally, DaRoone pulled the trigger and held it down for a straight ten seconds. The rifle popped backward into his shoulder numerous times, unleashing an infuriated outrage of bullets at the crowd. The woman absorbed two bullets which propelled her onto her back.

Nettled, Drux roared, *"SPRAY 'EM!!!"* DaRoone shut his eyes and waved his arms back and forth, allowing every bullet to make a severe impact with every Njenwire native. The people flew to the ground with their lives being absorbed by DaRoone. Finally, everything was silent, and the assault rifle dully clicked. DaRoone exhaled a horrified breath as he looked at the tragedy he created. Dozens of innocent people lay dead in their own suffering; their own blood, at the hands of DaRoone.

Drux sneaked behind DaRoone and placed his hand on his left shoulder. "Let's have a look," he said, then started toward the pile of dead bodies. The group followed, and the murderer trailed them all faint-heartedly. The bodies were sprung onto their backs and chests, necks were snapped in seemingly uncomfortable positions, blood, brain matter and other innards covered every corpse, and many still held their same appalled facial expressions that they displayed just seconds before the massacre. DaRoone stepped carefully through the sea of bodies until he discovered one luscious Babarin woman that was toward the back. She was light-haired and seemed to speak so highly through her amiable personality – a personality that came to a halt at the hands of a bullet. The woman's eyes were open, however. They were stagnant, unmoving, drying-out, hopeless and even more weighed down by the disappointments of Jaadakin County.

DaRoone squatted cautiously above the pretty woman and gleamed heavily into her once majestic eyes. He could feel her looking at him through this shallow glass pane that were her eyeballs. DaRoone could envision this nameless woman standing realistically behind these eyes, in a different realm; a plane of existence that was tranquil, a region that was only accessible through death. Even though DaRoone stole her life, he could see her mocking him, hopping with cheerfulness that DaRoone transported her to a better place. One that was far better than the one he was still in.

His visions were swept away with the sandy wind and the crunching sounds of the Ellmorian Blackguard group jumping on top of each body dominantly and skipping across their chests and backs. "DaRoone," Drux called as he migrated over to him. "This is our purpose," he spoke into his ear, "all these things were scums of Xenamus. The Jaadakins are the reason this planet is so upside-down. It is our *job* to correct it. It's what we do." DaRoone was quiet, staring into the same dry eyes, hoping to see the woman again on the opposite side. She was long gone, though. "*DaRoone,*" he raised his severe tone. DaRoone turned, sat on the ground next to the dead woman and the dozens of people he slaughtered. The empty, lifeless rifle rested mutely next to him. He could feel his own saneness slipping away from him with every person he murdered. DaRoone understood his deterioration. What was he to do of it, though? The worsening of the mind and the decline into a barbarous killer and survivalist was the only way to survive in Jaadakin County. Everyone was on this track to insanity, if they hadn't traveled down it already. It seemed to be the only way to live.

The Ctudd 8 rifle was dead of ammunition, the people around him had their heartbeats stolen from them, and the living Ellmorian Blackguard group around him was breathing, but they were dead. It seemed the new DaRoone was the only one living here, and it was difficult for him to hold a candle to his face and understand the true severity of his decline. But it was just about time for him to put the candle out.

***

Seventy-one jaros later.

DaRoone stood just outside of a metal cage. One woman and another man stood by his side. He was silent, listening to the griping pain from his four-fingered hand. DaRoone was unsure of what kind of torture he would impose next on his victim in this cage. He wiggled his right pinky, even though it was no longer there, and he thought of Drux and Zander Valem momentarily; he could hardly remember what it was like to feel emotion besides excitement from his sadistic and carnal tendencies.

The cage to his right was empty; DaRoone was finished with that inmate. His sanity had been lost for the past seventy jaros and the people he captured was his outlet for his fiery rage that always whisked through his blood. The people who worked for him were his mere servants. They understood that if they didn't adhere *exactly* to what DaRoone ordered, it would cost them a limb. DaRoone shut his eyes and listened to the starving, aching groan of a man that he captured and tortured for approximately two days at this point. He heard the uncanny music that glowed from this suffering man: Vlayn Par'Wil.

DaRoone let the sound of his torture baptize him, allowing his sinking mind to concoct the next torture scheme. *I'm going crazy,* DaRoone thought to himself, and he loved the thought of it. But Vlayn Par'Wil's eyes were filled with ferocity. He battled DaRoone from behind his bars. He wouldn't let DaRoone's heart beat any longer – not after what he did to Camrynn Ansheen.

-Eleven-

SILENCE

Thirty-four days later

Vlayn grew skinnier each passing day. He was used to being hungry; Vlayn's body was accustomed to battling diseases and germs. However, the last time he endured starvation like this was when he was alone with his brother and they were forced to cook and eat their father's limbs to survive.

Pramius bones surrounded Vlayn in the cage. His head spun in circles from the darkness and the pain of losing Camrynn heightened each day, but it was at its worst at night. He longed for her to be next to him again. He pled to Baleejus that she would return to this spiteful world and be by his side yet again. But Vlayn knew he was being ignorant.

DaRoone entered the room again. "thirty-somethin' fucking days and you still can't obey your master!" he shouted while walking with an odd gait. "You're an animal," he said, "Yuh gotta get in line – knuckle down on the orders." DaRoone exclaimed as he sent a piercing glare at Vlayn. "Tayreen!" he yelled into the air while continuing to lock eyes with Vlayn.

"*Yes, DaRoone!*" Vlayn could hear from the other room. Then, a soldier geared with firearms roped around his shoulder promptly greeted DaRoone with a small crate.

Vlayn got to his enfeebled feet, trying to get a better look at the crate, but it was too dark too see.

"You're either going to die, or obey me," DaRoone threatened over rustling noises from the crate. Vlayn glared heavily at this man; his tousled hair, his large, deformed nose, his under bite, his ragged, tattered clothing that symbolized his soul and how it was mottled with red, and the blood that seeped through his swaddled nub of a pinky. Vlayn hated it *all.* "All yuh had to do was prick up your little *fucking* ears and do what you were told, and what you were told was to simply say, *yes DaRoone.* Two words!!!" he screamed. "Yuh couldn't even do that. But no, no... Don't worry kinky Vlayn, you'll understand... let em' out," he ordered Tayreen.

Tayreen stepped inside Vlayn's cage and dropped the crate. Glithémien rained from the crate and instantly targeted a naked Vlayn. "Time to skedaddle!!!" he could hear DaRoone yell while Vlayn ran to the corner of his cage. He climbed the metal bars behind him, attempting to elevate himself above the critters that infested the floor. The glithémien hissed, chomping their fangs together on the floor below Vlayn. Their legs scurried along the floor and the venom oozed from their teeth. "Stop this!!!" Vlayn shrieked with fear. His arms burned as exhaustion hammered him down. He wouldn't let go; he wouldn't die.

"Just say it," DaRoone said as he caressed the stump of where his finger once was. "All you need to do is say it, and this will all go away," DaRoone said, then followed with a short titter.

"I'm going to fucking *kill* you!" Vlayn howled into the air.

"Nah, yuh won't, but the glithémien will in a matter of minutes. Your arms are going to get too tired and you'll fall to the floor, where the glithémien will stab you with their sharp legs as they swarm you. Their teeth'll rip at your weak Babarin skin and their foamy venom will empty into your blood. You'll soon feel them crawl inside of you. Shit, maybe you'll just die from suffocating underneath fifty of those things. But I won't let the glithémien eat your flesh for too long, no. That would be the easy way out of a mean, mean world that is Xenamus. The only way to leave this life is to leave it the way you lived it: painful, dreadful, and agonizing. *So*, I'll take the glithémien out. I'll starve you, let you bleed out from all the holes in your skin that the glithémien dug, and slowly allow the disease to wipe out your immune system… make you vomit your insides. I'll wait until you feel your psarrolii and stomach shrivel up inside you. I'll make you suffer. I can do that. I *will* do that. I promise, kinky Vlayn. I *promise*. This is me giving you my word." DaRoone ended his speech while Vlayn grasped the bars; his palms started to blister and he could feel his hands slowly sliding down. "All you need to do is say it! All you need to do is give your bitch-self a voice and *say it!*" he howled again.

Soon, the glithémien started forming a mountain; piling themselves atop each other, slowly making their way up the bars of the cage. "Stop this!!!!!" Vlayn screamed even louder. Tears filled his eyes as sheer agony tainted his voice. "Please!!!"

"Say it!!!!" DaRoone roared forcefully.

Still, Vlayn didn't say anything.

The darkness seemed to grow darker.

His breathing seemed to suddenly become slower.

The vision of Camrynn in the barren cage beside him seemed to grow more vivid. The image of her was revived, like it did days before. He could see her bright Babarin skin, her luscious hair. He could hear her soft voice, even if her deceased one wasn't uttering a word. And still, the voice of DaRoone only intensified amongst his daydreams.

"Fucking say it!!! You wouldn't be here right now if you would have just said it!!!" DaRoone shrieked.

Vlayn could see Camrynn just beside him now, as if she escaped from her own cage... as if she escaped from her own bindings of the past life she lived. She walked up to Vlayn unaffected by the glithémien scrambling along the floor. She wore stunning white clothing and dazzling necklaces with a sizable saurapine ring; all the trappings of extravagant wealth in the Kirbinian Galaxy. She placed her hand on his cheek. He could feel the warmth bleeding from the invisible hand. His eyes closed slowly – his treacherous surroundings withered away. It was as if he was transported to the tranquil home that Camrynn now lived in.

But all of a sudden, a shot fired off, landing right into the concrete wall beside him where Camrynn was standing. Her hollow figure disappeared. DaRoone stood outside the cage, lowering the pistol he just shot. "I'm going to keep shooting, closer and closer to your body until you fall, or until you say it!!"

Vlayn tried to raise his feet higher on the metal bars. The glithémien were slowly crawling up the cage and he could feel his exasperated body pulling him down.

"Say it!!!" DaRoone shouted again as he shot another bullet closer to Vlayn. "Say it!!!"

"*Yes DaRoone!!!*" Vlayn screamed with discontent.

"Lemme' hear it again!!!"

Vlayn grunted with agony and he closed his eyes, "Y-Yes DaRoone!"

"There it is!" DaRoone said with excitement. "C'mon Tayreen, get the body. This guy has had enough for now."

"Yes DaRoone," the man responded. Tayreen hastily spun around and walked down the hallway.

"Quickly! Before they kill him!" DaRoone shouted, then turned back to Vlayn, "See how easy it was?" he said, "All yuh had to do was say it," he added casually. "Finally, yuh shut up, yuh stopped pissin' and moanin'. Easy, ain't it?"

Vlayn was still clasped to the metal bars. DaRoone began to smile, revealing his decaying set of teeth again. He knew he tore Vlayn down, made him less than a man and stripped him of his dignity. After this was all completed, he would rebuild him into a robotic slave.

His arms and legs seared with pain from holding up his own body weight for such a long period of time. The large critters were still crowding the floor just beneath him. Soon, Tayreen entered the hallway again and approached the cage with a foul-smelling, rotting corpse. He tossed the body into the corner of the cage, opposite Vlayn.

Immediately, the glithémien halted their movement at the smell of death. The large insects instantaneously gravitated to the corpse and began their feeding frenzy on the rotten insides.

Vlayn hesitantly lowered his bare feet to the stone floor as he examined the glithémien herding over the carcass across him. As he stepped closer, his eyes flooded with tears, his face grew numb and his knees buckled. Chunky, dark red blood gushed out of the body, and Vlayn could hear the glithémien snapping the bones of the corpse with their fangs.

He snapped his attention over at the maniacal DaRoone, then back at the body on the floor. It was Camrynn. Her face was bruised and scarred, her clothes torn in all directions and represented complete violation, even in her desolate state. The critters smothered her entire body, enveloping the beautiful, sweet person she once was – the woman Vlayn was glued to, someone who could hold the weight of Xenamus and all its perplexities on her mere shoulders while assuring Vlayn was alright.

"Not so hard, aye?" DaRoone suggested excitedly, knowing he was winning.

Tayreen poured gasoline over the corpse of Camrynn. Vlayn watched intently, for his eyes thumped with rage at the sight of both these sinful men. Tayreen proceeded to set her on fire, immediately scorching the body, while disintegrating the glithémien that surrounded it.

DaRoone approached the naked Vlayn and threw his clothes on the ground. "Put your fucking clothes on, guy," he ordered. Vlayn equipped his clothes slowly; putting his pants and shirt on required too much energy for a debilitating Vlayn. "Now, who are you?" DaRoone pressed with an evil, underlying tone of malevolence and intimidation. He raised his right hand and placed it on Vlayn's cheek. Vlayn could feel the man's four fingers and the knuckle just above his pinky finger, where Vlayn chewed it off.

Vlayn cleared his throat, but didn't utter a word. Instead, his eyes were locked on DaRoone with the glare of animosity. His eyebrows lowered, and DaRoone felt his rage.

"Exactly," DaRoone whispered through the darkness. "That's because you aren't anybody. Your only purpose is to serve me. The only two words yuh should know how to speak is yes, and, my name: *DaRoone*… forget about your childhood, that Babarin I killed and how my people over here *roasted* her to perfection… forget about Ellmorr and the life of extravagance yuh *wished* yuh had. Forget about the High Clansees, Corvonn and Kirbside. Forget about the rest of the Kirbinian Galaxy. The only thing yuh should know now is your home, which is this cage in the darkness, your job, which is to be my pleasure, and your master: *me*," DaRoone's eyebrows raised, waiting for Vlayn's expected response. This man would never vacillate, but neither would Vlayn.

The only response he received, though, was absolute silence.

He lifted his palm from Vlayn's face and stepped back, "When I first saw ya, pal, you looked fucking *badass*. Not the punching bag type, nope, nope, *nope*. You were the duster *punching* the punching bag. Knew it was gonna be tough to *pull* you to the fucking ground. Yuh had the whole beard, goin'. Acting all tough in front of that sack that I put down," he shot out, pointing at the body of Camrynn. "I was shocked, though. You turned out to be nothin' more than an easy pick that anyone can push around."

Vlayn's eyes started tearing merely from the thought of Camrynn and from this wicked Babarin man speaking her name. "*I'm going to fucking kill you*," Vlayn promised, uttering every syllable. "I'm going to do whatever it takes to kill you," he added as he stepped closer to DaRoone. "I don't care how. Just as long as you're dead. *Nothing* will stop me from killing you. *Nothing* will."

DaRoone's face simmered with fury, "Nope!" he yelled. "Nope, yuh won't be doin' that. Obviously, though, you aren't on board with this and you have to be." His face grew heinous, cold, and consecutive with his severity. He didn't move a muscle until he jumped forward and took Vlayn by the neck and threw him into the metal bars that circumscribed the cage.

Vlayn shrieked with pain with his skull smashed into the thick metal bars. This didn't stop him though. Vlayn threw a knee into DaRoone's chest, instantly sucking the air from him.

Tayreen, DaRoone's slave, rushed into the room to his master's defense. This Babarin man wanted to escape his life of submissiveness to one man. If Tayreen failed at assisting Vlayn in killing DaRoone, though, then DaRoone would slice open his abdomen, yank out his organs – whatever he could get ahold of – and make him chew on it. Or worse, DaRoone would chop off each of the man's toes, cook them, then make him eat it. To take the safe route, Tayreen battled Vlayn alongside his leader.

Vlayn was taken down by Tayreen and was welcomed with a series of fists to the face. Soon, Vlayn was being choked by this man. He could feel his thumbs pressing deeper and deeper into his esophagus. Vlayn grabbed Tayreen's face, attempting to choke him in return, but he was unsuccessful. Then, he swiftly shifted his hands to his upper face. He began to dig his thumbs into his eye sockets.

Tayreen quickly shrugged Vlayn's arms off his face, protecting his eyesight, even though it was now fuzzy and his left eye sending poignant pains from the socket to the back of his skull. Vlayn's arms dropped to the stone floor weakly. He could see DaRoone rising to his feet in the darkness in front of him. His hair flopped from side to side as he gathered his bearings from his brief brawl with Vlayn. "That was fucking spine-tingling!" he could hear DaRoone exclaim. "Your worthless girl is dead! You're next, you arrogant piece of *fuck!!!*"

Vlayn's vision darkened, until a bright light shimmered into the blackness of the cage and a cold resurgence flooded his body. He was exiting this life. But he wouldn't give up yet. He sifted the floor with his hands, searching for something he could use to save his grim life, until he felt the pramius bones lying next to him. Vlayn took the bones and jabbed it into Tayreen's side, making him collapse.

Vlayn gasped, sucking in as much oxygen as his lungs could possibly attain. He immediately jumped to his feet, knowing DaRoone would attack him next.

And he did.

DaRoone quickly drew a knife and slashed it toward Vlayn. Luckily, he was able to avoid this attack.

But he wasn't able to avoid the counterattack.

DaRoone took a step closer to him and slashed the blade again, this time piercing Vlayn's stomach slightly.

Vlayn could feel his clothes slowly soiling with his own blood. DaRoone charged him, but he shimmied out of the way and was able to pin DaRoone against the cage wall instead. Vlayn wasted no time and stabbed DaRoone twice in the stomach with the bone. The first time penetrated, but the second forced the bone to snap in half. As a substitute, Vlayn took a strong grip around DaRoone's neck and slammed it against the metal bars of the cage several times. The rusty knife slipped through DaRoone's fingers.

Then, with all his might, he threw DaRoone to the side, knowing Tayreen would be retaliating any second.

Tayreen got to his feet and lunged toward Vlayn.

Off-balance and still trying to gather his footing after tossing the heavier DaRoone, got tackled to the floor yet again. Tayreen mounted Vlayn robustly and choked him again.

But Vlayn wouldn't give up.

In spite of the loss of hope, he just wouldn't give up his life yet. There were still a few things left to live for. And so, he shoved his fingers into Tayreen's wound, causing him to howl and lose his breath.

Vlayn threw his arms to the floor and began to sit up. He shoved his fist into the wound again, making the man even weaker. Tayreen fell to the side, attempting to regain his strength. Vlayn rapidly surged to his feet and started toward DaRoone's dropped knife. He grabbed the weapon and returned to the fallen Tayreen. He climbed on top of him, grabbed his neck, looked him deep into his eyes while driving the blade into his neck. Warm blood squirted from Tayreen's veins, soaking Vlayn's hands.

One second after, DaRoone pulled Vlayn off the lifeless body of Tayreen. He growled as he took Vlayn and threw him to the bars. Vlayn spun with a feverish haste with the knife tightly in his right hand.

DaRoone struck Vlayn again with another fist. Blood oozed from his cut lips and cheeks, heaving in agony. He held his lips momentarily, seeing his blood slowly drip from his face to his feet. He ignored it, though, and quickly stepped forward, attempting to jab DaRoone with the blade. But DaRoone side-stepped, avoided the strike, and hit Vlayn with a kick which forced Vlayn's feet to stagger slightly.

Vlayn stood stoop-shouldered and jaded from many, many restless nights, no food, and the absence of any light. He was aghast as he stood at DaRoone's doorstep. DaRoone struck Vlayn yet again. The small amount of hope he obtained escaped through the cracks of his lips.

Vlayn was the one equipped with a weapon. Somehow, though, DaRoone was about to take his life.

DaRoone started toward Vlayn again.

But Vlayn, with all the energy he had in him, jutted his arm forward and shoved the knife into DaRoone's torso, making him breathe a bit heavier. Blood seeped slowly from his chest, sullying his shirt, drenching Vlayn's hand, and coating the grip of the knife with his coppery liquid. It seemed that a stab to the chest was nothing to DaRoone.

But Vlayn didn't let up. This one jab gave him courage and the energy he needed. He ripped the blade out and stuck him again with the blade, then again and again into his stomach.

Blood cascaded from his body, drenching Vlayn.

DaRoone was wide-eyed as his life swiftly flashed. His minutes were limited now, and he understood the intensity of it all. His knees gave in and he tumbled to the floor of Vlayn's cage.

Vlayn pursued the man, though.

"I told you I was going to fucking kill you!" Vlayn screamed as he stared gravely into the eyes of a dying DaRoone. "You're *nothing*, you weak little duster. I *told* you

I was going to find any way to take your life. There's no hesitation when it comes to people like you," Vlayn murmured as he repeatedly took the knife out of his chest and pressed it back in. "I told you there wouldn't be a *shred* of a thought when it came to the worthiness of your life. And guess what?" he pressed, "I didn't take *one* second before I took yours," Vlayn finished.

Vlayn pulled the knife out from his chest and ran it once more into the open cavity of his body for good measure. DaRoone gagged on the blood that surfaced to his mouth. He tried to breathe, but his life was quickly ending. Vlayn shoved his hand into the wounds, grabbed whatever he could, and tore his stomach and ripped his intestines from DaRoone's body. He threw the innards into DaRoone's face, and slowly wobbled to his feet, dropping the blade onto the bloody mess below his feet. "*Never* forget who you are." Vlayn declared with blood masking his irate face, "*Never* let your guard down… If you listened to your own advice you wouldn't be dead," Vlayn rambled, out of breath.

Vlayn limped out of the cage and swung the door shut behind him. He heard DaRoone groaning from underneath the entrails that sat atop his face. He began to walk out of the stone hallway and into the light that he stared at for days and days; the light he envied for so long. He stopped in his tracks and looked back at Camrynn's cell. His eyes squinted, surprised that not a feeling of remorse, bleakness, or even depression overcame in. He was merely being naïve at this point, though, and he knew this. Adrenaline coursed throughout his body, and this was the reason for his coldness. Vlayn knew eventually the misery from the loss of Camrynn would rain down on his soul in due time.

He exited the hall and entered the next room. The smell of death, rotten flesh and blood filled this cold area. Body parts hung from the ceiling with blood dripping from the mutilated parts to the floor. Carcasses lay on old, wooden tables with sharp blades and scalpels accompanying the scene. Snapped and perfectly-cut bones were organized alongside these utensils. Heavy jackets with the symbol of two L's stitched on the sleeve were all strewn about the floor. Vlayn ambled over to the coats and examined them carefully. His coarse thumb ran over the sewed symbol, trying to come to grips with where he once saw it previously. Finally, it hit him: the Ellmorian Blackguard. Vlayn pulled his eyes from the apparel and began scrutinizing the room once more.

Food grew scarce in Jaadakin County. People sought ways to live and the last way to eat was to eat their own people. Vlayn stood solidly in the center of the eerie room with a dim light illuminating him, the blood and sinew soaking him and his clothes. The luminescence crafted by a large bonfire in the corner of the room whispered through the smell of death.

This was the light Vlayn was so envious of for all the days he was trapped in darkness. This light, though, was the source of cannibalism. It was the warrant to commit heartless acts of violence and sin. Vlayn was no different than this fire and those that ate the flesh that once roasted atop it. Indeed, he wasn't cannibal, but he held one identical characteristic. He was a sinner; there were times he drew blood when he didn't need to. DaRoone may have been a necessary killing, but Vlayn Par'Wil took the souls of some others that he could have spared.

This light was far more devious than it seemed at face value, acting as a tiny little light from down a stone hallway. Its weak flames and softer flashes of light mocked

Vlayn while he was trapped in the dark. It seemed like the frisky fire understood Vlayn's captivity and his torment.

He walked up to the fire, and it seemed as if the fire grew in size, as if it needed to stand tall against him. The flames grew and popped in his gaze. Vlayn stared at the beaming glow that the fire regurgitated.

Eventually he spun around and scanned the room. A small mound of sand sat adjacent the flames, accompanied by three rusty metal buckets. One was flipped over on its side, and the other two sat patiently on the ground. He murdered the man who once used these buckets, and now he was using them himself. He walked over to it slowly, glancing back at the fire every so often, ensuring it wouldn't attack him from behind. He scooped up a large bucketful of sand and dumped it over the flame.

The fire slowly began to die.

Vlayn retreated to the sand and scooped up more. He dumped the rest of it on the dying fire, permanently exterminating it.

The room soon grew morbidly dark and sinister. This darkness showed no hesitation as it instantly invaded Vlayn. Quietness didn't act as a bystander, though. It joined forces with the blackness and gnarled at Vlayn's skin as he stood in silence in this underground cove. Faint chatter came from another room; the rest of this Blackguard group hadn't the slightest clue that their leader was just killed.

Xenamus was a filthy planet filled with pitiless souls and others who were entangled by harrowed pain that was caused by their losses. The world pushed people to perform certain dark deeds that were necessary for survival – things that Jaadakins never saw themselves ever doing.

Life was a test on Xenamus. Those living after The Great Fall in Jaadakin County had to be resilient to survive; they needed the capability to channel their heartache to battle those around them to live.

The cages in this dark room grew more silent than ever as they held the last memory of the softhearted Camrynn Ansheen, along with the hundreds of other suffering souls that DaRoone captured before this couple.

Vlayn put an end to the continuous series of seized lives, though. He wouldn't allow the sins to continue even if he was as much of a sinner as DaRoone.

DaRoone made the greatest error of his life by putting Vlayn Par'Wil in his cage. He was just too strong to be apprehended – and he was strong enough to dominate this man and put a halt to the man's reign.

Vlayn continued onward. His mind bustled with thoughts but everything around him still seemed controlled by a dreadful, dreadful silence.

-Twelve-

WHISPERING PHANTOMS

Part I: THE BOG

Thirty-five jaros later

Witherhart was right at Vlayn's feet. He held his Troid submachine gun to his shoulder, ready to fire on any enemy, or merely any heartbeat. He was curious, though. Vlayn needed to see his hometown's deterioration jaros after moving out – jaros after the killing of his family.

Before entering the core of the city, Vlayn entered the vismal, or "the bog," in English. Witherhart, along with other major cities in Jaadakin, such as Ridgecall or Ambervale, was once a moderate city with commerce flowing through the streets, with people grooming their healthy lives. This was over one-hundred jaros ago, though. In current-jaro, disease and poverty sucked the cities into the ground.

Witherhart was one of the largest cities in Jaadakin, but when it was decreasing into poverty, so did its population. The number of people shrunk and as a result, the inhabitants grew closer together and they retreated to the center of the city, leaving hundreds of buildings empty. These hollow grounds were the very definition of the Vismal: the deflated, grim outskirts that surrounded the dying center of Witherhart.

Vlayn always studied the Vismal from his apartment window as a boy. He had a clear view of a portion of the Vismal from where his bedroom was stationed, where he could feel the dark loneliness creeping into his young, curious soul. Even still, though, it struck curiosity within the boy. All the jaros leading up to his escape of his hometown, he always had an increasing desire to explore the deceased buildings.

He finally was.

Vlayn energetically progressed up a set of stone stairs, jumping two steps at a time with his submachine gun raised solidly and the stock of the weapon pressing sturdily against his aching shoulder. Debris permeated along the stairs as his boots slid along the rubble with every increasing step. He exhaled heavily, allowing his warm breath to bounce against the metal stock. His finger lay tensely on the cold trigger, ready to release forty rounds into any detected heartbeat.

At the top of the stairs, trash and detritus littered the linoleum floor. A dining table was flipped on its side in the center of the room and a cold body sat up against the walls just below a set of windows. Vlayn lowered the weapon from his defensive state. It hung in his right hand as he leisurely walked about the room, inspecting the remains and the body. The musty, tacky smell made his nose tingle, and all he could realize was the close resemblance to his old childhood apartment bedroom. It wasn't exact. But it was far too close.

Beyond the windows, enervated buildings that once lodged life and endless deserts lay in front. Vlayn could see a touch of Shorewood from this height. He squinted his eyes, as if he was zooming in with binoculars.

A frigid shiver ran down his spine, for he could feel Enver Rodge staring at him from this distance, trying to shoot Vlayn in the head like Vlayn did to her many, many jaros ago.

Then, Vlayn spun his head toward the core of Witherhart, attempting to see his apartment building. He couldn't. All he could see was thick black smoke fuming into the sky and the smell of charred rubble.

Vlayn dropped the Troid to his feet and dropped to the floor, sitting upright next to the inert carcass. He peered emotionless at the dead body right next to him, mirroring the lifelessness next to him, almost envying it. He shut his tired eyes, letting the hunger and hopelessness of life wash over him. Vlayn felt his subconscious swim through the darkness of his mind as he drifted off into sleep. He could feel the expired presence of the corpse lying next to him as he slept. His inactive mind soon began dreaming of everything from the killing of Enver Rodge and DaRoone, to the happier days with Camrynn Ansheen. Then, his mind linked to just that: happier days. The days that were far too scarce. The days that stood out amongst the normalcy that the rest of the days *always* produced: survival, starvation, death, suffering, misery, and loneliness. Then, his sleeping mind jumped to the topic of death; his little brother, Tithen, falling into the lap of the Glithémien Disease. Vlayn's imagination transported him back to the very second in his life where he was forced by Xenamus to pull the trigger of a pistol that was pointed at Tithen's head.

Then, Vlayn's nightmare brought him back to the scene of his brittle, dying mother vomiting blood when he was just a young man. He watched her pass away and Vlayn was unable to do anything about it. No one was able to do anything, not even his father.

174

Vlayn's *father*.

Vlayn dreamt of his father and how he never wanted to disappoint him. When he tasked Vlayn and Tithen to find a doctor to examine their mother, Vlayn was determined to do just that and nothing less. He couldn't let his father down.

Footsteps banged against the stairs that were linked to the room Vlayn was asleep in. He didn't wake up immediately, though. He had fallen too far into his exhaustion.

The footsteps clamored along the floor once again, and finally Vlayn awoke. He scrambled for his Troid and locked it on the staircase in front of him and waited for the person to get to the top of the stairs. Vlayn didn't even get up. He sat on the floor, gun raised. He panted heavily and stoutly fastened his stare through his bloodshot eyes. His enthusiastic index finger lay softly on the trigger, ready to draw blood yet again.

The footsteps grew louder and louder as the person made their way up the stairs.

But who was it?

It had to have been another survivor, similar to Vlayn. Someone roaming the deserts of Jaadakin County, fending for themselves. Maybe they ventured into Witherhart hoping it was safe. If this was the case, they were most certainly incorrect.

An elderly Babarin man came to the top of the stairwell, turned, and eyed Vlayn with remorse. This was the suspicious facet of this look: it was solely a sorrowful one, and not mixed with the typical visual examination exchanged by two strangers. This was the one and only reason Vlayn didn't deploy a long string of bullets into this man. It was even more startling that this alone stopped the atrocious killing machine that was Vlayn Par'Wil. He stared heavily at this man while the weight of the Troid lowered his arms.

The old man straightened his newly-washed t-shirt and rearranged his silky white hair. Finally, he locked eyes with Vlayn again, and continued to send him a look of disappointment. Vlayn, in return, grew disgruntled at both the foreignness of this man and the maturing softness that he felt within him because he couldn't pull the trigger.

Silence inundated this empty building in The Bog, and a soft, chillier wind slithered through the debris of this floor. Vlayn was still seated, analyzing this man, trying to make sense of who it was. Across the room, the elderly gentleman was calm and also watched Vlayn's every move.

Suddenly, Vlayn raised the submachine gun and landed a few heavy bullets into the man's chest, right below the heart. Instead of toppling over in dire pain, followed by agonizing moans, this man didn't even take a step backward as a result of this blow. He simply absorbed the bullet and didn't even alter his facial expression.

Soon, though, blood started to stain his plush shirt. So indeed, this man was standing here. He was real. He must have been.

The man lifted his soiled shirt off his chest and watched his blood paint himself. Then, he placed his hands together, looked back at Vlayn and spoke in a rich timbre voice, "Son," he said.

Vlayn's face instantly lowered at the sound of his father's voice. His arms became weak and the weapon fell to the floor. He was horrified; the last time he saw his father, the man was just a bit older than Vlayn's current age. At this time, his father seemed to have aged sixty to seventy jaros. "Dad," Vlayn blurted out. "I–I shot you."

He shook his head, "No, son, you didn't." His father took one step closer to Vlayn and looked him up and down – observing his son's filth and utter corruption and decay as a living being. "But you did shoot many, *many* other people since my passing."

Vlayn tiredly propped himself against the wall and stared at his feet. "I had to, Dad," he said lowly, "It's all about survival now. It is. That's how it was when I was younger, too."

"Survival is different than merciless killing."

"Tha–That's what it costs. *Mercilessly* taking other people's lives to save your own. That's what I had to learn, Dad," he said anxiously.

"No."

Vlayn looked up at his father, whom towered above him. "That's what you taught me," he struggled to say. "Survival is life, that's what you said so that's what I did and *still* do."

"No, son," he replied with increasing frustration.

"No, Dad! You told me that one day I would have to do whatever it took to keep *my* family alive! *You* told me life was a test on Xenamus!" Vlayn finally peered into his father's eyes. Tears fell from his face, marking the first true emotion he felt for a very long time. "That's what I did. And I'm still living. I'm still *here!* I don't know if I want to be. But I still am… you told me that one day I'll change.

That I will adapt. I did. I can't apologize for that," he said coldly.

But his father didn't care. He squatted low to meet his eye line. Vlayn could see his cracking, timeworn Babarin skin and the glistening white hair that dressed it. "I also told you not to confuse pure survival with pure evil. You did, son." His father rose to his feet and began for the stairs.

"*Stop!*" Vlayn bellowed through his heightening cries. "Dad, I needed to do *anything* to stay alive. And Camrynn kept *me* alive and I lost her!!! I just couldn't take any chances. Please, Dad, *please!*" he wiped his eyes, looked back up at him and jumped to his feet. "You're the one person I don't want to fail," he whispered.

"You shot that boy straight dead in the face, Vlayn," his father said bleakly as he turned around. "You didn't need to. You ripped away the opportunity of life, even if it's a foreseeably tough one in Jaadakin County. As a father, it crushes me to see someone young pass on. It makes me think of Tithenkeen."

"Dad, it's not my fault he didn't live!" he shouted from behind his frayed rags that wept from his sweat and filth.

"*Everything* is your fault, Vlayn. And you *didn't* need to kill that boy that night," his father added with his bright, refined clothing that gleamed in the Xenamus sun.

Vlayn's face broke, his eyes oversaturating with tears, "I couldn't take the risk," he urged. "I couldn't. I–I've been through too much. I couldn't put mine or Camrynn's life at risk."

"Vlayn!" his father shouted. "The boy was on his knees. He was submitting. You both blindly and bitterly murdered him in cold blood. That isn't how I raised you, Vlayn. It is *not*. The strong who survive since The Great Fall are the ones who know when to kill and when to unionize with other sane Jaadakins. You need to see who you've become."

Vlayn slid down the wall and sat tiredly against it. He rubbed his face and his forehead, then looked over at his arsenal of weapons that sat silently on the floor next to him. "Maybe I didn't have to kill him," he murmured.

"You didn't need to, Vlayn, but you did. I've seen who you've become since you put down Tithenkeen. Vlayn, if I was alive, you would be the one man I would *never* want to become. I'm disappointed in you... you aren't a man... just stop fighting, Vlayn. You don't need to any longer, there is no reason to" with that, his father walked down the stairs, leaving Vlayn alone.

"Dad!!!" Vlayn screamed as his eyes sprung open and his chest lurched forward. The room was still and quiet, as if no conversation existed in here at all. The Troid was resting in his lap and not on the floor where he thought he left it. The corpse rotted away next to him and didn't budge during his sleep. "Dad!" Vlayn shouted again. He leapt to his feet and sprinted to the concrete stairs. No one was there. His head spun in circles, and still, no one was there.

Vlayn screamed furiously until his vocal chords almost snapped. He kicked the wall over and over again, then tore the slung submachine gun off of him and chucked it across the room. He ran over to the stairs yet again to check if his father was there.

No one was there.

Vlayn sprinted as fast as he could to the windows and stuck his head outside. "*Daaaaaad!!!!!!*" he roared painfully. "Please!!! Dad!!!"

No one was there.

The wastelands of Jaadakin County returned with quietness.

Vlayn ran back over to the wall and knocked it with a punch, then followed with yet another kick. This time, though, his foot went through it, breaking the solid ohbrizorne in the inner wall. Vlayn pulled his foot out angrily and tumbled to the floor, immediately smelling the mustiness of the decomposing chemical. The heartbroken Vlayn didn't care, though; he cried relentlessly while he rolled in the rubble on the floor. His grungy palms thoroughly rubbed his red eyes, for he felt the overwhelming loneliness of Xenamus yet again. "There's no one left!!!!" he howled. "Baleejus! Please!!!" he wailed while still covering his eyes. "I miss him," he mouthed while hysterically crying. "I miss 'em all. Why–Why am *I* the only one left?"

No Camrynn. No Tithen. No mother. No father. What was left? What was left to live for?

Ellmorr – a life better than his.

Vlayn inhaled heavily and exhaled his pain. He dropped his hands to the floor and stared at the rotting ceiling. He had to plot his next move. Right now, he was struck with heartbrokenness. Vlayn Par'Wil was a broken man with a mind that was slowly going haywire.

PART II: **SCORCH THE PAST**

The cobble road still ran throughout the city as sloppily as it did when he was younger. It didn't hesitate. It didn't alter. It didn't move slightly even through all the terror and violence over the hundreds of jaros of its existence.

It was persistent.

Vlayn made his way down this steady path. He knew where it led and he understood where it was taking him. The smell of charred rubble grew more intense with every step. The handle of the Troid was gagging by Vlayn's grip; he was alert; ready to kill if need be. The caffeinated natives of Witherhart dashed along the cobble road hastily, searching for the first scrap of food while avoiding a seemingly incurable Glithémien Disease. The same, massive tin signs were tightened into the concrete buildings that were confined to the cobble road.

JOIN THE ELLMORIAN BLACKGUARD AND LIVE AWAY FROM THE HORRORS OF JAADAKIN COUNTY! LIVE THE LIFE YOU'VE ALWAYS WANTED!

Vlayn still scrutinized the sign and its hypocrisy.

Another sign hung right next to it, screaming an opposite meaning.

STAND AGAINST ELLMORR it read, *STAND WITH THE JAADAKINS*

Vlayn's eyes lowered, wondering what duster or group of dusters actually took the time out of their lives to create, manufacture, and hang these signs all over the region. Who was trying to band Jaadakins together to rise against a negligent Ellmorr? What kind of person in Jaadakin County would do this? Who would be this *selfless?*

He took his eyes off the sign and down to his feet. Vlayn knew the risks brought upon by glithémien. At any moment, he could be bit by the critters, and his curtain would quickly fall. The risks were just as high as running into a group of people that were vowed to the Ellmorian Blackguard's beliefs. Such dangers were *always* present but it was more than ever at this moment. Witherhart, just like other major cities in Jaadakin were plagued by the disease. The danger was even higher for Vlayn than it was in the desert, but he kept moving down this cobble road.

The fears of being down on these streets were so prominent when Vlayn was young. He would watch the crazed people down below from his apartment. Jaros later, as an older, more experienced man, Vlayn walked the streets of his hometown seeming immune. *Nothing* could bring this true survivor down. He was venomous with a dauntless skip in his gait.

After much walking, his old apartment complex was in sight. Although, it was nothing Vlayn imagined it to be. The building, and many others around it, were burning ceaselessly to the ground. Heavy black smoke flew into the air, steel beams and concrete tore from the buildings and collapsed to the ground below it. The colossal flames reflected in Vlayn's glassy eyes as he examined the decay of his past. His thick beard and bushy hair seemed as if they were going to shrivel into embers from the scorching heat.

Suddenly, riotous mobs of marauders made way down the cobble road, cluttering the width of it to its brim. Four to five men stood at the front of the crowd, equipped with tall wooden pikes that were drowning in massive flames at the tips. Men and women would disperse from the crowds every so often. They pillaged through small shacks and buildings and would accompany the heinous crimes with blows to the heads or bullets to the chests of natives that were unfortunate enough to be stuck on the streets at the time of this ransacking.

Vlayn examined the crowd of devious thieves and murderers very closely. He could see through them: he knew that at least half of this crowd were once mentally sound, but later lost everything since The Great Fall, and turned to savagery like this.

Rage washed over Vlayn; he used to hide from these types of crowds. *Everyone* would hide from pillagers that would veer from the empty deserts and scavenge through major cities. This was the Blackguard.

Vlayn wouldn't run or hide anymore.

He wasn't a young boy.

The fifteen minacious men and women pummeled their way through the main cobble road like a tidal wave, bludgeoning anything either living or dead. They showed no care for glithémien either. They were almost invincible.

Vlayn sought a hiding spot behind the side of his apartment building and coughed from the noxious fumes of the fire from up above. He breathed heavily, hunger striking him aggressively. He raised the Troid and detached the magazine to check for ammunition: full magazine.

He powerfully crammed the magazine back into the weapon and used the built-in touchscreen to set the fire rate to fully-automatic.

Vlayn was ready to rid Xenamus of its atrocities, even if that meant he was one of them.

The group made their way closer and closer, hearing them chanting and shouting elatedly at making people suffer and bleed.

Vlayn spun out from the wall, swiftly locked his sights and held the trigger. The submachine gun recoiled energetically, springing backward. He maintained his hardy composure as he tore down the entire group. With such a small magazine, Vlayn ensured each bullet landed with every sinner in it.

And it did.

The first few collapsed to the ground lifeless as the rest scrambled to raise their weapons. Vlayn, being an experienced killer of Jaadakin, was nimble. He efficiently took a step back behind the concrete side of the building and stuck himself out just enough to precisely lock onto the group without exposing too much of himself.

Vlayn would no longer hide from these types of people. As a child, his father always ordered him to cower when a group similar to these men and women plundered the city. It was seemingly routine for Witherhart natives.

Vlayn was no longer a native.

Eventually, every single marauder was on the ground dead by the hands of Vlayn Par'Wil.

Vlayn stepped out into the cobble street with the flames dancing into the sky in front of him. The inhabitants of Witherhart came out of hiding and eyed him down with fear, both thankfully and submissively.

Just above him stood his old apartment complex. He peered upward, observing the window he once hid behind as an innocent and cowardly boy. Flames spit out of this window frame, but jaros ago, it was his safe haven; where Tithen and himself spent hours together talking through their childish imaginations. Discussing the wonders of the rest of the Kirbinian Galaxy and the city, Ellmorr.

Pretending they were as courageous as N.M.C. soldiers, or as important as the two High Clansees.

Vlayn wouldn't want Tithenkeen seeing him like this – a man murdering fifteen people within a span of seconds. Vlayn knew who he was becoming. He had no choice, though. He had become a product of Jaadakin.

The traditions of highly intelligent living beings were absolutely eradicated on Xenamus. And the ancient, instinctive lifestyles of past mortals quickly gained access to current lives and compelled those under this spell to resort to their barbaric, natural ways of life – survival. This, isolating the inhabitants of Jaadakin County from the Fraygen Plateau, and the rest of the Kirbinian Galaxy. Through his past, Vlayn grew to become one with those under this cynical enchantment.

-THIRTEEN-

A HEART BENEATH THE FLOOR

Thirty jaros later.

Vlayn trekked the deserts of Jaadakin County alone. A Nabbuu 88 pistol was holstered at his hip. A Flunklen 16 assault rifle was slung around his shoulder, exhausted of ammunition. In his left hand, he held the same miniature submachine gun, the Troid. The weapon's small, built-in screen alerted the user when it was overheated, out of ammunition, or needed to be cleaned. At this point the screen was softly beeping, flashing a red light, notifying the user it was out of ammunition. Next to this red flashing light, the screen displayed another warning sign: this one showed a blinking orange light, letting the user know it needed to be serviced. Evidently, the needs of the Troid weren't going to be fulfilled anytime soon.

Vlayn's head dropped backward as he walked. He stared blankly into the dusty Xenamus atmosphere. He admired the dimly-illuminated planets in the sky above him. From this distance, they were merely balls of light. These points of lights were planets: the water-covered planet of Anceykik, and the conflict-driven planet of Bactra with a bloody war being fought between the immense Akafayl Gang and the N.M.C.

Vlayn didn't know very much of other planets in the Kirbinian Galaxy – he was tethered to Xenamus. Space travel was a fairly common activity among people in The

Galaxy, both rich and moderate. For Vlayn, he was far too poor to get out of Xenamus.

Then, the blaring lights of Ellmorr shined in his eyes.

They could travel anywhere they want, Vlayn thought as he studied the distant lights.

But Vlayn was stuck in place in these apocalyptic deserts of Jaadakin. His last chance was Ellmorr; trying to make it into that city, finding out what the cure for the disease was, and seeing how the wealthy lived above the chaos. He lost everything else around him: Tithen, Camrynn, his mother and father, his hometown of Witherhart burned his past away. The only reason he still wanted to live was for just that reason.

The Fraygen Plateau and the immense city atop it seemed so far. It seemed so unachievable. It seemed like the people on it were in a different universe than him; as if he wasn't good enough. Blinding fury flooded his mind at the sight of the shimmering light.

The past sixty-four jaros consisted of just Vlayn Par'Wil; mourning over Camrynn. He ventured all across Jaadakin County – Ryokard, Njenwire, Ambervale, all the way back to Kepembold and many small camps in between. He never once took on a companion, neither intimate nor formal. He developed acquaintances throughout the jaros, but would never travel with anyone else. Since, Camrynn, he wouldn't.

Vlayn religiously traded with other dusters in exchange for food, weapons, or Credits. When he wasn't trading, he killed; he murdered unnecessarily. He took people's lives if they crossed him the wrong way or irritated him. Most importantly, he mercilessly slaughtered those that reminded him of Camrynn even in the slightest. He also grappled with himself. He tried to figure out who he had become since the latter years of his childhood. *It was always going to happen,* Vlayn thought, *to kill and not to trust anyone was the only way for me to live. I started my life fine, but it just wasn't going to be that way 'til I died. The way I am. I was always going to turn out this way.*

Later, a small settlement appeared in the near distance. The star was setting rapidly in the sky and the lonely Vlayn needed to find shelter. The star grew increasingly weak and Vlayn could make out the perfectly spherical outline of it as it sat lofty in the bronze sky. After a mere thirty minutes the barren village sat at his doorstep. He equipped his Nabbuu 88 pistol defensively. Any type of threat could lie before him. He took soft steps forward with caution. He panted and his bottom lip quivered from time to time. His right hand trembled faintly with exhaustion as it bore the heavy weight of the pistol.

He was ready to make someone bleed.

A row of wooden shacks stood before him; each one covered almost fully by drifting sand. He observed each structure; some had large prints on them saying: *Laxryy Tavern* and *Laxryy Bank.* Evidently, this settlement was empty for many jaros, just like many others in Jaadakin County. This town went by the name of Laxryy, and Vlayn knew he was going to search each shack for anything useful. He already knew the outcome, though. This village was already pillaged countless times. Over and over. It was drained. There was nothing left here, just like everything else. And yet, his stomach still rumbled from hunger, his tongue was still arid, and the bizarre motivation to keep moving was still alive.

A small light flashed quickly from the top of a shack through the crisp darkness of the nighttime sky. It caught Vlayn's hungry eyes and it drew him closer. He raised the rusty pistol high, switched the safety off, and was ready to fire. He opened the creaky door to the first story of this structure carefully, beginning to survey the floor. Sand encompassed the first story almost completely, with the smell of paper, dust, and jaros greeting his nose. Blackness filled the room with a small glimmer of light from the bustling city of Ellmorr in the distance.

Vlayn breathed slowly. His weary arms swayed from side to side. He felt his eyes slowly beginning to shut, but he shook his head vigorously, knowing his fatigue was slowly taking him over. Indeed, he was tense. But thinking of his past assuaged these nerves, and thus kindling a confident anger to kill.

Slow-moving footsteps scraped along the floor upstairs. Vlayn stopped in his tracks as he sensed the nearby foreign heartbeats like an animal sniffing out their prey. He knew there were people right above him, and those people knew he was downstairs.

Vlayn slowly shifted toward the wooden staircase. Each stair was bent downward and creaked with the weight of his body. The emptiness of this shack and Laxryy as a whole found a home in Vlayn's heart. His hands gripped the pistol even tighter; did he have to kill every single living being at the top story of this decrepit shack? Did he have to kill every single heartbeat he sensed just to survive another day?

Vlayn was so accustomed to being on the move at this point in his life. He jumped from place to place without a home. He was used to this nomadic lifestyle. And he was even more familiar with having to kill at the sight of anything breathing. After so many jaros of exercising this, he started to grow tired of killing and constantly travelling.

He didn't want to kill anyone at this moment. He knew he needed to and he couldn't let this weakness make him soft. If Vlayn let it, a knife would eventually be driven into his neck.

He had to kill. Vlayn had to remind himself of this. It always came down to survival and that was all Vlayn understood at this moment.

Vlayn carried himself up the stairs with caution, unsure of where the enemies exactly were. He finally reached the top story where five men were huddled together, all mobilized with machetes and knives.

Vlayn's eyes speedily widened, resulting in the raise of the pistol to one man, and followed with a shot without hesitation. A bullet wedged itself into one of the man's skull, causing it to burst into fragments and painting the wall with blood behind it. Adrenaline surged through Vlayn's body and combatted his lassitude. He pointed the pistol at the next marauder and landed another bullet in his chest, propelling him backward against the wall.

"Stop! Stop!" another man hollered.

Shockingly, Vlayn paused his killing spree and breathed heavily with the Nabbuu 88 locked onto the next man.

"We're obviously outnumbered," the Babarin man expressed in a thick accent. "You've got the guns, we only have sharp objects."

Vlayn's feet were locked in place with the two machine guns drooping from his shoulders as the pistol was still aimed at the man's head from across the room. Vlayn breathed steadily and his mouth hung ajar from underneath his beard. He could hear the walls creaking with age and sandy dust falling through the slits in the ceiling above him. He didn't flinch. He didn't even move a muscle. Vlayn was sparing these last three men.

"It's better to team up than to survive in Jaadakin County alone. You should know that better than any of us just by the look of ya," the man added. Then, he glanced at the other two men while he lowered his machete. Eventually, the other marauders followed.

Vlayn still kept the Nabbuu locked on the man. His facial expression didn't stir. "No," he repudiated bleakly. "Anyone can survive out here alone."

"Didn't say it was impossible, *friend*. It's just easier with others," he suggested, "Cling onto hope. Alone, hope is impossible to find. But now, you're the only one with the gun," the man said.

Vlayn stared at the men from behind his pistol. He didn't flinch, "kick the weapons to your sides," he demanded. "I don't lower this until you do." And so, the man nodded and kicked the machete to his right with his arms still raised. The other men did the same. "I want all of you to keep your arms raised. Walk to the wall *without* the windows." The three men stood mutely. "I'm the only one with the gun, so do it."

The first man glanced over at the other two men to his left. "We have nothing to lose—"

"Now!" And after that sharp command, the men ambled to the wall, where Vlayn shouted, "turn around! Face the damn wall!" The dusters did as told, and Vlayn finally drifted toward the center of the room. He analyzed the shanty room quickly – as much as a capturer could. It was bleak, as if everything that had once dressed this floor had purposefully been wiped clean. It's foundation, though – the wooden floorboards wept inward from hundreds of jaros of neglect, as well as its walls. The intense Xenamus sun sucked them dry. They didn't stand a chance. But the lights of the metropolis peered into this room, shining on the backs of these men Vlayn held hostage. "The first duster all the way to the left – back yourself up to me. Keep your arms raised." This man began walking backwards cautiously, wary of Vlayn.

Vlayn started frisking his body with his left hand, with the pistol steady in his right. He was thorough, ensuring he was completely unarmed. "Go back," he commanded, then ordered the middle man to step out. He began frisking this duster. Vlayn noticed his bald head as he patted him down, "Do you shave your head, or something?" Vlayn mumbled, then let out a weary sigh.

The man glanced backward to Vlayn, "What?"

"I guess you don't," Vlayn retorted. "Get back to the fucking wall." The last man stepped backwards to the center of the room, where Vlayn searched him. It was excruciatingly hot in this shack, and this duster's warm, salty sweat didn't even stream down his cheeks. They got caught in the thick, bushy curls of his hair. "You're protective," the man suggested, "You're careful. I can respect that."

"Don't talk to me."

The man sighed. "It's not easy to trust other Jaadakins, I know that. But like I said, it's better to team up out here. We wouldn't kill you." But Vlayn chuckled, stood up, and turned the man around, where he looked deeply into his eyes. "That is the biggest lie I've ever heard," Vlayn said. "There is only one reason why you're standing in front of me right now: you have killed. And you would kill me at the first chance you got. Only thing is I will never give you the opportunity to."

The man grinned, "Arith Kan," he introduced as he stuck out his hand, "And you?"

He looked into this man closely. He tried to unfold his manipulative personality, but he wasn't quite able to yet. But he wouldn't back down, "Vlayn Par'Wil," he shuck Arith's hand steadily, showing no weakness.

"Plan on staying in Laxryy for a while?" Arith asked, but Vlayn didn't answer. He didn't even flinch; he may've even stopped breathing in the moment. Vlayn's eyes were steadily locked on Arith's.

Arith smiled, then started for the window sill. The other two men began leisurely taking a seat on the floor up against the wall. Vlayn was still planted into the floorboards, vigilantly holding his Nabbuu.

"Well we don't plan on staying for a while," Arith laughed while leaning against the window sill, "Jus' easy to see people comin' from here."

Vlayn looked over at Arith, "Have you had anyone else sneak up on you like I did? Shoot two of your group?"

"Yeah," Arith countered. "Four others, actually, probably a jaro ago. They were Babarin men. Looked like real survivors of Jaadakin, you know the type when you see one. They're pretty easy to take down. 'Nother two Babarin women came up on us about half a jaro after that, shot one of our guys, threatened me, then left Laxryy."

Vlayn scoffed, "Babarin women are the toughest of the brood of Jaadakin County."

"That's damn true," he cackled. "You, though… We heard you come in, but after that you were as silent as Zaxraan Arn."

"Took down these two bastards," Vlayn uttered, referring to the lifeless bodies on the floor.

"I didn't really know 'em,'" Arith replied. "Meet Babarins along the way. Either kill 'em or pair up." The man moved over toward a window sill and sat on it. The nighttime wind blew against his back through the shattered window frame with the endless desert landscape sprawling itself out behind Arith.

"And you paired up with those guys," Vlayn supplemented to Arith's sentence, beckoning to the corpses.

"Damn true. That's why I don't really care to know their names. People last as long as their ability to survive out here."

"I know," Vlayn said, "That's the only reason I'm still alive today," he eyed Arith deeply, mastering a face of stone while he analyzed this man.

Arith bent over and rifled through his burlap sack, provoking Vlayn to reach for his holstered Nabbuu cautiously. Arith raised his eyes to the defensive Vlayn. "Easy," he mumbled softly with a snicker, and finally, after much scrambling of his filthy hands, he eventually drew a bottle of whiskey and two glasses. He grinned at Vlayn gently. "Nothing to act irrationally about," Arith said, then poured himself and Vlayn a glass, ignoring the other men.

"Ever have?" Arith questioned.

"No," Vlayn replied, lowering his shaky hand from his weapon. "What is it?"

"Whiskey," Arith replied joyfully.

"Whiskey?" Vlayn inquired after he took the glass and smelt the liquid cautiously. He leaned up against the sagging wooden wall, near Arith.

"Just for us, though, not for them guys," Arith added, referring to the two other men sitting across Vlayn and Arith.

"Fuck off," one man returned.

Arith grinned sneakily from behind the glass. "Try it," he urged.

Vlayn slowly drank from the glass. His head immediately recoiled from the drink as he forcefully swallowed it. "Fucking Baleejus, man. What is this?" he demanded repulsively.

Arith snickered harshly. "Whiskey, I told yuh what is was."

"Where'd you find it? It's like I'm drinking eejiff.'"

"Right here," he responded enthusiastically. "In this tavern. It's human shit though. And don't tell me it tastes like fucking fuel for land cruisers," he tittered.

"It does," Vlayn said. "Tastes like eejiff."

"Well it's a human drink. Comes from Earth before it was all fucked up. Used to be brewed on Earth but after that whole nuclear bombing shit over there and humans were moved to Zidonian in our galaxy, they brew whiskey on Zidonian. Bless 'em. Don't know what I'd do without it," he said cheerfully, downing the rest of his liquor and immediately refilling his glass. "It's cheap shit, but fuck it – not like we got many options."

"This fucker drinks it five times a day, *at least*," one man pointed out from across the room.

"I like what I like," Arith declared while he raised his glass and smiled. "What can I say? Aren't I right, Vlayn?"

Vlayn glared at Arith with odd confusion and defensiveness. "We don't see too many humans on Xenamus," Vlayn said quietly as he stared out of the grimy window pane, adjacent Arith. The talk of whiskey didn't interest him. Instead, he scrutinized Jaadakin, and he judged the lights of Ellmorr viciously. The light from the monstrous city shouted from across the darkness of the desert. It glistened into the hollow, decrepit room that these malevolent men dwelled in. Each one was uniquely diverse. Different personalities, voices, appearances, and most importantly, histories. However, regardless of their differences, each one was adversely cold to their surroundings and the outsiders to their inner soul; a soul that was bruised and nearly inexistent at this point in their long lives. Each one similarly had a soul such as this – one that was both deprived and starved of true life. This was an explicit outcome of life in Jaadakin County.

"Na, you don't see humans," a man from across the room put in. "You don't even see Kirbinians, and that's the largest race in The Galaxy."

"It's all Babarin," Arith said.

"It is," The man replied.

"If you see *anyone* that isn't like us, keep a hold of them," Vlayn chuckled, "'cause that's a rare sight."

"Indeed, it is," the man said.

"What's your name anyway, guy?" Vlayn asked to the one across the room. He could see and even feel the man's coarse, grey patchy beard, his blistered skin, his stress wrinkles, and his glowing, bald head that was soddened with sweat.

The man shrugged, "call me whatever you want."

"I'm not gonna do that so just tell me your fucking name," he demanded aggressively. "What, you don't have a name?" Vlayn said, laughing falsely.

"What's the need for names, buddy? Do I *need* a name to kill someone? Do I *need* a name to stay alive?"

"Watch your fucking tongue," Vlayn threatened, then the man sneered sarcastically.

Vlayn sprung to his feet, dropped the glass on the floor, and drew his Nabbuu 88. "Laugh again I fucking swear," he ordered angrily while stepping in his spilled whiskey. "I'm not takin' any shit, I'll kill you." He glanced over at Arith to his left, who sat calmly on the window sill.

"Do it, I can care less," Arith abetted, sipping from his glass. The man sunk into a placid state. His eyes didn't shift at all. His eyebrows raised slightly, though, and spoke, "gonna do it?" he asked mildly.

Vlayn said after short thought, "Na. Not going to waste the ammunition on you." He lowered the Nabbuu 88, but still kept his eyes on the man.

Arith took another sip and exhaled with force. "That's always the excuse," he joked, "honestly, this late in the game," Arith started, "with all the loved ones gone, doesn't matter who dies around me. I don't even know 'em," Arith told him. "I don't even know you," he added, gesturing toward the man across him.

"No," Vlayn said, "it don't matter. You're right."

"Everything is black and white, now," the man stated across Vlayn and Arith. Vlayn inspected the frail, sparkling moonlight against the man's face as he stared at the floor beneath his fatigued body. "What do you mean?" Vlayn asked tiredly.

The man raised his heavy head to Vlayn's face, "Everything's black and white – I can remember the days when I was younger, living in Ryokard with my mother. We'd play catch behind the butcheries –" "The *what?*" Arith jumped in.

"The butcheries," the man repeated, then formed his fingers into a rectangle as he explained himself, "it was like a set of buildings where the infected were killed off," he told them. "We played almost every day. Kept the ball in my bedroom and when we didn't play, I admired that fucking ball. It spoke to me differently than all the misery around me did. We played every day, until it all changed."

Vlayn crossed his arms as he listened diligently.

"What changed?" the seated man next to him asked.

"You all know," the man retorted. "We've all experienced this change many, many times before. Everything becomes black and white – dull, uninteresting, *dark.*" He rubbed his eyes quickly and gazed at his shoes. "Used to love that ball even when I didn't play with it. Eventually my mother's health fell off, so we didn't play. *I* fell into the depression of Jaadakin County, too. The very few things I found interesting in this fucking *horrible* planet grew so black. That ball held no meaning anymore."

"What happened to your mother?" Arith asked.

Vlayn glanced over at Arith strangely, "She fucking died, idiot. What do you think happened?" he shouted out.

The man nodded silently while rubbing the top of his head.

"'Cause everyone you love fucking dies in the end," Vlayn murmured. "There's no such thing as *happiness—*"

"It's a fake word," the man across from him interrupted. "It holds a false meaning. It's a delusion for cowardly people who can't accept the suffering of life. They fall in love with that delusion. And they die."

"It's *all* about survival," Vlayn declared, "That's what life is. You can try to fucking switch it up and *make believe* that life is more than that, but it just isn't. Living and fighting becomes the only thing we understand. It comes to the point where I can still *hear* the heart of everyone I once loved beating wherever I go. No matter what, it's all about survival. It's all about keeping your guard up…" and just then, Vlayn became silent, feeling DaRoone's presence lurking over him. Vlayn read the dirt and grime along his sweaty forearms. He thought of everywhere he had been over his lifetime – everyone he met, all the people he had killed. Was it worth it?

"That's the only reason why we are still here today," Arith agreed while he poured himself yet another glass of whiskey.

Vlayn looked over at him expressionless as he nodded. "If you get the *privilege* of watching everyone you kept close to your heart die a painful death, you change, like you said," Vlayn motioned to the man across from him. Then, his eyes dropped to the floor as the thought of Camrynn made a hefty impact on his thoughts. "The pure sadness takes you over," his tired, monotone voice continued, "the *sadness* is the only substance you can feel living inside of your dead body. Your face sinks into your skull and *always stays* in that vacant state. *Smiling* becomes a chore, and everything grows black and white," Vlayn finished as he glanced over at the man. He pulled on his beard and ran his fingers through his hair. "That's what Jaadakin County does to all of us."

"I couldn't have described it better," the man said. "Life was so much different back then – when we were all younger. The Great Fall was so much more recent. Fuck, our folks may've been alive just before The Fall, who knows?"

"People didn't even understand that there was a disease spreadin'," Arith reminisced. "Maybe it was better that way; people not knowing. Maybe if we didn't know, we would've had more of a reason to live."

"When I was younger," Vlayn interjected, "people in Witherhart were still so used to how life was before The Great Fall. I mean, my parents were born just after The Great Fall, but their parents were alive in the wealthier days of Jaadakin. So my parents were raised that way."

"My mother lived before The Fall," Arith told him. "I never met my father, but I'm sure he did, too."

"Most of people's folks nowadays lived before The Great Fall. Like I said, it was even more recent when I was younger. Give it another thirty jaros and Jaadakins won't be teaching their young about their history, current news, nothin'. *We* were raised that way," the man emphasized.

Vlayn rested his hand on his holstered pistol and rearranged his stance to alleviate the pain from his tiresome soles of his feet. "What's your name?" he asked the man.

"I told you."

"Na," Vlayn countered. "You have a name. You just don't want to say it because it will bring you back to a sad, sad time."

Silence.

"Truth is, there is no time that's *sadder* than right now," Vlayn started as he examined every person in the room. He could feel the Ellmorian lights staring him down from behind. "As every single day passes, everything just grows more depressed. Saying your name will bring you back to a sad time, sure, but it isn't worse than *right now*."

Arith looked over at the man, eyebrows raised, "So, what is it?" he asked, equally as curious.

"Endeen Hades," he said softly.

"Endeen *Hades*," Vlayn repeated as he stared deeply into the soul of moroseness and death. He pulled himself off the wall and began to turn toward the window behind him. "We all have a story," Vlayn said as he looked at the enthusiastic lights in the night sky. "And regardless of the person, the story is filled with a tragic fucking ending. We're no different," he muttered.

Arith sipped his drink in the midst of the heavy grief that stuffed the room. The room was bleak. There were merely a couple arthritic floorboards and four spiritless men of Jaadakin County that witnessed and done too much. "What's the goal here?" Arith asked everyone.

"Whatcha mean?" Endeen responded.

"Ellmorr is the fucking goal." Vlayn stepped in, glancing at the city in the distance.

"Aggressive, aren't ya?" Arith implied.

"Ellmorr's a pipe dream, pal," the other man said.

"It is," Arith said, reinforcing the man's statement.

Vlayn looked back at the group heinously. "None of you at least want to try? To see what we've been missing out on our whole lives? To see what kind of fucking city has been watching us suffer all these jaros?"

The group was silent.

"You're all weak fucking people."

"Watch what you're saying," Arith threatened.

"There's nothing else to fucking do!" Vlayn shouted with anger. "There's nowhere else to go! Nothing left to see! All we fucking do is run and run and *try* to survive! Day after day! Trying to avoid death and glithémien! Trying not to *starve!* It's over! Let's fucking try! There's nothing left to do!!!" he howled with bloodshot eyes, pointing to the elegant city in the far distance as it was elevated angelically above the devastated lands of Jaadakin County.

The three men all got to their feet, eyes widened. None were afraid, merely befuddled by Vlayn's passion.

"Might as well," Arith blurted out through his boozy breath.

"We're not too far," Vlayn added calmly.

"The Sheethmarr Pass is close," Arith suggested. "That'll be the only way to make it up there. The rest of the walls of the plateau are just too steep to climb."

"N.M.C. uses the pass to get up the plateau from Jaadakin," Endeen put in, "we'll get spotted."

Arith snickered. "How often do they use the fucking Sheethmarr Pass? How often does the N.M.C. come down to Jaadakin County?"

"Okay, okay. I get it," Endeen replied.

"How *often* do yuh see the fucking N.M.C. 'round Jaadakin?" Arith continued to ask snidely.

"Shut up. Both of you. Baleejus, man, just stop talking." Vlayn ordered. "We will get started in the morning."

Then, he turned back to the ruined window. He peered out at the nothingness of Jaadakin County, then his eyes naturally met the boundless metropolis of Ellmorr, sitting majestically on the Fraygen Plateau.

-Fourteen-

FOOL'S PARADISE

Part i: LAST HOPE

Half a jaro later.

Sweat flooded Vlayn's face. His hair fell into his eyes as he breathed heavily. The steep terrain leading to the flat Fraygen Plateau became increasingly treacherous with each step the four took. Regardless, Vlayn, Arith, and the men scaled the Sheethmarr Pass. It was steep for these dusters, but not for the land cruisers that unfrequently used it. Of course, none of them had climbing experience. One missed step would certainly be the end. They would risk anything, though, for the last hope they had. "Keep going!" Vlayn shouted to the three as he scaled the pass. The group climbed and walked the lofty terrain for hours already, and behind them lay the empty, subsiding desert of Jaadakin County.

Laxryy could be seen in the near distance, and even a sliver of Ryokard from this lofty perspective. His past: the killing of Tithenkeen, the sight of his mother lying dead in the Witherhart apartment, hacking at his lifeless father's limbs just to feed himself and his brother, hearing Camrynn, the Babarin woman whom he loved dearly, getting raped and killed, being trapped in a dark cell for days; he could feel every single moment of his past. He could feel the pain, devastation and the helplessness. All of these events stared at him as he climbed the Fraygen Plateau, as he attempted to leave his own horrors behind.

Vlayn didn't want to get sucked back into that terrifying vortex that was his life. He never wanted to live in that constant cycle again: surviving, starving, killing, losing loved ones, feeling excruciating pain that sucked the life out of his heart, and doing it all over again.

Vlayn *couldn't* endure all of it again.

He climbed faster, for he felt his past bolting up the cliff behind him, seeking to cave his skull in if it caught up to Vlayn. Arith and the men tried to keep up, but just like Vlayn, they were all exhausted.

Vlayn could feel his past tugging at his soiled coat as he climbed higher and higher toward the wealthy city. His excessive number of weapons swung from his shoulders like a swing, blowing in the ferocious wind. They flew into his bony ribs and hips, leaving bruises and small cuts and scrapes. Vlayn didn't care, though. His focus was steady and no amount of pain would alter it. He *needed* to escape Jaadakin County. But the words of his father when he was a young man rang into his mind like a dinner bell, *"The life we have… is the life we have. We can't change it. We can only accept where we are, and fight every single thing that tries to take us down…"*

Vlayn didn't want to believe those words when he was that age. He didn't believe it at first. Although, after jaros and jaros of fighting in Jaadakin County, killing strangers each passing day, fighting life with Camrynn, avoiding the Glithémien Disease and the Ellmorian Blackguard, and scavenging for food and water, he finally did realize that this was the life himself and all the inhabitants of Jaadakin

County faced. There was no changing it. There was no fighting it.

As each day became more agonizing than the last, as his soul darkened by the hour. All he could ever think about was how he pled to his father, hours before his death, that there was hope for everyone. The young, naïve Vlayn truly believed there was. But every second of his life after he uttered that sentenced only proved otherwise. Even after one-hundred thirty-eight jaros later he still felt embarrassed that he said such a thing.

The young Vlayn Par'Wil still lived in this callous, cold-blooded killer, though. The optimistic, upbeat boy was still *there*, somewhere underneath his skin. After hundreds of times of Jaadakin County proving to Vlayn that there was no hope, that there was nothing to live for, he still believed for some reason. Even after being as alone as a person could be, he knew there was some sort of life worth living out there in The Galaxy. *Somewhere.*

So, he climbed quicker.

Escaping Jaadakin.

The sky was gloomy and cheerless, as if it knew Vlayn had snapped; life of Jaadakin County brought this man to the brink of madness. He was a product of the deserts.

Vlayn exhaled heavier, heaving himself up the perilous, rocky wall of the Fraygen Plateau.

Hundreds of people died each jaro from scaling the side of this plateau, attempting to make it to Ellmorr for a better life than what Jaadakin served. Vlayn knew this. He would do anything to find hope. To merely understand *what it was* and what the term simply meant. Maybe there wasn't an ending to his depression – to his insanity that drove him to climb up to the Fraygen Plateau.

The top was finally reached. Vlayn hauled his body upward, elevating himself on the plateau. He gasped for air as the thick, intense heat overcame him. His hair drooped onto his face, but he instantly wiped it and his sweat away. He then reached for Arith's hand and pulled him up. Arith then reached for the two men.

Vlayn stood and wobbled slightly, taking in the brilliant sight of Ellmorr which was now close by. Forever, for his entire life, Vlayn dissected Ellmorr. He gawked it from afar, judging the lights and the wealth and deceit that it shielded behind their walls. There was always a colossal distance between Vlayn and Ellmorr, as if the city was hiding from the blood-thirsty Vlayn. Now, though, he was close – closer than ever. The distance had shrunk and Vlayn was here, but he didn't rejoice. In fact, he felt nothing at all. Camrynn was gone.

Fort Ashfall, the galactic base home to a squadron of stationed N.M.C. troops was standing right before their feet. Beyond that stood the strapping city, a pinnacle of the entire Kirbinian Galaxy, home to power, success, commerce, fame, wealth, pleasure, gambling, and tourism. Its lofty skyscrapers punctured the atmosphere, creating a second city above the dusty clouds. Air skimmers flocked through the sky in the distance, reaching the highest point in Xenamus' atmosphere, and where the highest superstructures of Ellmorr stretched to. The lights danced in the air, parrying the star's rays of light. The black security walls stood fifty feet tall, both guarding and circumscribing the affluence from the animals of Xenamus: those of Jaadakin County. They shot out of the ground and revolved the metropolis. Only the tallest of structures were able to be seen. Each building was lit up happily, displaying the productivity of its people. From Vlayn's distance, at a quick glance the city could look like a big ball of light. But if analyzed, one could see people living comfortably in the narrow, pointy skyscrapers.

Vlayn didn't see any of these things, though. All he could see was a deceiving city, home to greed and people that slept each night on their Credits and turned their eyes away from Jaadakin County. The cure to the disease was hiding behind those precious walls somewhere. He knew it. His family could still be with him if it wasn't for Ellmorr's arrogance and its inhabitants. Camrynn could still be here. Turmoil struck Vlayn.

"It's gonna be tough," Arith noted. It's a straight shot to Ellmorr," he added exhaustively. "Fort Ashfall is right there. They'll see us crossing Fraygen. They'll stop us. Kill us."

"There's no point," a man stepped in. "This is fucking stupid. Ain't no *glithémien cure*."

Vlayn flared. He spun around, took the man by his neck and threw him into the rocky surface of the plateau. "There *is* a glithemien cure, don't say there ain't!!!" he bellowed as he punched the helpless man in the jaw.

Vlayn stepped back from the three men, his sharp, brown blades of hair flowing in the wind and the flat floor of the plateau hiding nothing, and revealing everything it had. "I'm going! This is our last hope! There's nothing left down there!" he wailed, pointing down to the hollow deserts of Jaadakin. The crisp hills of gold sand went as far as the horizon and partially hid Laxryy. "The major cities are *falling* to glithémien! Everyone is dying!!! We're gonna die too if we stay there!!! This place is sitting above us *all*! Living without worrying!!! While we gotta live every day suffering!!!" his eyes began to weep, but he jerked his coat together and wiped his eyes stiffly. "They do *anything* for

Credits – carelessly making those fucking U.V. Suits and selling it to Jaadakin just to get wealthier!"

The men stood with their feet rigidly planted into the ground. No one flinched even in the midst of the roaring winds that accumulated at the edge of Fraygen. They kept a safe distance from Vlayn – a man who had reached a point of hysteria – a point he couldn't return from because he couldn't remember who he once was in the beginning. "I'm done letting Ellmorr mock me from afar! Watching me suffer! My family died because of them for hell's sake! Maybe if the Clansee cared about the whole planet and not just the Fraygen Plateau, then they would be *alive!* Maybe all of you wouldn't have such terrible lives! I'm going!!!" A poignant hunger pain rippled through his veins and his vision was blurred and sideways; but he could still see the men nervously observing him. He exhaled heavily through his parched lips while his hefty beard cloaked any struggled verbalization his face may have made.

Arith took a hesitant step forward, "Buddy…" he started.

Vlayn's eyebrows lowered as tensions grew and his face loosened. Dull aches were hidden behind his pupils as they were locked on Arith's, holding an unmatchable anger in them. He was in a daze of fury as Arith stood right in from of him. Finally, though, his eyes gravitated to Fort Ashfall in the distance. Massive black walls surrounded the fortified complex. Advanced turrets were mounted on the walls, sitting idly in one place as they were able to detect any unrecognized movement for miles.

The only settlement besides Ellmorr was Acri and it was a mere trading outpost for N.M.C. patrols to stock up on ammunition, food, water, and U.V. suits for soldiers who were not Babarin. The rest of the plateau housed

N.M.C. bases to protect the sole place that kept The Council interested in Xenamus. The rest of Fraygen was heavily enforced by N.M.C., assuring there were no possible threats that could bring Ellmorr down.

Only a few were successful in the trek across the plateau without being spotted by N.M.C., and Vlayn was ready to be one of them.

"Don't try to calm me down," Vlayn muttered. "If you aren't as angry as I am, then you don't understand how Ellmorr is using you – letting you rot."

Arith took a step closer to Vlayn. "There's no point in going back down now," he assured him. "But I need to know you haven't lost your fucking mind. I need to know you won't get me killed."

Vlayn exhaled slowly through his lips; his anger heightening. "If anything, you'd be the one getting me killed. Not the other way around. I'm not responsible for you," Vlayn told him as the elegant Ellmorr stood lofty behind him, "*Never* let your guard down. *Never* forget who you are... probably the best advice I was ever given," he said, staring deeply into Arith's exhausted eyes. "And that's the only way you're making it to Ellmorr."

PART II: NO HOPE

Half a jaro later.

The flat terrain of the Fraygen Plateau seemed boundless to an empty Vlayn Par'Wil. However, an end was most certainly coming, and it was coming at any moment.

He watched the rocky floor as he sped over it. His head sat back against his seat, and all he could hear was an angelic, female voice that wasn't there, and real, indistinct chatter amongst N.M.C. soldiers in the front seats. The whirring noise of the land cruiser he was in spoke over these soldiers as it bottled across Fraygen's landscape. An odd banging sound was drizzled lightly over this loud whirring of the cruiser; almost like a shrewd machete tapping gently on a dumpster full of fecal and body matter. It produced an overall, repugnant sound that Vlayn couldn't swallow.

Without doubt, the galactic army obtained premium, upmarket land vehicles and air skimmers, such as the Voxx brand, even on destitute planets like Xenamus. No model or make, regardless of its cost, could handle the constant heat, or the morbid natives of Jaadakin without getting a few kinks in the motor.

All Vlayn could feel was the pain and loneliness that was bred and built into a monster in him. It was assembled by the darkness and depression of his hopeless life.

There was no hope.

He tried to find it, but no one could ever find anything that didn't exist. He began to cry and Arith looked at him coldly, then retreated back to minding his own business.

The emptiness inside Vlayn ate at him each day. It seemed it had completely indulged him. The devil was invisible but it was there, living under Vlayn's skeleton.

There was nothing left in this life.

Everyone he loved was dead.

Why must he be alive long enough to experience each loved one's death? Why him? Vlayn's head dropped forward and he stared cock-eyed at a particular soldier in front of him. All he could realize was his appearance:

Clean skin.

Conditioned hair.

Polished N.M.C. armor.

Fully nourished.

Then, he studied himself.

Saturated, grungy skin.

Disheveled hair.

Torn, ruined clothing.

Nearing death because of starvation.

Two separate lives, and Vlayn caught onto this very quickly.

"Glithémien," he mumbled softly to the soldier, but the man didn't answer. The soldier kept his eyes steady on the plateau they ventured across, as the air skimmer moved at a firm one-hundred miles-per-hour. Arith glanced over at him with growing frustration. And after a short silence, Vlayn added, "That's right," he said louder, fishing for a response. "Ignore me."

"*Vlayn,*" Arith urged, "Shut your fucking mouth."

"You're killing us," Vlayn started to say casually, for witnessing and almost experiencing death was his norm. "You know that, aye?" he pressed, but an overwhelming heaviness coated his voice, revealing his hopeless state of mind which sucked the intensity from his words.

The soldier finally turned to Vlayn, who was sulking in a suppressed state of bottled choler in the backseat of the Voxx C-25, which wasn't notable for its spacious interior. "Yeah, now you look at me," Vlayn uttered boldly, while staring into the man's eyes. Then, he raised his tone, "You're kicked up here on Fraygen smokin' paylian, while millions of people below you are dying because of glithémien."

The soldier hadn't replied. He simply watched Vlayn's irate movements while he strangled the grip of his holstered Nabbuu Type-V, an expensive sidearm that charged every time it was holstered. This soldier's Nabbuu was fully charged, so it could knock off Vlayn's head like a golf ball getting smacked off its tee.

Finally, the edge of the plateau was up ahead, and Vlayn worriedly took notice. "Now, what're you gonna kill us!?" he hollered. The C-25 slowed to a complete halt enormously quick, and the soldiers exited the vehicle with the doors shutting promptly behind them. They began speaking to one another outside and glancing back at the men inside the skimmer.

"Good plan!!!" Vlayn screamed through the window, spitting on the glass. "Might as well off us now, because, fuck, we're gonna be dead soon anyways!!!" The soldiers heard Vlayn's muffled wails from outside, but they turned their heads away carelessly.

Arith lunged forward onto Vlayn and threw fists into his chest. "Watch what you're fucking saying!!!" he shouted.

Vlayn retaliated by throwing Arith off of him and starting swinging at his face. Finally, Endeen got into the mix, trying to break the two up by posting his arms in the middle of them. "Stop!" he ordered, but the two didn't listen. "They're killing us!!!" Vlayn screamed with teary eyes.

The soldiers threw open the doors and jerked Vlayn out by his coat collar. One solider shot his foot into Vlayn's abdomen, and followed by strenuously pulling him closer and closer to the edge of the plateau. The powerful, beaming headlights of the Voxx C-25 shined strongly onto Vlayn and the few remaining feet of the plateau, then the light dissipated into the air above Jaadakin County.

Vlayn squirmed in the soldier's tight grip, until he slipped himself out of his coat and took a few steps back with his hair blowing wildly with the strong winds.

Vlayn looked forward at the black, ominous figures of the soldiers as the overwhelming headlights shined onto their backs and burned Vlayn's corneas. He could hear Arith and the other men also being dragged toward the edge to his left, and he knew his fate.

"Don't do this," Vlayn insisted with his arms raised innocently in the warm winds, his feet nearing the edge, and his back facing Jaadakin County. "You don't know what it's like down there!" he shouted, "The Glithémien Disease is fucking killing us!!!"

A soldier stepped closer to Vlayn, "What did you say?" the man asked him aggressively.

Vlayn also took a step forward and shouted with intensity, "You know exactly what I said!" Another soldier stepped in and yanked Vlayn farther away from the human soldier by his t-shirt.

"No, no!" the soldier countered. "Wyth," he called to the N.M.C. soldier that defended him. "I don't need you to fight for me. What I need you to do is get those three other dusters off my plateau while I deal with this one." Wyth kept her gaze on Vlayn, displaying her unending resentment toward Jaadakin natives. Then she started for Arith and the others.

"Now, you listen to me," the man started as he walked up to Vlayn's scarred face. "I've never believed I was a conceited soul," he said. "I do my five jaro patrols on Fraygen, take my half-jaro hiatuses and go home to Liberta. But even Baleejus knows I will never let some Jaadakin speak to me the way you've done –"

"No other Jaadakin had the chance to speak to some privileged man living on Fraygen," Vlayn countered lividly. "Glithémien are *killing* us down there."

"*Glithémien,*" the soldier repeated. "Do you hear yourself?" Vlayn's head retracted slowly. His eyebrows loosened and his eyes widened. "No one knows what glithémien are. Now, I dunno how much paylian you've been smoking, but there ain't none such thing as *glithémien,*" the man struggled to pronounce the word. "You're on your way back down," and with that, the man stepped in to grab Vlayn, but he counter-stepped and started sprinting.

Vlayn could see the enormous city of Ellmorr in the distance. The metropolis' lights flickered repeatedly from its skyscrapers, illuminating the plateau all around it, and clashing harshly with the darkening copper sky.

Vlayn ran and ran, knowing the soldiers were after him. The hard blisters on his soles smashed with the rocky surface beneath him, shouting painfully with every dashing step he took. He could hear Arith scream his name, *Vlayn, Vlayn, Vlayn,* but the only thing he focused on was his scurrying feet. Vlayn could almost hear the soothing commotion of the Ellmorian people conversing with one another, the sound of the traffic made by the land cruisers on the Ellmorian roadways – the sound of civilization and society. He could taste the blissfulness of the immense communities. Even from twenty miles away and behind intimidatingly tall, secured walls, he could hear. And all he wanted was to find hope.

Civilization was close. Vlayn was the closest he had ever been to it. His mouth salivated at the thought of it. He craved true life for so long, and he was so close.

Suddenly, a powerful boom rang out. While sprinting, Vlayn turned around, only to see the N.M.C. soldiers' guns drawn, chasing after this fleeing duster. Vlayn tripped and tumbled to the ground, landing on his shoulder. The soldiers quickly crowded around him, ready to fire. But Vlayn viciously coughed up the dust and sand he swallowed from his fall.

"To your feet," the man in charge ordered.

Vlayn stood, shirt sullied, torn, and dripping of sweat. His hair unkempt and tears swelling in his eyes. He raised his arms with Ellmorr sitting calmly behind him and the sky dimming slowly above it all. The city observed another Jaadakin getting executed for attempting to gain entry.

The city's energetic lights skipped quietly in the sky for jaros. For jaros they did. Nothing affected it. Nothing altered its tempo or its colors. Nothing could stop it. Not the Glithémien Disease, not merciless murders, not kindhearted killings that were deemed as necessary. Not the fall of Jaadakin County. Nothing could. Vlayn's lips quivered and he shut his eyes in defeat. Jaadakin County broke him.

"Please!" Endeen bellowed. "There's no need to waste the ammunition! Ju–Just throw us off! We'll die or not! Either way there ain't no chance in us getting back up here!"

One soldier glared at Endeen while pointing his gun at Vlayn. Endeen could see Vlayn's frozen face and his pupils locked onto the pistol that was aimed at him. If he was able to, Vlayn would empty out this man's insides and hang the empty carcass up to dry.

Just like Vlayn, Endeen could kill if the need arose. He could defend his life. He knew that if he was thrown off the edge and survived, and Vlayn was shot in between the eyes, Endeen would need someone as adapted as Vlayn in the group. He needed Vlayn to live. Endeen bargained for his life.

The soldier thought momentarily, until he looked over at Wyth and nodded confidently. The soldiers made their way to Vlayn and the group and began pulling them to the edge of the Fraygen Plateau, ready to throw them off.

Wyth dragged Vlayn closer to the edge with her pistol aimed at his back. Wind flew up the wall of the plateau, hissing through the air. Vlayn's grimy hair flew backward and his beard fluttered with the wind. He could feel himself being submerged by this soldier into the reminiscent pain and suffering of his past; as if someone was thrusting his skull underwater.

Vlayn was so close to finding hope, and to finding the cure for glithémien. He was *so* close to finally figuring out how his mother, father and beloved brother could have lived. But he never even made it to Ellmorr, and no one in the city or anywhere else on this plateau even heard of the disease.

Vlayn got pushed closer and closer to the edge of the plateau as the N.M.C. soldier was shoving him off without any hesitation or shred of a thought.

It didn't matter that Endeen negotiated with the N.M.C. soldiers. Vlayn still screamed, "Please!!!" Vlayn rarely begged for his life. He believed it was demeaning, as if it was too low for him. Vlayn was at the highest side of the spectrum in Jaadakin County. He was the strongest. He was the most capable. He was the most intuitive warrior of these deserts. If he wasn't, he would've lost the first battle for his life and he wouldn't have made it this far.

All he ever did was fight and win. This time, though, there was no more fighting. He was willing to do anything to stay on the Fraygen Plateau and avoid going back down into that condemning force field that subdued its natives into a life of misery, hardship, and an unending war that pinned its people against each other for their gloomy lives. This was the nature of Jaadakin County. Vlayn was going to beg and do anything to avoid going back there.

Then, he looked over to see Arith and the other men also being pushed off the plateau by the armed N.M.C. soldiers.

Vlayn fell to his knees on the rocky floor. "Please!!!" he whimpered.

"It was your fault for even attempting to gain access to Ellmorr and the plateau," Wyth told him rigidly. "This was inevitable," she added, "you may live or die from this fall, but either way, never attempt coming back up here," she said, throwing another solid kick to Vlayn's ribs.

"Please!" Vlayn tried shouting again. His voice was so worn out, though, that the word barely escaped his lips.

The wind squealed louder as he was flung closer to the edge with each kick to his ribs. He closed his eyes for a moment, wishing life could have been different. He wished he was never born in Jaadakin County. All he could feel was the constant pain from the absence of Camrynn; maybe all he needed was Camrynn for him to be reasonably happy. Maybe he didn't need to chase Ellmorr for an untroubled life.

Vlayn was ready to go from this place. He was ready to see Camrynn again.

His eyes were closed, feeling himself being lifted by the soldier from his arms as the wind blasted him with even more force.

Vlayn gave this life all he could.

But there was simply no hope.

There never was.

Then, the tight clench around his arms was gone and he could no longer feel the gradual decline of the plateau's edge. Then, he started falling from the solid, rocky surface of Fraygen; an angelic, exalted ground that lodged wealth, prosperity, and most importantly, hope.

That was merely a brief period of time that Vlayn experienced this – and it was a morsel of what hope actually was in Ellmorr and Fraygen. He should have known better, though. He shouldn't have been so ignorant.

Vlayn's eyes opened and he stuck his arms out to break his fall. Vlayn wanted to die. There was nothing left. It was only instinctual to catch himself, though. He fell a few feet until he collapsed onto the rocky cliff and began to flop down the wall of the plateau.

Arith fell near him, tumbling downward simultaneously with Vlayn. They barked painfully as their limbs collided with the jagged terrain. The two eventually slowed as the steepness levelled out. The two other men landed near Vlayn and Arith and gasped in an excruciating pain.

Vlayn sprung to his feet without hesitation nor consideration for his bruises and injuries from the fall. He glanced up toward the top of the plateau. He could see the N.M.C. soldiers' heads peering from the top, seeing if Vlayn and the group were dead, or made it to the bottom.

They hadn't though.

The four of them stopped falling a quarter of the way down the cliff.

Vlayn's head spun around, staring a few thousand feet below him to the start of Jaadakin County. Then, his eyes met Arith's.

Vlayn was caught in the middle of answers and depression: the Fraygen Plateau and Jaadakin County. It was as if he was in a waiting room. As if some unknown, all-powerful life-force was watching down upon him from afar, controlling his life with strings. It was at this point where this supernatural being was trying to decide what to do with Vlayn Par'Wil:

To show him what a safe life was behind the security of Ellmorr. To allow Vlayn to feel what it was like to live a simple day without having to look over his shoulder. To demonstrate that life wasn't completely miserable, and drowning in appalling pain and heartache wasn't all of life. It could be more, and it was more for those on the Fraygen Plateau, and much of the Kirbinian Galaxy.

The second decision: inhaling him back into life in Jaadakin County. Obligating Vlayn to face the struggles of life and submerging him back into the terrible agony that was tagged along with the loss of each loved one; a pain which he felt each waking second in the lands of Jaadakin. To continue to bound him to the inevitable rule of thumb: *draw the blood of others so you never see your own.*

These were the evident two choices that an almighty being in some other universe could choose. It was a clear path that Vlayn was heading down.

The wind blew roughly, throwing Vlayn's hair from side to side as his head hung low into his hands. He breathed heavily as his palms shielded his disheartened face. He could feel a gnawing pain in his shoulder and a long laceration ran up his forearm from the fall, emitting blood that dripped down his arms.

There was no hope for anybody.

"We need to climb back up!" Vlayn shouted with fury against the increasing winds.

"We can't!" Arith returned, "N.M.C. is *right* there, they'll put a bullet in our heads the next time they see us!"

"I don't fucking care!!! We *need* to try!" Vlayn exclaimed with heightening grief.

"No! We aren't going back!"

Endeen and the foreign man began making their way closer to Arith and Vlayn. They stuck close to the cliff wall, walking on a narrow ledge.

Vlayn's face was grave and somber as he analyzed the three men that stood before him. Then, he began for the wall and scaled it.

Arith ran over and pulled Vlayn from the wall, forcing him to the ground. Vlayn ripped Arith's arms from him and immediately sprung to his feet, taking hold of Arith. He shoved him against the wall, screaming with angst. "I'm going to do whatever the fuck I want!!!" he shrieked.

"You're going to die!!!" Arith screamed back.

One of the men jumped into the quarrel and detached Vlayn from Arith, throwing him to the side.

"What?! You're all going to let Ellmorr mock *all* of us!? You're just going to stand by, letting Ellmorr watch you all *rot* in those fucking wastes that we live in!?" Vlayn bellowed. He stood stoop-shouldered, still regaining his balance after being thrown off Arith. "We're just going to let Ellmorians smile and laugh and *eat*, all while we struggle to find a scrap of fucking food and watch everyone we love die!? A Blackguard group will catch up to us at *some* point down there and will execute *all* of us. We will *all* eventually catch the Glithémien Disease and our insides will bleed through to our eyes and mouths! Our bodies'll cave into itself!!!"

Arith and the men simply listened as the strong gusts of wind blew them off balance.

"We're all dying!!!" Vlayn howled with watering eyes. "There's nothing left! Life is *over* don't you understand that!?" His eyes dropped to his feet, exhaling heavily. "There's nothing left for any of us," he finished quietly.

Vlayn slowly raised his head. His voice was ragged and hoarse. He summoned all the strength he could muster, and uttered, "There is just no hope for any of us..."

-Fifteen-

KILL TO LIVE

The atmosphere dimmed as nighttime approached, lowering a lazy, dusty fog over Laxryy. And quickly, the darkness seized this lonely town. Vlayn and the three men tiredly ambled down the center of the barren graveyard that was Laxryy; they had nowhere to be, and Vlayn was just too succumbed.

The weapons hung from his twinging shoulder as he walked with his wobbly gait. His hair hung in front of his eyes but he didn't have the energy to shake it. Exhaustion and hunger wasn't even a factor, even though he felt it sharply coursing through him all the way to his fingertips. He could feel the misery everywhere. But his distrust of these deserts and the agony that it caused him was more debilitating. Vlayn hoped to contract the Glithémien Disease so he could suffer just the way his mother, father, his brother, and the love of his miserable life, Camrynn, did. Should he just end himself?

The four migrated to the building in which they squatted in prior to their unsuccessful venture to Ellmorr. It had been almost an entire jaro, and Laxryy hadn't altered an inch. Vlayn stood silently on a creaking, leaning porch. He perched on the edge with the Jaadakin sand sitting two inches below his toes. He observed his darkening surroundings and the abandoned shacks of Laxryy around him that lowered into the sand even farther with each passing jaro.

The usual desert heat wasn't eating his skin like it usually did, making him sweat incessantly. Instead, the nighttime air was nippy. Vlayn shoved his hands into his pockets, exhaled quickly and looked over at Arith and the two men.

Arith lit the paylian roll in his mouth, sucked in the smoke, then blew it out swiftly. He passed it to Endeen, who stood comfortably in the sand. His grimy head caught the moonlight and shot it back out into the silent atmosphere. Vlayn peered off into the distance toward Ellmorr yet again. He could feel the city ridiculing him as always. He walked a few steps off the front stoop, clasped his hands together lividly and cracked his knuckles.

He looked up at the three men standing in front of him. Arith still smoked the paylian roll calmly, living his worthless life, and living out the nothingness that it served.

"Ever since I was young," Vlayn began in a croaky, monotone voice, "always thought yuh had to kill to survive — that there was *no* other way to live." Arith, Endeen, and the man examined Vlayn carefully; each syllable spoken, the way his bottom lip dropped aggressively when Vlayn grew irate about the topic, and how his glassy eyes were narrow and angry. "Then there were a lot of jaros when I thought I was wrong..." He walked a few feet closer to the three and pressed on, "Met someone I loved. She showed me that there was more to this fucked up life; showed me that yuh didn't have to kill to survive. She saw my flaws, my weaknesses, the unending pain inside my chest. Sometimes I could see her eyes in the eyes of others. Hear her voice carrying with the wind. She was perfect. She wasn't broken like me... I'm a stunted Babarin." His eyes returned to the glaring lights of Ellmorr and a frigid shiver ran up his chest under his soddened t-shirt and the coat that covered it. Vlayn could see air skimmers circling

227

the bustling city from his perspective. They were mere dots in the sky from this distance, but he knew what they were.

"But then she fucking died..." Vlayn continued, "she suffered from the disease and fell by the hands of another *animal*... but that was the day I realized I was so fucking wrong... Yuh gotta' kill to survive." Then, he lifted his grungy t-shirt to reveal his lower stomach. "See this?" he asserted while pointing to a long, uneven scar that ran from left to right across his stomach. "I almost died from this scar. A man named DaRoone got me with a knife. Didn't even feel the pain at first. I was fighting to live at the time. You *gotta* kill to live. That's the only way in Jaadakin. Maybe not them..." he said, motioning to Ellmorr, "maybe not *anyone* else in the Kirbinian Galaxy, no other planets except us. We just got the shit end, and it's *all* because of Ellmorr," Vlayn exclaimed in a raised voice; a voice that soon transitioned swiftly into a hush one, "Maybe if that fucking city wasn't so greedy, maybe if they cared 'bout the rest of Xenamus, then she would still be here. They don't know what glithémien are, sure. But they got the power to change something."

"How the fuck is it Ellmorr's fault?" Arith questioned.

Vlayn's eyes started twitching potently as he glared at Arith. He could feel the expiration of the man's life, even if he was still breathing. "Because if they fucking considered us, then glithémien wouldn't be taking down the major cities on Xenamus. That's why and that's me putting it lightly!" Vlayn moved closer to Arith's face, almost ready to exterminate all three men.

But Vlayn wouldn't. At least he wouldn't at this moment. He knew this was *his* crew. They would always listen to his command. They wouldn't be leaving him because they knew they wouldn't survive without him. Vlayn knew they would do his work.

He took a step back from Arith and glanced up at the second story of the Laxryy shack. He scoffed, spit into the sand, and murmured, "I'm goin' up," he told them as he held the Nabbuu 88 tightly in his right hand. "Got that booze from the other day?" he asked Arith.

"The whiskey?" he returned. "That was half a jaro ago."

"Yeah, whatever. The booze. Do you still have the booze?"

"I do, but you aren't getting it."

Endeen jumped in, "you still have that shit?" Arith parried, "We've been locked in Ashfall for a half a fucking jaro!" he shouted at him.

Vlayn rushed forward, pushing Arith to the side and reaching for his backpack. Arith stepped back and faced Vlayn, "Back the fuck off," he threatened.

"Give me the fucking booze," Vlayn asserted, then threw a fist into Arith's ribcage. Finally, when his defensive behavior was dismantled, Vlayn shoved his hands into the backpack and retrieved the whiskey. "Like I said," he began while he strangled the neck of the bottle, "I'm goin' up," he started for the dilapidated front door. Using his seething anger, he kicked open the door and started up the stairs. He breathed in the murky air, making his way through the darkness. He walked into the brightness of the second floor and he could see the moonlight shimmering into his eyes. But when he got to the top, his pace came to an immediate halt at a startling sight: an N.M.C. soldier laying in the corner of the room, closest to the broken window frame. A rusty C.C.N.T. 90 assault rifle rested by his legs. One leg, though, was swathed in bandages. The man's body was restrained by N.M.C. armor and his neck was slanted in a seemingly uncomfortable position.

Vlayn grinned maniacally at the sight as he retreated into the darkest corner of the room, opposite the unconscious man. Vlayn stared at him, knowing he was finally in control.

-Sixteen-

VENGEANCE IS NECESSARY

The N.M.C. soldier slowly awakened. The man's eyes
softly opened to a broken window. Monotonous blond
hills of sand were beyond the window frame, with a soft
shimmer of the blue moon twinkling through the broken
shards of glass. A lazy, sandy fog hung over Laxryy, with
the rambunctious noise of voices from down below
penetrating his eardrums as he woke. He peered down at
his assault rifle that lay underneath his weakened leg.

He tiresomely rolled his head left along the wall he
leaned on. A faint outline of a figure in a dark corner of
the second floor took hold in his eyes as he immediately
sensed a presence. The soldier swiftly tussled for his
weapon in fear of this invader.

But the figure began to walk; footsteps grew louder
and louder until it stopped right in front of the soldier's
sprawled legs. The ominous figure stood above him. The
seated N.M.C. soldier got hold of his rifle, but it was far
too late. He met the monstrous, murderous eyes of a
savage of the wastelands: Vlayn Par'Wil.

The man was frozen at the sight. He stared at this
figure who was a stranger to him, while Vlayn returned the
stare with hungry eyes.

Vlayn raised his Nabbuu 88 pistol on the seated
soldier.

Darkness coated the atmosphere heavily and the second floor of the shack was half illuminated, partially masking Vlayn's face.

"N.M.C., huh?" the hoarse voice of Vlayn asked. "I met some of you recently. You people truly are the lowest walks of fucking life."

The soldier didn't answer. Instead, he glanced down at his C.C.N.T. 90 assault rifle, and then out onto the town of Laxryy. Three other marauders stood outside of the shack and they appeared thirsty for more blood to the N.M.C. soldier. He looked up at Vlayn, "does it matter?" he responded.

"Yes, it certainly does. Me and my group need to make sure soldiers won't come after us."

"N.M.C. soldiers will never be in search for you. There's millions of other heartless killers out here in Jaadakin County. You aren't special," the man said insultingly. "It don't matter," he continued as he glanced over at Vlayn. "Out here, people don't care who it is they're killing. It's blood and it doesn't matter whose blood it is," he stated bluntly.

Silence.

The man peered outside again, "I know the code you people follow. And I've only been talking to you for thirty seconds."

"Pretty daring to be speakin' to a random guy like that... what code is it?" Vlayn asked condescendingly.

The man ignored Vlayn's remark and answered without hesitation, "The one that says, I don't care who you are, what gender you are, or what race you are, if you have what I want, I'll kill you and take it."

Vlayn laughed and let out an enthusiastic smile, "You are certainly right," he replied. "Take off that armor, *I want it.*"

With no alternatives, the man undressed his armor, enabling Vlayn to assert his dominance. The man was dressed in his civilians and sent a chilling glare to Vlayn Par'Wil; one that matched Vlayn's gaze.

"And here you are… listening to that… *code*," Vlayn said as he kicked the gear to the side then looked Bardolf up and down, nothing but a sheathed energy dagger on the soldier's hip.

He noticed Vlayn's staring. "Soldiers keep it locked on their sides underneath their armor," he told him. Vlayn scoffed and smirked wildly. "Keep it on you if it makes you feel safe. Tellin' you, though, it won't help." Then, he walked to the corner of the room where he started scratching his beard, revealing his irritated state.

"Here," Vlayn exclaimed from the other side of the room, "Bourbon. Found it downstairs… it is a tavern, yuh know." He handed a glass to the man and poured some for both of them. Vlayn took a large sip and murmured through the alcohol, "Sit back down," he demanded. The glass was tightly clasped in his left hand while he strangled the firearm in his right. Vlayn took another sip then raised the glass to his eyes to admire the alcohol. "Imported straight from Zidonian! But before that, Earth," he said excitedly.

They both simultaneously took another sip of the alcoholic beverage.

Here, these two men sat. This stranger was right across from the sinister devil himself: Vlayn. He didn't need to know exactly who Vlayn was. He could comprehend all of it. He knew of the dozens of people Vlayn had slaughtered, how many sins he had committed, and how many other heartless acts of violence Vlayn Par'Wil had attested to. It was drawn all over his face. The number of sins emphasizing by the hour. And yet, Vlayn carried himself weightlessly – or at least that was how it appeared to this man.

Vlayn was a product of Xenamus.

"What are you, anyway?" Vlayn asked brutishly, interrupting the soldier's thinking process.

"What do you mean?" he responded guiltlessly as he forcefully swallowed the stale bourbon.

Vlayn chugged the rest of his alcohol then immediately refilled his glass.

"What *race*? Yuh look like an idiot," he cackled viciously and flung his pistol around as he spoke, "It's like three races in one."

"Human and Kirbinian race. But race doesn't matter," the man said quietly as he swallowed more booze.

Vlayn's face drastically transformed when the man said this, "Race matters… I'm Babarin – obviously," he responded, "What other race do yuh run into that isn't Babarin or Kirbinian on this planet? Sure as hell not human."

The soldier's hand slowly migrated to the wound in his thigh, grasping it in pain and caressing it slowly. Finally, he spoke, "what are you trying to say about the Human Race?" he asked daringly. Vlayn stood ominously above him, glaring down at him with one eyebrow raised. "I'm saying they're weak."

"Really?"

"Really."

The soldier paused, then took a bold leap, "Well I can tell you I can kill you just as well if I was Babarin," he said as he looked away from his glass and into the eyes of this savage.

A sinister tension exacerbated even further in this room, and Vlayn dreadfully glared into the man's eyes for almost a minute straight. One would expect a sinister chuckle, but he didn't move a muscle. He scrutinized this man, contemplated the worthiness of his presence, while writing out his death in his head. Then, he spoke in a plain tone, "Don't worry," he whispered slowly, "I'll put a bullet in your head when we are done with this conversation," he insisted without making a single facial expression. Not a blink, not a squint, not even the slightest movement of his mouth. Nothing. It was like the words effortlessly blew through his ajar lips.

The soldier stared right back at Vlayn and started laughing, then sneered at him challengingly.

"I'm Vlayn Par'Wil," he introduced, still not flinching. "You?"

He glanced up at Vlayn, "Bardolf Marow."

"Nice to meet you, Bardolf... *Marow*. Unfortunately, you'll be dead soon but that's beside the point." Vlayn sipped from the glass, then lowered this conversation to a more civilized level. "What are you doin' out here anyway? Laxryy ain't got nothin' to offer."

"I've got no idea," Bardolf replied.

"You're N.M.C. though, right?"

Bardolf nodded.

"Where you stationed anyway?" Vlayn inquired.

"Does it matter?"

"Not really, I suppose. Then again, nothing seemed to matter to you. First you say it don't matter if you're N.M.C., then you're saying race don't matter, now you're saying it don't matter where you're stationed," Vlayn stated as he stared into Bardolf's eyes as if he was trying to uncover some deeper meaning.

"You grow up here? On Xenamus?" Bardolf asked politely, quickly turning the direction of this dialogue. And surprisingly, Vlayn answered, "Whole life."

"How's the life out here?" Bardolf asked.

"Horrible. I'm used to it though. Was born out in the city of Witherhart; that place was a dump just as much as Laxryy. Of course, the place is much bigger. After all, it's a major city. Whole life I've been always used to constantly moving from one place to another. Seeing someone out in the open desert, and just outright killin' em'... just to avoid any conflict. Then I rifle through the corpse. All of that just becomes normal procedure... *daily routine*," Vlayn explained.

Bardolf had no response so he nodded and finished his alcohol. Vlayn rested his glass and raised the bottle as a gesture for a refill. Bardolf leaned in and Vlayn filled his glass. He observed Bardolf through the dusty glass as he was seated on the floor, watching the bronze liquid fill it. Then, Vlayn turned to the outside world of Xenamus. The light chatter of Vlayn's crew from down below crept into the silent shack, nettling him even more.

Bardolf took a small sip; watching the amount he drank while Vlayn inhaled each glass he poured. He then reached into his pocket and pulled out the last remaining picture of his family. He started smiling foolishly at it, so he covered his mouth with his hand. But his left eye started tearing and his smile swiftly dissipated. Bardolf turned the picture over and saw a handwritten message on the back. Vlayn turned and instantly noticed him holding the sentimental picture. Vlayn moved toward Bardolf and swiped the picture from him. He held it up to his face to get a better look. Bardolf quickly sprung to his feet. "Isn't this cute!" Vlayn shouted excitedly.

Bardolf struggled to get the picture back from Vlayn, pushing his body against his, sprawling his arm out to grab it. But Vlayn stepped back a few feet and raised his pistol, "Sit down!" he screamed violently.

Bardolf stood defenseless, tears swelling his eyes. He backed up, leaned against the wall and slid down it in defeat.

Vlayn scoffed at Bardolf's defenseless state. So, he pulled out a lighter with his left hand, while he placed his pistol on the window sill. He held the picture high and lit it on fire. Vlayn continued to gawk at the flames. The orange light reflected off his crusty skin and then he dropped the picture on the wooden floor planks below him. "Don't move," Vlayn ordered, "let it burn."

Bardolf stared at the blazing picture. A tear ran down his face and he sniffled a few times. Vlayn continued to smile while chuckling sinisterly as he sipped the alcohol.

"Can't believe you ain't dead yet." Vlayn murmured into his glass.

Bardolf sat for a moment, wiped his face, and carefully responded, "I can handle myself."

"Na, I'm not even talking about that," Vlayn changed the subject despite this sorrowful moment for Bardolf, "I mean what yuh just said is a lie. If you were out here day after day and not cooped up safely in your N.M.C. base I'm sure you would be slaughtered quickly by someone like me or my guys. Still, though, I'm talking about the heat. It gets *hot* out here. I mean, I'm Babarin so I can withstand it. You, though, would melt, or worse, you'd just get sun poisoning. What, the N.M.C. don't give you a U.V. Suit?"

"It's already built in under the armor," Bardolf responded softly after sipping his bourbon. The picture was charred and crumbled through the wooden floorboards.

"Wow," Vlayn said in false excitement, "can't wait to use that," he added menacingly as he took a swig of the beverage. "You know what a U.V. Protection Suit is, right? Protects you from the extreme heat."

Bardolf took his eyes from the picture, "of course I know."

"See, it just annoys me," Vlayn began, stepping closer to the seated Bardolf. "Yuh got all of Jaadakin County suffering. We're out here fending for ourselves."

"I'm not all human," Bardolf mentioned, cutting him off. But Vlayn didn't seem to care, "And then, you got Ellmorr sittin' pretty on top of the Fraygen Plateau," Vlayn's voice raised with disregard of what Bardolf mumbled. "Those pitiful, *gleaming* lights shine all day and all night from that city. People from *all* over the Kirbinian Galaxy travel to that damn city... Ellmorr just reminds us that we aren't rich and we're living a hopeless life!" he wailed.

Then, he began to pace in rage. "Those U.V. suits," Vlayn started up again, "is the–the *essence* of lies – some of the suits don't even work – U.V. Company knows this, too." The pace of his croaky voice quickened, "I mean, they gotta know! And yet they *still* sell the suits because they know people will buy them!" He stopped his walking and faced Bardolf, who was witnessing Vlayn's madness first-hand. "But who cares right?" the speed of Vlayn's voice rapidly increased as if the words were tripping over themselves; "If you're not Babarin you need a suit for protection against the heat." Bardolf simply sat in utter confusion as he attempted to listen to the conglomerate of words spewed by a raging Vlayn.

Vlayn retreated to his glass and tightly grasped it. "I don't care about the people getting sick from the heat! It just gets to me that the U.V. Company is constantly profiting, even from broken U.V. Suits." Vlayn leaned back onto the wall across from Bardolf. He peered out of the broken window frame onto the dark, barren wastelands.

The two men could hear the faint conversations from Vlayn's crew down below. "And obviously, all the money Xenamus makes goes straight to the city of Ellmorr," Vlayn finished when the glass under his tight grip shattered. Glass fragments exploded into the air, propelling the whiskey upward, splashing onto Vlayn's coat. He inhaled sharply and clenched his fist, feeling the lingering glass particles in his palms puncturing his skin. He glanced down and exhaled painfully, wiping his hand on his thigh, rubbing the blood off. He bent down, grabbed the bottle by the neck, clutched it tightly in his bloody palm, and started drinking it straight.

Silence resided in the second floor of this ravaged shack and the grinding voice of a tired Vlayn spoke again. This time, though, he migrated close to Bardolf with the gun still drawn on him, and knelt down to get on his level. He spoke as soft as an unrefined voice could, "Your opinion on the city of Ellmorr?" The stale smell of whiskey echoed from his tongue with every word, which was mummified in an immaculate irritation.

Bardolf fixated his eyes on Vlayn nervously. He knew this was a form of intimidation, but Bardolf could see Vlayn's erratic behavior. The humanistic accent in his voice was more prominent than ever before, "I definitely don't resent it like you," Bardolf declared boldly.

"How could you not?" Vlayn challenged him bitterly. "There's that massive city on top of the Fraygen Plateau," Vlayn explained while pointing to the outside world of Xenamus. "*Millions* of people up there – *safe* from the rest of Xenamus. You don't agree, *human*?"

"I'm a Kirbinian," Bardolf reciprocated with power mustered behind every word.

Vlayn grinned with satisfaction, knowing he got to Bardolf, "Really?" he started, "because just before you said you were human," he asserted combatively.

The room suddenly grew darker. Vlayn was still in Bardolf's face, steaming with a fury that powered his body like coal in a steam engine. Bardolf simply blinked as a response to this statement and tilted his head as a gesture for termination of this conversation. This signal was rejected.

Vlayn spoke, this time it was softer than ever. "Seems to me you are unsure of what you are," he paused to see if he was getting a reaction out of Bardolf. "Or," Vlayn continued, "you are unsure what you want to be. You're damaged, *human*."

Vlayn impatiently waited for a response.

Nothing.

"Never seen anyone so uncertain of their race... must be a tough life... who are you? Who is... *Bardolf Marow*?" Vlayn sprung to his feet and resumed his pacing. He walked slowly with each step while he hummed maniacally. Then, his voice raised into a loud voice with an intimidating overlay, "One second you say how you're a human. Then the next you boast about how you're all Kirbinian as if you're trying to be patriotic of this galaxy or something." Vlayn stopped in the midst of his pacing and turned his head toward Bardolf. The room began to brighten; a new day was gradually approaching over the lonely desert.

"Yuh know what?" Vlayn continued, "Uncertainty shows weakness... especially in an N.M.C. soldier... oh no, no, no, no, no... you don't want to be uncertain, Kirb. Or human, should I say. *Damn*."

Vlayn walked toward Bardolf, who was now slacking back against the wall. Bardolf stared at the ruined picture that was now shriveled on the floor by his feet.

Vlayn whispered, "Are you weak... Bardolf? Me personally, I think you are." Bardolf finally spoke up, "You're a manipulative fool."

Vlayn continued without care, "I'm sure them wealthy Ellmorians over there wouldn't accept you," he shouted out louder, cutting Bardolf off. "You can't be anything more than some petty front-line soldier for the N.M.C... no one knows who you are, *Marow*. You think High Clansee Corvonn and Kirbside know who you are? They don't. They're all clueless, anyway. Leaving planets like Xenamus to rot," his scratchy voice mumbled.

Vlayn peered out at the dark desert once more. His aching eyes instantly snapped onto the prestigious Ellmorr sitting on top of the Fraygen Plateau. "Trade, food, salvation. All of it up there in Ellmorr. Gambling, too, I hear… oh, and how can I forget? The people in Ellmorr have cures for diseases." And suddenly, his voice transformed, "Diseases like glithémien… diseases people in Jaadakin County have… Diseases that will kill people down here!" he wailed, even though he knew this wasn't true.

"What disease are you even talking about?" he asked contentiously. "I don't even know what in the hell you're talking about –"

"The disease that's killing everyone!!!" Vlayn screamed until he felt his throat burning. Bardolf cackled, though, "That's killing everyone down here, maybe. Not up there, though. No one knows what that is on Fraygen – I certainly don't. But what's occurring to me is that you've just lost your *fucking* mind. Something is driving you crazy. So you pin this disease onto Ellmorr to make yourself feel better about something that *cannot be fixed*… Or let alone paid any attention to… This *glithémien* disease… No one in Ellmorr knows, because no one cares enough to know."

Vlayn's face was solidified as he dazed off. His breathing labored; Bardolf's words slapping him hard. But his insanity repositioned itself in his mind, allowing him to continue, "All those people up there on the Fraygen Plateau sleep comfortably at night behind those goddamn walls, without a worry in The Galaxy – under the protection of you fools, the N.M.C…" Vlayn took a step close to Bardolf, looked him up and down, summoned saliva, and spit on his feet.

Bardolf kept his composure; breathing in and out and biting his bottom lip with a hardening face. "I'm a bigger man than you," he told him. Vlayn spun around, smirking and scoffing. "The bigger man is the one who survives by the end of this night. We both know who that'll be," Vlayn said.

Bardolf's chest rose as he fumed. "Yeah," he said with a tattered voice. "I know who it will be."

Vlayn stared outside again, and his voice raised, "those lights that shine at night are there just to remind the rest of us, people like *you* and me, those lights remind us of how bad *we* have it. And I know how it is down here. You don't!" he wailed, still staring off into the distance, "you think you do! You don't!" he then looked into Bardolf's eyes, "that's why *I'll* be the one leaving this place tonight!!!"

Vlayn exhaled sharply, his eyebrows lowered, and he could feel his lassitude in every movement he made. "Major cities are in poverty," Vlayn pressed on, "I remember living in Witherhart. We prayed we would get a scrap of food for the day. Prayed a merchant vehicle passed by. Yeah, it's a major city, but the major cities become ridden with plague and violence and death. Who the hell wants to stop by? Nobody even had the Credits to purchase from passing merchants anyway. People traded their companions for food."

The situation became strange for Bardolf, some time ago a gun was pointed at his head. Now, Vlayn was in a daydream as he recited his past. Bardolf saw an opportunity to escape, but for some reason he didn't, as if something was restraining him to this dilapidated shack.

He *wanted* to hear Vlayn's story. Almost as if he wanted to know about the man who was keeping him captive.

Vlayn rested the gun on the decaying wooden window sill and continued, "one day… jaros ago, when I was younger… cannibalism spread like the plague throughout my hometown, Witherhart. No food or water for days. So many corpses strewn across the roads, hanging from balconies, tossed in alley-ways… cluttering the city. The hell were we supposed to do? Lay down and die like the rest?" Vlayn dropped his eyes to his feet. A tear ran down his face, but he quickly wiped it away. He cleared his throat, rubbed his beard, wiped his eyes, and spoke, "My brother and I… we ate our father."

Bardolf was shocked. It recently started becoming customary for Jaadakins to eat others – food was even scarcer than it was seventy jaros ago. For an N.M.C. soldier, though, living away from the terrors of this county, he was befuddled; he lifted his head slowly, eyes widened. But he felt no pity for Vlayn.

"Our mother…" Vlayn hesitantly continued with a gruff Babarin voice that had screamed too far for too long. A voice that had spoken too many hopeful words. A voice that was disappointed in the past. A voice that had learned time and time again that hope was never alive. Vlayn began with vexation, "Those fucking desert bugs. They stick to the goddamn ground and they *follow* your scent til they tear the skin from your eyes. It wasn't necessarily the hunger that killed her like everyone else."

Then, a heavy silence weighed the room down. The gallant lights from Ellmorr silently illuminated the shack and the depressed, empty settlement of Laxryy as it sat lonely in the desert. Vlayn's voice was clearer and calmer than ever, "We woulda ate her if we could," Vlayn said.

"We didn't want to. We *had* to… survival… that's all it comes down to. It always comes down to that. After that, I killed my brother. He caught the disease, like my mother. He woulda suffered. I needed to put him out… had to. Ever since, I've been on the move. Without a family. Alone. Jumping from one place to another… it fit. I got used to it."

Bardolf tried to stand while grasping his wounded leg in pain. Vlayn took notice and paused until he asked a question that he had already answered himself long ago. And he knew this. "Do you needa kill in order to survive…?" he mumbled to a bewildered Bardolf. "Never forget who you are," Vlayn added. "Never let your guard down. Remember that."

Bardolf's C.C.N.T. 90 assault rifle still rested on the floor next to his feet.

Vlayn studied the weapon for a brief period of time, but long enough to see the words "Claeen Company Nabbuu Type 90," engraved sharply into the side of the barrel. He continued, growing irate once more, "See, those people in Ellmorr don't know how good they have it. They haven't had to do the worst kinds of things just to stay alive! Ellmorians haven't had to do things they never thought they would do! Major cities – close to death! And what does the Clansee do? Nothing! He continues to fund Ellmorr and leaves the rest of us to suffer!" Vlayn was out of breath; his long hair drooped in front of his eyes and the energetic lights from Ellmorr, over forty miles across the empty desert, caused his sweaty skin to glisten. He turned to Bardolf and sent him a piercing glare.

"This isn't about me," Bardolf said. "This is about *you*. *You're* damaged. *You're* weak. You want vengeance on Xenamus because of what has happened to *you*. This isn't

246

about me. And you're alone, and I don't know you, but I *know* that. You lost anyone you ever enjoyed or loved. And those people outside – they're just foreign assholes who are following you into some dark fucking abyss. The county is falling all around us, but lunacy and rage isn't as unavoidable as you probably made yourself believe."

Vlayn's breathing grew noticeably louder, "You speak of me as if I'm too far gone... As if I'm Altkin."

Bardolf waited a moment, then spoke softly, "Altkin is dead. But there's still people in this galaxy that are just like him... you *are* too far gone."

The two continued to make eye contact.

It seemed as if time had slowed.

Vlayn swiftly reached for his pistol and shot three bullets; one for each of his crew down below: Arith and the remaining men next to him. The three flopped into the sand, stuck with a bullet in their backs.

Time seemed to move even slower as the noise of the shots rang throughout the hollow desert of Jaadakin.

Vlayn immediately spun, locking the pistol on Bardolf, ready to draw his blood.

But Bardolf leapt forward and swiped the weapon off of him, pushing Vlayn's arm to the right, avoiding sudden death. But Vlayn still pulled the trigger, missing Bardolf and striking the wall instead.

Bardolf's ears screeched and a rippling pain was sent through his skull. Despite his lightheadedness, he charged in toward Vlayn in self-defense and threw him up against the wall.

Vlayn, now pinned up against the wall by Bardolf, struggled to lift his pistol that was clasped by Bardolf's torso. "*Raaahhhh!!!!*" he screamed next to Bardolf's left ear, trying to raise the pistol, but Bardolf pressed his torso into him, making it nearly impossible.

Bardolf started tussling Vlayn for the pistol, and now Vlayn was merely trying to keep it out of his hands. Both barked forcefully while Vlayn was still pinched against the wall. As a result, the pistol eventually flung from his grip and was knocked down to the floor. Bardolf left Vlayn. He turned and sprawled to retrieve the gun, but Vlayn grabbed him as he was bending down to reach for it and threw him to the side, pulling the muscles in his lower back.

Vlayn followed through and quickly got on top of him, mounting the half human-half Kirbinian man. His back stung in pain, but he began to throw a flurry of fists at Bardolf's face anyway. His cheek ruptured, spewing blood. He forcefully pinned Bardolf down by his neck and choked him hastily. Struggling to escape and in need of oxygen, Bardolf unsheathed the energy dagger that was attached to his hip. He quickly jabbed Vlayn in his side with the dagger and Bardolf instantly sat up and gasped for air.

Bardolf ripped out the dagger that was wedged into his foe's side. Just like the pistol, this, too, was fought for.

Vlayn still mounted Bardolf and the two both gripped the energy dagger, struggling to get hold of it. The dagger was held up in the air, swaying from side to side and under control by both men. But Vlayn's grip was severely weakening; blood rained from his side, forcing him to bellow.

While gripping the energy dagger with Vlayn, Bardolf threw a forceful elbow to his face, knocking him to the floor. Despite the constant flow of blood from his cheek, he attempted to mount Vlayn.

Vlayn refused. He quickly leapt to his feet and charged Bardolf, leaving a trail of dark blood behind him.

The weakened Bardolf stood his ground against Vlayn.

Both men grunted, especially Bardolf, who was knocked back a few feet from absorbing Vlayn's stiff shoulder that was thrown into him.

They tussled yet again, until Bardolf shoved Vlayn off of him.

Punches were quickly ping-ponged, igniting a continuing apoplexy within their bodies and minds. It stimulated them to work harder – throw a quicker punch, perform a swifter takedown – anything to survive.

Vlayn tackled Bardolf yet again. This time, Bardolf was more defensive.

He collapsed to the floor, but resisted the mount once more. The two lay on their sides, struggling to mount the other to gain control while the floorboards creaked in stress to the weight.

The men seemed to be in their own ring of violence, for the eerie quietness of the desert kept its distance.

Blood gushed out of their wounds, soaking the wooden planks. Vlayn pressed against Bardolf. He was in full control and began hammering away at Bardolf's face. The N.M.C. soldier's face quickly swelled until Vlayn was able to draw even more blood from his cheeks and forehead with his knuckles. Then, Vlayn placed both hands on Bardolf's neck, laying all of his weight down onto him.

Unable to breathe, Bardolf squirmed. He was quickly running out of oxygen and Vlayn simpered at the view from above him.

Bardolf's face started turning blue as his vision blurred. His hearing was faint and the only thing Bardolf could see was the sinister face of the crazed man, Vlayn, right above him. Bardolf soon lost control of all the muscles in his body as his breathing was severely labored.

Death was upon him, and he knew it. Blood showered down from Vlayn's face onto Bardolf's. His eyes began to roll to the back of his head, but Bardolf fought to keep his focus on the enemy: Vlayn Par'Wil.

It seemed as if his hearing dissipated completely, but a turbulent shouting from the damaged Vlayn still ran into his ears.

As a last resort, with almost no oxygen or energy remaining, Bardolf pulled Vlayn down by his sweaty, bloody shirt, and threw a weak punch to his face.

No effect; Vlayn shrugged it off.

Vlayn was still close to Bardolf's chest. So, while suffocating, he reached for Vlayn's face and jabbed his thumb into his eye. Almost instantly, Vlayn's grip loosened and he fell from his mount in pain. Bardolf breathed in a surge of adrenaline; he shoved the damaged Vlayn off him, who was roaring from his punctured, bleeding eyeball. Bardolf pinned Vlayn to the floor, mounted him, and threw fist after fist at his forehead and temples. His blood painted Bardolf's sharp knuckles. His mind could only do its very best to conjure images of what he looked like at this moment; bedraggled hair, blood-stained, mud-caked hands, his mouth hung open, tongue salivating for blood, just like the man he battled. All while sitting on the chest of Vlayn, whose ruptured eye oozed of gelatinized water that was mixed with sticky blood.

Bardolf immediately swapped his hands to Vlayn's neck, choking him and screaming in his face, "I don't know why you choose this life! You do this to yourself!" he howled with all his might.

Vlayn groaned from underneath the choke, and he pressed into Bardolf's gunshot wound in his right leg. Bardolf tried to shrug the pain, but it was unbearable. He sunk to the ground and yelped.

"I've got no choice!!" Vlayn responded with equally as grating of a voice.

A pool of blood enveloped the two foes. The wooden planks suddenly caved in and the two men fell through the floor, landing on the first level. They both viciously coughed and tried to breathe amidst the dust that floated everywhere. No light had penetrated this room, for the desert floor itself swallowed this level of the shack. Only shimmering rays broke through the slits of wooden planks that boarded the windows. The two men continued to fight for their lives and ignored their surroundings. Bardolf stood and leapt off his pristine leg, bashing into Vlayn with his shoulder and knocking him down into the almost one foot of sand that filled the floor. Being so feeble at this point, Vlayn limply collapsed to the floor and tried to regain his bearings. His skull smashed into the sand and he could feel his eyeball turning to mush and leaking from his eye socket and sliding down his cheek.

Bardolf, just as exhausted, stumbled toward a fallen Vlayn.

"I wanted a brawl!" Vlayn bellowed while lying in the sand. Then, he drew Bardolf's pistol that was retrieved after it was dropped in the beginning of the fight and later fell through the collapsed floorboards. From the ground, he aimed it the now defeated, defenseless Bardolf. The gun swayed in the hands of the weakened Vlayn. After a little hesitation, he fired. The recoil blew Vlayn's frail arm backward. The bullet blew into Bardolf's torso, and he failed.

Bardolf flung into the sandy floor and he could hear Vlayn struggling to get to his feet while growling in misery. Blood poured out of the gaping hole and was instantly soaked by the sand. Bardolf held the wound as tight as he could, as if retaining this amount of blood would help. After all, there were so many other wounds and holes in Bardolf's body where blood was still flowing out of. How much blood was left? How much more could Bardolf bleed?

Vlayn stood above Bardolf. He lay there, half dead. Vlayn fired another shot, this time in his right shoulder. It barely penetrated the skin, though, so not much blood was emitted. Still, it was another hit on Bardolf. They both gasped heavily, covered in each other's blood, and their own. Bardolf attempted to rise to his feet, but Vlayn kicked him down, and he began writhing.

"*We...*" Vlayn muttered through the grueling pain he felt from his popped eye, "we need to do the worst kinds of things just to stay *alive*." Vlayn dropped himself on top of Bardolf, mounting him again and holding him still. Even though Bardolf was practically dead, Vlayn needed to see his soul fly from his chest.

He raised the pistol to Bardolf's head. Bardolf, barely able to move, simply stared back at Vlayn, suffering, hardly able to breathe for he gargled on his own blood.

"I had no choice as to what life I wanted to live!" Vlayn howled. Although, he yelled as if he was trying to convince himself.

The two men stared at one another momentarily.

Vlayn kneeled there expressionless as the pain from the fight, the intense trauma from losing his eye, the loneliness of this world, and the loss of Camrynn stifled him. His face was smeared with blood and his hair was disheveled. There was nothing left for this man. What if he made it out alive? Where would he go? What would he do? No one he loved was alive. He killed his crew. He didn't even have those strangers to keep him company. The bleak, grim world of Xenamus would simply prop itself back on this one-eyed man's shoulders, reminding him of the suffering he would quickly endure from the isolation; reminding him of the immortal Glithémien Disease, pillaging through Jaadakin County's people.

This planet was a trap. It would take away every single person Vlayn loved with the help of the disease, but wouldn't take Vlayn with them. Xenamus wouldn't allow this. It would hold him at a distance, making him watch each person he loved disappear with this deadly illness.

What was left for Vlayn Par'Wil?

Still, though, there was that connotation – that thought process to *keep living*. Even if there was nothing left.

Vlayn was ready to take another life.

Bardolf sifted his hand through the sandy debris on the floor while pinned to the ground. Finally, he could feel something he could use. He thrust a shard of wood to Vlayn's side, making him yelp and subside to the floor next to Bardolf.

Bardolf scrambled to his feet, slipping in the sand and collapsing to the floor before fully ascending to his feet. He saw Vlayn thrashing his body back and forth in agony. Vlayn couldn't scream, for he had no more voice left. Bardolf picked up Vlayn's Nabbuu 88 and rested the tip of the barrel on Vlayn's forehead.

The two men were still. Vlayn lay in his own pool of blood with a wooden plank wedged into his side, one eye, and multiples gashes. And Bardolf, with a gaping hole in his right leg, two gunshot wounds, and a strangled neck.

Bardolf stared solemnly into the eye of the fallen, revengeful Vlayn. He wondered what Vlayn Par'Wil experienced throughout his life. What drove him into madness. What he had to endure. What he had to do just to keep himself and the ones he loved alive, and what the ones he loved had to do to keep Vlayn alive.

He put those thoughts to rest, and spoke in a shrewd voice, "Never let your guard down," he muttered, and pulled the trigger.

- EPILOGUE -

BLOW IN THE WIND

The sky breathed softly, its breath blowing against the frail old shacks, making them creak with age. Dusting sand blew through the parched village, clicking against the wooden walls of the abandoned homes. This blowing sand held its secrets – it buried voices. But the blowing sand had been everywhere, witnessing everything. Every act of bloodshed, every act of cannibalism, every act of rape, every time someone lost their breath. Not one Jaadakin could catch these blowing grains. Dusters tried, but no one could.

In Witherhart, people cried, their faces stuck in wilted positions. Loved ones pulled from their laps. The city of previous wealth and civility before The Fall, now burned. And the sand continued to blow in the wind.

In Ryokard, people starved, futures nonexistent. People kept their eyes behind them as they beat on against the dusty wind, wary of a horde of glithémien or a dangerously unhinged Jaadakin that lost who they once were, after they lost it all. And the sand continued to blow in the wind.

In Woodvale, dusters pranced around energetic fires at the base of the Klapaytch Mountains. They lived in their idiosyncratic minds. Glithémien scarce, but humanity amongst Babarins scarcer. And the sand continued to blow in the wind.

In Shorewood, a new dictator controlled the village, but he didn't differ from Enver Rodge's rule. Dusters were raped, others eaten, others maimed for pleasure. And the sand continued to blow in the wind.

In Ellmorr, people smiled, families abundant. Ellmorians stepped into the bustling metropolis' streets, joyously reached into the air and ran their fingers through the hair of the wealth. They would overhear rumors of Jaadakin County suffering, but no one knew why and not one person showed any interest. Some would convene at the highest point of a skyscraper above Xenamus' gloomy sky. Their bodies furnished with thoroughly cleaned and pressed clothing with their rings or necklaces crafted from glistening saurapine that reflected the somber sky. They would speak of their business jargon while sipping Karelis from glasses made of pure crystal. The view would be magnificent for them; the communities of clouds sitting a few hundred feet below their walls of windows.

On clearer days, the wealthy could look out of these panes and through the hot sky and see a sliver of Jaadakin County. But no one thought twice. No one questioned what was going on down there. They only thought of themselves, while the sand continued to blow in the wind down in Jaadakin County.

XENAMUS

PLANET DESCRIPTION

Xenamus consists of six major cities, five established N.M.C. bases, one space port and one major manufacturing factory stationed on the Fraygen Plateau. As with many other planets in the Kirbinian Galaxy, the governmental breakdown is as follows and is listed in descending order of command:

Clansee: Acuura I

It is the Clansee's duties to not only oversee Xenamus and its operations, but the other planets in his/her sector of the Kirbinian Galaxy. As with other Clansees in The Galaxy, Acuura I is directly under the High Clansees of the Kirbinian Galaxy, Kirbside and Corvonn, and he is also a member of The Family (see glossary entry *Corvonn*, p. 264).

Elder: Kafenstag

This is a very high position in the Kirbinian galactic government. The Elder is given authority of a planet and takes on the responsibilities of being the head of all judicial and executive functions.

Senior: Kimbr Thorne

The Senior on every planet acts as an "assistant" to the Elder. The Senior typically takes on many responsibilities of the Elder jaro-to-jaro, and frequently usurps the Elder's position when he/she convenes with their Clansee on the Imperial Planet of their sector. When Elders retire or get promoted to Clanseeship, Seniors are usually next in line to fill the Elder position. Senior Kimbr Thorne is a very busy Babarin woman. However, it is likely that she is involved with much of the scandalous activities that Elder Kafenstag is allegedly involved in as well; one activity is funneling Credits to the city of Ellmorr instead of dividing the funds appropriately among all of the major cities.

Leader: This position is the most abundant in the galactic economy for there are innumerous openings. Leaders act as figureheads over a specific city on their assigned planet. The number of Leader positions varies based on each planet and how many major cities there are. Considering most major cities on many planets in the Kirbinian Galaxy are massive, they require one person at the top of the chain, supervising the city's activities. Xenamus has a total of six Leaders. Although, due to the glithémien epidemic, five out of the six major cities are collapsing, forcing the people to sheer survival and making the Leader position almost superfluous.

<u>Cities and Their Leaders</u>

Ellmorr: Sheethmarr Laken

Witherhart: Teetin Kal

Woodvale: Ashir Mez-Mire

Ryokard: Lezzerrake

Ridgecall: Julith

Ambervale: Ratakeen Tejenkay

PATHOLOGY OF GLITHEMIEN

The name glithémien is actually derived from the desert insects that carry the glithémien plague. Glithimite (the insects) are members of the Glithacoro family and are of the type Cordus. Glithacoro are composed of pathogenic insects whose members inhabit a wide range of planets. While most of these insects are found on sparsely populated planets, the glithémien are home to the deep deserts of Xenamus, a moderately populated planet.

Little is known about the insect as it spends the majority of its life nested underground, but once every ten Xenamus jaros, glithémien surface themselves to mate. It's at this point the sentient population is most vulnerable to being attacked by a horde of glithémien (glithemai), thus starting the cycle of the plague. When the disease (pathogen) enters a body it immediately begins to mutate and integrates components from the body's cells into its own make up. This is hypothesized to allow the glithémien to exponentially ramp up its cell division thus expediting the process. It begins to move through the body's venial structure or transport system until it reaches the heart, or the equivalent pumping organ for a different species. It begins a process known as tardun corpus, which forcibly slows the rhythm down to nearly two pumps per minute. This drains the body of energy and forces it to stay in one place.

GLOSSARY

Acri: Besides the city of Ellmorr, Acri is the sole village on the Fraygen Plateau. Acri is an outpost for N.M.C. patrols to stock up on ammunition, food, water, and U.V. suits for soldiers who are not Babarin. The village sits approximately

Acts of Baleejus: A holy book that tells the history of Baleejus, his time in the Kirbinian Galaxy, and how he rose into The Soke and battled Zaxraan Arn. The book is also known for its many quotes from the God himself. Its first publication dates back to the Middle-Pre Jaros. In current-jaro, the book's circulation hangs in the hundreds of billions all across the Kirbinian Galaxy.

Akafayl Gang: One of the largest gangs in the Kirbinian Galaxy, with the Saaxon Gang being the largest. Currently, the Akafayl prove to be deadly and merciless. The organization stretches all across The Galaxy, but there is a conglomerate near the Bactra and Weraxon area. The gang is known for the destruction of cities, burning and crucifying people, and many other crimes. There seems to be no apparent goal of the Akafayl. Rumors suggest, though, that they're owned by the Saaxons.

Allameen: This is known as the underworld; a dimension below The Galaxy where the worst kinds of people go after death.

Altkin: The former leader of the immense Honcheen Empire in the early jaros. Son of the feral Allibbar Quatin, Altkin superseded his father and took the Honcheen Empire onto Kirbinian World to apprehend the planet and its people in Jaro 7. After many jaros of keeping the

Kirbinian People enslaved on Kirbidia, the Kirbinians rebelled for their freedom, starting the planetary rebellion that eventually rewarded the Kirbinians with victory and marked the death of the Honcheen Empire. Altkin disappeared at the loss of the war and the Honcheen Empire. Rumors are spreading in current-jaro that Altkin is still alive – hundreds of jaros after the defeat, roaming the vast Kirbinian Galaxy, plotting his vengeance.

Ambervale: A major city in Jaadakin County. Just like the rest of the cities in Jaadakin, Ambervale, too, is suffering in the ways of food, water, and the Glithémien Disease.

Anceykik: An Imperial Planet in the Kirbinian Galaxy. Anceykik is most notably known for its absolute water-filled surface. With no land, all civilizations are underwater – both under the sea floor and floating above it. Anceykik is extremely popular for its mining excavations. Rare minerals and substances were found underneath the sea floor, which sprouted the enormous amounts of mining by galactic excavation companies.

Babarin: A fairly large race in the Kirbinian Galaxy. These people dwell all throughout The Galaxy. However, the majority inhabit hotter climates such as the planets of Xenamus, Weraxon, and Bactra. Unlike many other races, Babarins have high resistance to the heat that planets such as Xenamus serve.

Bactra: A Sub-Imperial Planet in the Kirbinian Galaxy. Bactra houses a massive lava lake, named Zfihjaal, that equals the size of a typical ocean found on other planets. Land sits beside this lava ocean. Bactra has been in a state of consistent peacetime for a while. Although, it seems that may change. The Akafayl Gang recently entered the planet and has established several bases across the lands. No violence has begun, thankfully, but the mere presence deems worry amongst inhabitants. In addition, the notorious Saaxon Gang also established a base on Bactra. It appears the only safe location is Nekron, a city in the middle of the Zfihjaal Lava Lake.

Baleejus: A God generally believed in by the Kirbinian people. However, many other races adopted Baleejus as their God.

Clena 441: A compact, single-burst pistol. Although it contains a small magazine, it's powerful and reliable. The pistol originated on the planet of Siskilian in jaros 205-217, when the Saaxon Organization invaded the Western Isles of the planet. The Council on Kirbidia was resistant to sending N.M.C. troops, for the galactic army was spread thin across The Galaxy, so Elder Ortaz Dardeck (see p. 258) began arming the planetary army in case the Saaxons pushed into the Eastern Sector, where the majority of the Siskilian population resided. The Eastern Sector of Siskilian was of generally moderate households. Still, the Siskilian Private Army was at a disadvantage and wouldn't be able to stand up to the Saaxon's force had they invaded.

Determined to construct a reliable, yet powerful sidearm to protect the soldiers of the Eastern Sector, Siskilian engineers Masha Kadeen and Ly'Lith Clena built the first model of what was soon to be the Clena 441 with heavy inspiration from the famous Nabbuu 88 pistol, which was born two-hundred jaros prior. With a few jaros of work, the final product of the Clena 441 was pushed into the arms of Eastern Sector soldiers. Roughly three-hundred jaros later, the Saaxon Organization has yet to push out of the Western Isles. However, Elder Ortaz Dardeck is seeking further assistance from Clansee Jexteen (see p. 258) and from neighboring planets to make an initial attack on the Saaxons.

Corvonn: High Clansee of the Kirbinian Galaxy and brother to High Clansee Kirbside. Corvonn is a Kirbinian man born in the late Pre-Jaros on the planet of Kirbidia. Corvonn was born with a specialized and rare blood form, which over time, mutated into something called Somatic Powers; where he grew into the ability to summon the environment, like wind or lightning in the sky and use it at his disposal. Almost every Kirbinian person is born with this type of blood, but very few are born with blood of this power and quality. The select few who are born like Corvonn are members of what is known as The Family. This is a group of people of differing races who also serve in high positions in the galactic government.

Credits: The main currency in the Kirbinian Galaxy. They are hundreds of thousands of other forms of currency across The Galaxy, but Credits, formally and unpopularly known as Kesganeen Shae, are directly distributed from the galactic government and are the most widely used and accepted.

Dsaar: The largest subdivision of the N.M.C. (see p. 271). Independently, each dsaar functions as its own military. Each dsaar has anywhere from ten to fifteen fleet ships depending on their location and the number of comprised soldiers. Out of the roughly one billion N.M.C. soldiers in the Kirbinian Galaxy, approximately five-hundred to six-hundred million are stationed in space on these dsaars. The largest dsaar is known as Zavrynth. It is stationed in the inter-planetary region between Zenokian and Fandosan (planets). It consists of thirty-two fleet ships which houses roughly ten million N.M.C. soldiers.

Dufe-102: A uniform assault rifle that is generally used throughout the Kirbinian Galaxy. The 102 is an older model in the Dufe series, with the Dufe-EB23R being its successor. Along with many other rifles, the Dufe-102 is a popular firearm amongst gun fanatics in The Galaxy. It is sturdy, reliable, cheap, and quite easy to obtain under the eyes of the galactic government.

Earth: Planet Earth entered a massive nuclear conflict between the United States and Russia in the year 2038. In Earth's history, this event was known as the Russo-American Nuclear Effect, lasting from years 2036-2038. Marking the end of the Nuclear Effect, the utilization of both countries' nuclear weaponry, it caused catastrophic annihilation of Earth's landscape and much of the humans. After many years of sitting in a destroyed world, the Kirbinian Galaxy entered the planet's atmosphere, curious to see what the planet could offer. After realization of Earth's destruction, Kirbinians transported near uncountable amounts of humans to the empty planet of Zidonian – a planet in the Kirbinian Galaxy with a climate much similar to Earth's pre-nuclear war.

Now, Earth is desolate with only an estimated population of two-hundred to three-hundred million people across the globe. After seventy-one years, humans are still picking up the pieces, rebuilding civilization the way they believe is correct.

Elder Kafenstag: Kadeen Kafenstag (see p. 258) is seen as a cruel Babarin man amongst many Xenamus natives. Kafenstag oversees the planet of Xenamus. In the both authoritative and powerful position of Elder in the galactic government, Elder Kafenstag funds all revenues to Ellmorr, as opposed to the declining Jaadakin County, to make it attractive to the rest of the Kirbinian Galaxy. The metropolis of Ellmorr is believed to be the only link to the galactic government, the High Clansees, and Xenamus' relativeness to the rest of the Kirbinian Galaxy. Elder Kafenstag and his superior, Clansee Acuura I believe

Ellmorr should be the utmost priority, not the suffering Jaadakin County.

Ellmorr: One of the wealthiest cities in the Kirbinian Galaxy. The city sits atop the Fraygen Plateau and is guarded every second by the N.M.C. Ellmorr boasts with its tall communities of skyscrapers, its gambling, nightlife, museums, theater shows, movies and other forms of entertainment, excursions across the plateau and more. The metropolis has grown so large, many galactic companies transferred their headquarters to the city, purchasing entire skyscrapers to operate out of. People from all over The Galaxy travel to Ellmorr to witness its elegance – thus, proving more of a priority to secure it from the horrors that are occurring below in Jaadakin County.

Flom: An Imperial Planet in the Kirbinian Galaxy. Flom is actually a two-planet system. Hundreds of jaros ago, Flom's moon was close to crashing into its planet, The Council established an anti-gravity system to keep the moon locked and at a distance from the original planet of Flom. Now, its original inhabitants eventually migrated to the moon as well as Flom. The planet of Flom is known for its massive agriculture and farming of a variety of produce, vegetables, etc. All the agriculture that is farmed is transported up to the moon, and from there it is shipped to hundreds of thousands of other planets in The Galaxy through the many space ports that is stationed on Flom's moon.

Flunklen 16: A widely-used assault rifle. Like the Nabbuu and Dufe, the Flunklen has grown to become a very popular assault rifle over the jaros within the N.M.C. The Flunklen 16 is the oldest of the trio – Flunklen 16, 17, and the Flunklen BDM. In its heyday, the Flunklen 16 had widespread use amongst the N.M.C. and even the S.A.F.U.

In current jaro, however, it's more of a deceased weapon, considering the newest model – Flunklen BDM is used more often. The Flunklen 16 was considered efficient and packed a heavy punch. Now, when being compared to modern weaponry, the 16 proves to be considerably cumbersome and recoils heavily.

Fort Ashfall: One of a few large bases stationed on the Fraygen Plateau on the planet of Xenamus. Unlike many other N.M.C. bases found on other planets in The Galaxy, Fort Ashfall has a strict, clear-cut goal – to keep anyone from Jaadakin County down below away from the affluent city of Ellmorr.

Fraygen Plateau: The single raised region of land above the deserts of Jaadakin County. On this plateau is one of the wealthiest cities in the entire Kirbinian Galaxy: Ellmorr. Additionally, the Fraygen Plateau is heavily guarded by N.M.C. troops and protects Ellmorr against wandering natives of Jaadakin.

Gasoline: After the nuclear fallout on Earth, the Kirbinian Galaxy later entered the planet's atmosphere during an exploration mission. After short investigation of the ruined Earth, The Galaxy took a large portion of the remaining Human Race from the dangerous conditions that Earth was in and moved them onto the planet of Zidonian in the Kirbinian Galaxy; a planet that was initially desolate. After hundreds of jaros, humans along with the natives of the Kirbinian Galaxy began to excavate Zidonian and discovered petroleum. Humans, being familiar with this substance, adapted this black liquid into gasoline, using the same techniques that was used before the nuclear devastation on Earth. Since then, gasoline had grown to become a recurring substance used in The Galaxy.

Gatald: A meager settlement in the deserts of Jaadakin County on the planet of Xenamus. Like many other tiny settlements, Gatald was established after the glithémien outbreak in Jaadakin County to get away from the infested major cities.

Glithémien Disease: A deadly disease that is plaguing the deserts and major cities of Jaadakin County on the planet of Xenamus. With a simple bite from a glithimite, one will begin to suffer from symptoms within a few hours. Symptoms begin with a slowed heart rate, high fever, weakening of muscles, bleeding eye sockets, and eventually the decaying of the lungs and sometimes other organs. Symptoms set in quickly, but it can take up to two days for an infected to die. Currently, there is no known cure for the Glithémien Disease. Although, there are rumors circulating that the city of Ellmorr on the planet of Xenamus has a cure, but isn't releasing it to Jaadakin County.

Glithémien: Small creatures that inhabit the deserts of Xenamus. They generally live in packs and move very quickly across the ground. They have many legs, varying from six to twelve, and four, massive fangs that bulge from their mouths. Their venom oozes from their razor teeth constantly, and it seems that just about every species in existence beside glithémien are susceptible to the disease they carry.

The Great Fall: The swift decline of Jaadakin County into turmoil after the Glithémien Disease plagued the cities and civilizations. Prior to The Great Fall, Jaadakin County was managing fairly; Commerce coursed through the deserts. There was enough food for the majority of Jaadakin County natives. However, the disease mutated so quickly that Jaadakin scientists couldn't determine a cure, or even its origins, before it ransacked the entire region. The Fall was relatively recent, thus the older generation of current-day lived before it, thus raising and educating their children during the chaos of Jaadakin County.

Gronotine: A natural substance found in the extensive cave networks underground mainly on the planet of Tabascuu. Gronotine is generally mined by the Human Trade Guild (H.T.G.) and ships this substance to many planets across The Galaxy. Gronotine is widely used – ammunition, explosives and even expensive jewelry. In the recent jaros, however, gronotine has been being laced with the extremely addictive narcotic, opium, to create gronotine-opium, a drug almost two-times as powerful and addictive as opium.

High Clansee: Highest obtainable galactic government rank. Currently, two Kirbinian men occupy this position: Corvonn and Kirbside and have obtained this position since the birth of the Kirbinian Galaxy. These men are replaced upon death and the replacements are chosen prior to death and remain anonymous. Essentially, High Clansees are "leaders" of The Galaxy and oversee all Clansees below them.

Human: One of the many races dwelling in the Kirbinian Galaxy. Humans originated from the planet Earth in the Milky Way Galaxy. However, after nuclear destruction on the planet, the remaining humans were discovered by the Kirbinian Galaxy and moved to the planet of Zidonian in their galaxy.

Jaadakin County: The main region on the planet of Xenamus. Jaadakin consists of hilly deserts to flat stretches of sand. It houses five out of the six major cities on the planet. Jaadakin currently sits in extreme poverty and is being plagued by the deadly Glithémien Disease.

Kirb: An abbreviation for "Kirbinian," and a commonly used nickname for Kirbinian people.

Kirbinian Galaxy: An immense galaxy that houses hundreds of thousands of inhabited planets and stars, mostly overseen by the galactic government. In comparison to the Milky Way, the Kirbinian Galaxy is quadruple in size and is divided up into five sectors.

Kirbinian World: The capital of the Kirbinian Galaxy. Also nicknamed "The Mother Planet," and, "Kirbidia." This planet is one of the wealthiest. Officials and Clansees convene on this planet to discuss important matters with the two High Clansees.

Kirbinian World's climate is similar to Zidonian's and Earth's, being moderate with cyclical seasons.

Kirbside: High Clansee of the Kirbinian Galaxy and brother to High Clansee Corvonn. Kirbside is a Kirbinian man born in the late Pre-Jaros on the planet of Kirbidia. Kirbside was born with a specialized and rare blood form, which over time, mutated into something called Somatic Powers; where he grew into the ability to summon the environment, like wind or lightning in the sky and use it at his disposal. Almost every Kirbinian person is born with this type of blood, but very few are born with blood of this power and quality. The select few who are born like Kirbside are members of The Family. This is a group of people of differing races who also serve in high positions in the galactic government.

Konlax: Sub-Imperial Planet in the Kirbinian Galaxy. Konlax is well-known for its beautiful landscapes, mountain ranges and vast oceans. Only the richest of The Galaxy live on Konlax, with thousands of estates and mansions skewed across the lands.

Laxryy: A meager, desolate settlement in Jaadakin County on the planet of Xenamus.

Liberta: This planet neighbors Xenamus. It is one of many Sanctuary Planets in the Kirbinian Galaxy. Sanctuary Planets are designated planets that are directly funded by

Kirbidia and the two High Clansees. They house many
N.M.C. veterans and those currently serving, as well as
people who work on the planets to serve the troops.

Nizer Marine Corps (N.M.C.): The Kirbinian Galaxy's
primary army. The N.M.C. is spread across The Galaxy,
with bases stationed on almost every planet. The N.M.C. is
headquartered on one of Kirbidia's moons. Unlike the
S.A.F.U. (see p. 274), the N.M.C. is not at the disposal of
the two High Clansees. For the N.M.C. to be deployed
into a galactic region or a planetary region for military
operations, a war council (see p. 275) must be convened,
and there must be a seventy percent majority vote.

Nabbuu 88: One of the most popular and famous
weapons in Kirbinian history. "Nabbuu" is a popular
weapon model in regard to side-arms. Currently, there are
three models of the Nabbuu: the 88, the 99, and the Type-
V. The Nabbuu 99 had a very short lifespan and didn't
make much of a presence in the eyes of the N.M.C. The
Nabbuu 88 is not only the eldest Nabbuu model, but it's
also one of the oldest firearms ever created in Kirbinian
Galaxy history. The Nabbuu 88 has grown to be one of
the rarest weapons ever. Obtaining a Nabbuu 88 is
considered an achievement, but also can be sold for
hundreds of thousands of Credits.

Nydek Urlon: The most notorious and most wanted
criminal in the Kirbinian Galaxy. Urlon is known for his
immense heists and brutal killings. He has been wanted for
jaros, but the N.M.C. nor the S.A.F.U. are able to find him.
Rumor has it he is stationed on the planet of Onafactus,
masked by the jaro-long rainstorms on the planet.

Ohbrizorne: A chemical used in walls for insulation. Once
the inner wall is coated with ohbrizorne, it foams then
eventually hardens to the surface. In warmer climates, it's

typically mixed with asbestos to keep heat out. A primary downfall to ohbrizorne is that it requires annual inspections and upkeep to maintain its efficiency. When it isn't maintained, it begins to wither away and emit toxic fumes.

Opalenium: An industrial gem used in the manufacturing of the blades of tree cutters, specifically the blades that cut the extremely hard and dense trunks of the Eucalonus trees. Opalenium is turned to molten and mixed with other compounds both synthetic and natural to create a liquid to create or coat saw blades for loggers. The saws are massive blades the size of 200 feet to cut down the Eucalonus trees that have a height of over 400 feet tall. The lumber is used to create a near exponential amount of lumber for The Galaxy.

Paylian Roll: Similar to cigarettes, paylian rolls are extremely popular in the Kirbinian Galaxy. Paylian Rolls are smoked and usually give the user a light head-high. These rolls contain paylian – a natural, gooey substance found on the trees on the planet of Tabascuu. Paylian is generally used for medicinal purposes, but they also largely contribute to the manufacturing of these Paylian Rolls. There are a few hundred popular Paylian Roll brands, with one being DarkWagen, as it seemed to monopolize over the market in Sector 1 of The Galaxy.

Pramius: A fish-like creature typically found in the oceans of Reft, Siskilian and Sayt-Lok; planets that are very much comprised of large bodies of water. Like any raw fish, pramius should be cooked, due to the fact that risk of contracting a disease is very high. The pramius is one of the more common fish in the water, like fluke or azbeck.

Reft: A wealthy planet in Sector 1 of the Kirbinian Galaxy. Much of the planet's wealth can be attributed to the deep-sea hunting of kamuu whales generally in the Blaikkhall Ocean. The meat of these whales sells for thousands of Credits across The Galaxy. Reft is also popular for the Nakafed Continent – where many of the wealthy people of The Galaxy settle down in the cities of Daarankeen and Vaalinkail.

Ridgecall: A major city in Jaadakin County. Just like the rest of the cities in Jaadakin, Ridgecall, too, is suffering in terms of food, water, and the Glithémien Disease.

Ryokard: A major city in Jaadakin County. Just like the rest of the cities in Jaadakin, Ryokard, too, is suffering in terms of food, water, and the Glithémien Disease.

Saurapine: This is recognized as one of the most precious minerals in the entire galaxy. It is coveted by the highest echelons of society but only the most prestigious can afford to dawn this symbol of power. The stone comes in a variety of forms but the most popular is azure blue or a translucent white.

The only known location where Saurapine exists is deep within the mantle of Stion Kor (planet). The gemstone is created from the combination of a unique thermal reaction in the core with rapid mantle convection that completely sub ducts the surface in a mere hundred jaros. Though this alone is not enough to produce Saurapine; many studies produced from the PanGalactic Institute of Geology show that elements found in Saurapine do not exist nor are created on Stion Kor. Instead, researchers have proposed the frequent bombardment of outer system asteroids introduce the materials necessary for Saurapine to be created. Thus, the culmination of all these processes make Saurapine one of the rarest gemstones in the entire galaxy.

Specialized Advanced Fighting Units (S.A.F.U.): The S.A.F.U. serves as the reserved, elite army of the Kirbinian Galaxy. Unlike the N.M.C., the S.A.F.U. is considerably smaller in size and its soldiers are trained almost every day. Noc, a large asteroid in the corner of The Galaxy, is the central headquarters for the S.A.F.U., where much of the troops live and train. The soldiers are often transferred to planets of extreme climate across The Galaxy, pushing the soldiers' boundaries of conditioning, stamina and strength, creating the toughest of soldiers. The S.A.F.U. is rarely deployed by the High Clansees, but they are always on standby.

Shorewood: A small settlement nearing Witherhart, on the planet of Xenamus. Like the village of Gatald and others, Shorewood was established after The Great Fall to escape the chaos of the major cities.

Siskilian: A Sub-Imperial Planet in Sector 1 of the Kirbinian Galaxy. Not only is this planet prominently covered by the vast Yarintail Ocean, but the immense Saaxon Gang has recently conquered the Western Continent, controlling its major cities and sea and space ports.

The Soke: A mystical dimension that exists above the plane of the Kirbinian reality. It is mostly shrouded in mystery, as only certain individuals have a higher attachment to the dimension. A plethora of cults and religions exist around the Soke, those of which include the chantry of Baleejus and Zaxraan Arn. It's also the way ships travel through hyperspace, through the Soke lanes, or "levels." The higher the level, the quicker the travel. Many believe that after death, they live on in the Soke.

The Council: The name for all the top, powerful officials in The Galaxy. It includes all of the Clansees and the two

High Clansees. The Council routinely convenes in The Palace on Kirbidia to discuss planetary, political, civil, and many other matters in their galaxy.

T-Bomb: A small, crude explosive device frequently used by Akafayl suicide bombers. Their composition varies, but all bombs have a slim coating of raw, unprocessed tocsin, which proves to be highly reactive.

Tocsin: This is a metal that is primarily used in the construction of spacecrafts. This metal is found in abundance on the planet of Hexx, where imperial and private mining operations take place.

Troid: An inexpensive and unreliable submachine gun. Most certainly, the Troid doesn't fair well against other submachine weapons in its class like the Ctudd A-12, or the Yanitt L-5. However, it still packs a steady punch and stands confidently for the job when it's called upon. Critics, however, feel the Troid resembles plastic, labeling it as inefficient after much use. A small computerized screen on the side of the gun proves convenience to users, especially the N.M.C., with its notifications for low ammunition and service.

U.V. Suits: Protective armor that defends against the powerful rays of heat on the planet of Xenamus. Every race, with the exception of Babarin, should equip a suit when on Xenamus, Weraxon, or Bactra. Currently, there is much controversy that companies, such U.V. Company produces carelessly-crafted suits that doesn't work.

War Council: A gathering of the High Clansees, the Clansees that are members of The Family and the Supreme Commanders of the N.M.C. The War Council convenes bi-jaro to discuss the routine military activities of The Galaxy. Meetings typically occur in The Palace on Kirbidia, but can take place elsewhere. Occasionally, an emergency session is summoned for urgent military operations.

Whiskey: Liquor that originated from the planet of Earth. After the massive excavation of humans from Earth to Zidonian, brewers immediately started crafting the booze after their arrival in the Kirbinian Galaxy. After hundreds of jaros of humans brewing the alcohol on Zidonian, it grew to become a popular beverage amongst those of The Galaxy.

Witherhart: A major city in Jaadakin County on Xenamus. Once a massive bustling city similar to current-day Ellmorr, it is now a dying village, with its people holding onto life and the rest dead at the hands of the Glithémien Disease or starvation.

Woodvale: A major city in Jaadakin County. Just like the rest of the cities in Jaadakin, Woodvale, too, is suffering in terms of food and the Glithémien Disease. Unlike the other major cities in Jaadakin, though, Woodvale is neighbors with the Klapaytch Mountains. Much of Woodvale consists of uneven, hillier terrain with cooler air temperatures. Thus, climate doesn't agree with glithémien. The disease is indeed present in Woodvale, but not nearly as much as the rest of the cities in Jaadakin.

Xenamus: A Sub-Imperial Planet of the Kirbinian Galaxy. Technically, Xenamus is one of the wealthiest planets in The Galaxy, with thanks to the city of Ellmorr. Besides this bustling city, the rest of the planet – Jaadakin County – sits impoverished with little food and medicine to defend against the Glithémien Disease.

Zavrynth: The largest dsaar is known as Zavrynth. It is stationed in the inter-planetary region between Zenokian and Fandosan (planets). It consists of thirty-two fleet ships which houses roughly ten million N.M.C. soldiers.

It was initially commissioned during the jaros following the Kirbinian-Honcheen war, making it the oldest dsaar that is still operational. The dsaar earned the title, Zavrynth, after the annihilation of the Zkarian imperial fleet and the disintegration of the empire. The Zkarian government system was known as "Zavrynth." The name was later stolen by the dsaar after their success. Zavrynth later went on to fight in almost every N.M.C.-fought war.

Zidonian: An Imperial Planet in Sector 4 of the Kirbinian Galaxy. Zidonian houses a climate extremely similar to that of Earth's, pre-nuclear fallout. The planet endures a cyclical change of seasons, however it isn't predictable; summer can last an entire jaro, while winter can last for a measly month, for instance. Zidonian is also well-known for the presence of the Human Trade Guild (H.T.G.). The H.T.G. is one of the largest companies in the Kirbinian Galaxy. The guild's main focus is mining and transporting the natural substance gronotine to planets all over The Galaxy. However, the guild is involved in transporting many other goods as well. Currently, though, the H.T.G. is involved in the alleged manufacturing and distribution the highly addictive narcotic, gronotine-opium.

About Nick Ercolano

Nick Ercolano was born and raised on Long Island, NY. His interest in writing began at the early age of nine when he wrote poetry. Through many years of writing and photography, he was able to publish his first science fiction work, _Vengeance_ in 2016, and a separate work, _Corruption_, in 2017. Through inspirations of other literary works and life in total, he is able to craft stories, characters, and create different universes that surround such characters. You can find his latest publications online.

www.nickercolano.com